D0498014

# DOUBLE
## OR
# NOTHING

Center Point
Large Print

Also by Meg Mims and available from
Center Point Large Print:

*Double Crossing*

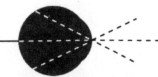

**This Large Print Book carries the
Seal of Approval of N.A.V.H.**

# DOUBLE OR NOTHING

## Meg Mims

CENTER POINT LARGE PRINT
THORNDIKE, MAINE

This Center Point Large Print edition is published in the year 2013 by arrangement with the author.

The text of this Large Print edition is unabridged.
In other aspects, this book may vary
from the original edition.
Printed in the United States of America
on permanent paper.
Set in 16-point Times New Roman type.

ISBN: 978-1-61173-898-8

Library of Congress Cataloging-in-Publication Data

Mims, Meg
Double or Nothing / Meg Mims. — Center Point Large Print edition.
pages cm
ISBN 978-1-61173-898-8 (Library binding : alk. paper)
 1. Elopement—Fiction. 2. Murder—Investigation—Fiction.
  3. San Francisco Bay Area (Calif.)—Fiction.
  4. Historical fiction. gsafd  5. Large type books. I. Title.
PS3613.I591997D69 2013
813'.6—dc23
                                    2013032823

# Dedication

I thank God for guiding me through this book. Love and thanks to my husband and daughter for their unfailing support, and to my long-time CP—you always believed in me. All my thanks to Western Writers of America for honoring Double Crossing with a Spur Award. I'm so blessed.

*". . . whatever you do,*
*do it all for the glory of God."*
*1 Corinthians 10:31*

*'Be ye therefore merciful, as
your Father is also merciful . . . forgive,
and ye shall be forgiven.'*
Luke 6:36-37

# Chapter One

## 1869, California

I jumped at a screeching whistle. Men swarmed over the distant slope like bees over a wax honeycomb in a mad scramble. "Good heavens. What is that about?"

Uncle Harrison pulled me out of harm's way. "They're almost ready to begin the process of hydraulic mining," he said and pulled his hat down to avoid the hot sun. "You'll see, Lily. This is far better than panning for gold in a creek bed."

"I can already see how destructive it is, given the run-off," I said, eyeing the rivulets of dried mud that marked each treeless incline. "I've read about how the farmers can't irrigate their fields and orchards due to the gravel and silt filling the rivers—"

Water suddenly gushed from two hydraulic

nozzles in a wide, powerful stream. The men's bulging arm muscles strained their shirts, their faces purple with the effort to control the water. I turned my gaze to the ravaged earth. Mud washed down into the wooden sluices, where other men worked at various points to spray quicksilver along the wide stretch. Others worked at a frantic pace to keep the earthy silt moving.

An older man with a grizzled goatee and worn overalls held out a canteen. "Have a sip while you're waiting, miss," he said. "A body gets mighty thirsty out here."

"Thank you."

I sipped the cold, refreshing ginger-flavored liquid that eased my parched throat. Dirt from the canteen streaked my gloves. Not that it mattered. At least the spatters of fresh mud wouldn't show on my black mourning costume and riding boots. Two days of rain earlier in the week had not helped.

The kind man offered the canteen to Uncle Harrison, who brushed it aside with a curt shake of his head. Steaming, I bit back an apology. The man had already headed back to his position near the sluices.

Bored of watching the ongoing work, I wandered over to several horses that stood patient in the sun and patted their noses. A tooled leather saddle sat atop one gelding's glossy brown hide, and the silver-studded bridle looked as rich. The horse gave a low whicker in greeting. If only I'd pocketed a few carrots or sugar lumps from breakfast.

"You're a beauty. I wish I could ride you for a bit."

The gelding's ears dipped forward. One of the men left the knot of others in a huff. His dusty open coat swung around him as he stalked, spurs jingling, and closed the distance. He passed by me with a mere tip of his wide-brimmed hat and untied the reins. The horse pawed the ground, jittery, as if sensing the man's foul mood while he mounted. I noted his scowl. Was he upset that I'd dared touch his property? A scruffy beard and thick black mustache hid his mouth. He rode off, keeping the gelding's gait easy, down the gully toward the Early Bird's entrance.

"Who was that?" I asked a miner.

The worker wiped sweat from his forehead with a sleeve. "Señor Alvarez? He's got a burr under his blanket as usual. Pay him no mind, miss."

I rubbed the remaining horse's flank and glanced around the mining site. My uncle continued to chat with the foreman close to the shack near the head of the sluices. Another section of the wooden troughs was raised from the ground further north at a different bank of earth. My curiosity increased. I walked to the sluice and stared down at the filth in the bottom. No glints of gold flecked the bits of rock and slag. I had no idea what quicksilver looked like either. This whole business seemed crazy, although Uncle Harrison disagreed.

In the distance, pines smudged the lower half of the Sierra's tiny white-capped peaks. To the west, gray clouds threatened the pale blue sky. No doubt rain would soak everything again by morning. My uncle had mentioned how winter was wetter here than back home in Chicago, or even St. Louis. I hadn't known what to expect for autumn in California. Now that it was close to October, the stands of golden aspen on a ridge high above sported various shades of green, gold and hues of orange.

Homesickness overwhelmed me. I longed to see the brilliant shades of orange, red and yellow oaks, the thick forest of elms and birches behind my father's house in Evanston. To ride along the shoreline of Lake Michigan's navy waters, and watch the snow falling fast on a chilly winter's day. I wouldn't even mind listening to Adele Mason's endless chatter about the latest dinner parties she attended with her many beaus.

It seemed like an eternity since I'd crossed two thousand miles of prairie and mountains on the Union and Central Pacific railroad. Donner Lake had resembled a sapphire jewel nestled among pristine snow fields. Perhaps it was frozen already.

I shivered, remembering the darkness of

Summit Tunnel. It also brought back the delicious memory of feeling safe, nestled in Ace's strong arms. Feeling the sudden shock when his tongue sought my own . . .

"Miss? It's dangerous standin' that close to the sluice. Over yonder is best."

Guilt flooded my heart. Nodding to the man, I twisted around and glanced in the direction he indicated. My uncle remained at the shack. "Will they ever stop talking business?"

"Doubt it." The miner was the same one who'd offered me water earlier. He carried a roll of canvas slung over a shoulder. Shrugging, he swiped his muddy goatee and cheek against his burden's nubby surface. "Reckon they'll yammer on for a while more."

"Thank you. I'll be careful."

"Sure thing, miss."

He passed by and handed the canvas to a pair of men. They unrolled it and laid the fabric inside the wooden sluice. I walked across the shifting ground, trying to avoid the worst of the mud's damp patches. One claimed my uncle's shoe when we arrived that morning. I'd fought hard not to laugh aloud, watching Uncle Harrison hop about on one foot, so comical with his blustery red face. At last a worker retrieved his shoe, mud up to his elbow, half his face coated as well. My uncle had not thanked the man for the rescue, either.

On higher ground, two workers held long

snaking hoses that spurted water at the high bank. Two others sprayed quicksilver over the sluice. It didn't look like anything but dirty water. I sighed. This entire trip had been a waste of time. Uncle Harrison resented the questions I'd peppered the foreman with and ignored my opinions on how the operation damaged the countryside. Why had he suggested I tag along in the first place?

I should have stayed back in Sacramento. My sketchbook drawings needed work. I had yet to finish anything I'd glimpsed during the journey on the train. Etta had brought all my watercolor supplies from Evanston, and most of my books too.

But I didn't want to read or paint. A deep melancholy robbed me of energy. Nightmares haunted my sleep, of the deep ravine and the lizard I'd caught, of the sandy slope I climbed on Mt. Diablo, desperate to escape my father's killer. Of being trapped, with no way out, and facing death, and of seeing that shocked surprise . . . and hearing the gunshot.

Self-defense, as Ace claimed. My uncle and the sheriff agreed.

Poor Ace. He'd felt bad afterward, forced into a cowardly deed. I had never shot anything except a badger with Father's Navy revolver. Missed, too. But I'd tried to protect my darling pet lizard's clutch of eggs in the garden back home. The thought of shooting a human being turned my stomach. I suppose stabbing someone wasn't any less of a sin. Heavy guilt weighed on me. Had it been self-defense? I shuddered at the memory.

As Mother used to say, it was water under the bridge. Nothing I might say or do now would change the past. But I'd rather avoid making such a horrible choice again.

Instead I trudged toward the shack. The foreman held a large piece of blueprint paper between his hands while my uncle pointed at various sections. Two other men argued with them, their heated words carrying over the whooshing of hoses and creaks and jolts of skeleton wagons over the rutted ground. Most of their argument was peppered with technical jargon that didn't make any sense. Even Chinese sounded more familiar.

"We haven't made enough headway," said a man in a tailored suit, whose gold watch chain glinted in the sun. "I say we dig out the ridge all the way."

"You take that ridge down any more than we have and we'll never get equipment to the furthest point of the claim, over here," my uncle said and prodded the map. "That was Alvarez's advice. He knows this land better than you, Williamson."

"I agree, it's too dangerous," the foreman said.

"I'm the engineer! Are you implying I don't know my business?"

"I'm saying it's stupid to undermine that ridge. You're being a stubborn coot."

13

"You're a fine one to call me stubborn—"

Good heavens. I reversed direction and headed back toward the sluice. They were sure to argue for another few hours. I wanted to ride that horse, even if it meant hiking my skirts to my knees and baring my ankles. The poor animal looked like it needed a good run, or at least a trot over the rough ground. I had to do something productive or I'd go mad.

Steering around the same boggy patch of mud, I cut close to the sluice. A blood-curdling yell halted everyone. I whirled to see the entire bank of earth, a huge avalanche of mud, rocks and two large trees root-first, rushing straight for me. Someone grabbed my waist from behind. I found myself sprawling head-first in the wooden trough. Other men shouted. The mine whistle screeched in my ears, so loud my head throbbed.

Spitting gravel, I struggled to my knees. The tidal wave of mud and rocks hit the trough, rocking me backwards, and then pushed it off its moorings. I screamed when the miner was swept off his feet. Reaching out, I grabbed for his hand—he lost his grip and vanished. A large boulder slammed into the trough and almost tipped me off my perch. I fought to keep my grip on the wooden edge. At last the massive mud-slide halted.

Somehow I found myself staring up at a huge tree trunk that hovered over my head. The thing teetered in the wind. Terrified it would crush me, I held my breath. Several workers waded waist deep into the mud and threaded ropes over the tree's boughs. Two dozen men scampered from all directions, pulling and tugging, until the huge trunk slid backwards a few inches.

"Hold still, miss! We'll get you to safety quick as a wink."

"There's a man buried somewhere! Please try to save him first!"

The crew, grunting and panting, lugged the tree out of harm's way. Two other men lifted me off the wooden sluice's remnants. The younger one carried me up the slope toward the shack and set me on my feet. I sagged like a limp rag doll into Uncle Harrison's arms. White-faced with shock, he stripped off my gloves and chafed my hands.

"Are you all right, Lily? Say something!"

"That worker was buried alive. He saved my life—"

"Hush. They'll find him."

Together we watched the workers dig and scrabble with bare hands at the massive runoff. Horrified, my body shaking, I prayed hard that they'd find him before it was too late. My uncle pushed me onto a camp stool. Once he thrust a clean handkerchief into my hands, he forced a drink down my throat from his silver flask. The brandy burned its way to my stomach. I almost retched, but it calmed my jangled nerves. Uncle

Harrison wiped my face and neck before he departed. Shivering, wet and muddy, I glanced down at the cotton cloth in my hand. Brown grime stained it along with streaks of pale pink. Blood.

I mopped my neck again, aware now of the stinging pain below my earlobe, and scraped away tiny bits of gravel. My uncle had left his flask. I tipped it against a clean spot on the handkerchief and dabbed my flesh. That burned as well.

A worker pushed me back onto the stool when I stood. "Better rest, miss. You look ready to faint, and we ain't got any clean clothes for you."

"Have they found that poor man yet?"

"They will. One way or another," he said, his tone mournful. "This ain't the first accident we've had at the Early Bird."

Mortified, I clenched a fist. "How many others have been hurt? Or killed?"

"I better not say."

He stalked toward the crowd, who continued to clear rocks and a second tree trunk from the muddy runoff. I heard a shout. Five men jumped to assist a sixth who called for help. They lifted a prone figure between them. My heart quailed at the sight of a huge splinter of wood protruding from the man's blood-soaked shirt. I turned away, tears blurring my vision. I could have suffered the same fate if not for his courage.

The poor soul. He'd been so kind, offering a drink of ginger water, even warning me away from the sluice. He'd given his life to save mine. How could something like this happen? And he had not been the only victim to this destructive mining practice.

Numb, I staggered to my feet and hunted down the foreman. "What was the man's name, the one who died? Please tell me. Does he have any family?"

"Hank Matthews." The worker swiped mud from his bearded cheek. "Wife and three kids from what little I know."

I marched off to find my uncle, ignoring the growing stiffness and itch of my filthy clothes. He was busy consulting with the engineer and three other men, supervisors no doubt, given their clean clothes. Uncle Harrison turned to me at last.

"We must send money to Mr. Matthews' family," I said, "for the funeral, and to care for his wife and children—"

"We will discuss the matter later."

"I insist that we support his family! It's the least we can do. He saved my life, you must see that—ow." He'd snared my arm and pulled me aside, his voice lowering.

"We cannot support every family of all the men who've suffered accidents," Uncle Harrison said. "They knew the risks. They chose to work at the Early Bird."

"But—"

"Enough, Lily. I said we'll discuss it later."

He marched me back over the rough terrain to the small camp. Someone brought a real chair and placed it inside the "store," a crude canvas tent shelter. Two wooden barrels covered with a plank served as a counter. Fifty pound burlap bags of flour, coffee beans, sugar, salt and dried navy beans lined the shelves, along with tins of pepper and saleratus. Another man brought a wooden bucket of clean water. I washed my face, hands and neck, weeping in silence over Hank Matthews' death. He'd died in a horrible fashion. How many others had suffered similar fates or life-threatening injuries?

At last my uncle arrived to fetch me. I stood, exhausted and dejected. "I'd like to find out where Mrs. Matthews lives—"

"That's not important now. This landslide will set back production for a few weeks," he said, "but that can't be helped. Forget what happened, Lily."

"I cannot forget such a tragedy! I won't forget."

Uncle Harrison shrugged. "Suit yourself. It's time to return home."

Furious, I followed him toward the coach we'd hired in Folsom earlier that morning. My stiff skirts and jacket rustled with every move. I refused his help and climbed inside on my own. For the past month, my uncle declined to read reports in the newspapers about farmers who complained how their orchards and soil were ruined by silt and gravel from the hydraulic mining runoff. The Early Bird was only one of over a hundred or more sites in the high hills surrounding Sacramento. Now I'd seen the truth of the destruction first hand. Somehow I had to get through to Uncle Harrison. To him, the accident meant nothing.

I had to take matters into my own hands.

Etta flung the door wide. "Miss! What in the world happened—"

"A bath, please, as fast as you can prepare it."

I pushed past her into the house. The ride to Folsom had been bad enough, along with the short trip to the railhead at Roseville. Uncle Harrison gave in when I rejected his offer to find a hotel and have my dress sponged. I'd borne the scrutiny of several late night passengers on the train to Sacramento with wounded pride, and in extreme discomfort. My skin crawled, my muscles ached to the point of agony. I wanted to scream with impatience.

Once upstairs in my bedroom, I stripped every bit of clothing off with a weary sigh and tied a wrapper around my waist. My whole head itched, as if plastered in place. I pulled several hairpins out and dislodged a hunk of dried mud. Ugh.

Etta knocked. "I've heated water. Let me have your clothes, miss."

"There's no use salvaging them."

"Now, Miss Lily. Your uncle explained everything, and it's not your fault." She bent to gather the filthy clothes. "I'll get you something to eat."

"Hot tea, with milk and sugar, thank you. I'm exhausted. I need to sleep."

"You received a letter, miss. I left it on the dressing table."

"I'll read it tomorrow."

Etta held out a small bowl with creamed paste. "Your favorite scrub—lavender, honey and a bit of oatmeal. Cover your face and hands with that, and I'll mix some fresh beeswax with rose hips and almond oil when you're done."

I sank into the hot bath water in the screened alcove. Once I scrubbed all over, Etta washed my hair and brought fresh water to rinse all the dirt out. She poured a mixture of rose-scented mineral oil and massaged it into my curls. The room's cold air sent shivers up my spine. I slipped into my nightdress, slathered my face and hands with salve and crawled into bed. It seemed the minute my head hit the feather pillow, I woke to tugging on my scalp. Etta sat beside me, comb in hand. Mid-morning sunlight streamed into the room.

"I'm sorry, Miss Lily. I couldn't see all the tangles in your hair last night," she said. "You'll never grow it long again if I have to cut snarls out."

Flexing my sore limbs, ignoring the pain, I

yawned wide. "I don't care—" Yawning again, I hunched down while she tugged and pulled. "Go ahead and cut it short."

"That's silly. Your future husband wouldn't appreciate that."

"I will never have a husband."

"Didn't Mr. Mason marry that young lady you met on the train?"

"Yes, Kate Kimball." I hadn't been surprised at that news when the telegram from San Francisco arrived last week. "She's better suited to be his wife than I ever was."

"That doesn't mean you won't find a suitable young man to marry."

I didn't bother to answer. Etta clucked to herself and left the room. I rolled onto my back, yawning again, too tired to rise. Disappointment lingered inside me when I recalled Kate and Charles' news. They hadn't asked me to witness their vows or invited me to a small celebration. Not that I'd expected them to host a lavish wedding. But I had lost the chance to share in their happiness. Perhaps they assumed I wouldn't leave Sacramento, being in mourning for Father. They were wrong. Wearing black wouldn't have stopped me. Friendship and loyalty meant far more than the customs of the day.

California wasn't as exciting as I'd expected. I hadn't made friends in the neighborhood. Most women here were either elderly or married with children, few my age. Uncle Harrison often missed meals, and only returned home to sleep. Thank goodness Etta had arrived from Evanston to keep me company.

I stretched, working out the soreness in my shoulders, back and limbs. Boredom had driven me to visit the mine yesterday. Now boredom struck again, harder than ever. Kate would be cooking breakfast for her new husband right now. To think a few months ago, Charles had wanted me to marry him and fund his mission trip to China. I snatched up the letter that Etta brought last night and slit the envelope with a hairpin. Kate's scrawled handwriting covered every inch of the paper, both sides. Father had often written letters to Mother during the War like this, the inked words smeared a little, and difficult to decipher.

Padding barefoot over the rug, I curled up on the window seat. Thick gray fog shrouded the city streets below, and a scent of mildewed leaves invaded the room. A horse-drawn milk wagon clopped over the cobblestones and halted, its outline faint. The driver scurried toward the porch with a wire rack of bottles. He walked back with the empties and vanished. At last I turned my attention to Kate's letter.

*Dearest Lily, I hope you are well . . . we are so happy, even though we haven't a penny to our name. At first we had to accept the kindness of strangers, staying two days here and another elsewhere. But our ministry has grown here in San Francisco. We hope to build a permanent church in Rock Canyon. The poor come to us, and bring whatever they can to share a meal every Wednesday and Sunday. That's when Charles preaches the Word. He is winning souls to the Lord's work every day . . .*

Charles? Preaching, when he never had the courage to speak to Father back in Evanston! Had he changed that much? To think I might have slept on the floor in a stranger's house next to a husband—but no. My inheritance would have guaranteed a hotel room, a house, and passage to wherever Charles wanted to serve as a missionary. But that door had closed. I was thankful, too, because Kate proved a better choice for him.

She'd made no mention of Ace Diamond. What was he doing now?

I let out a long breath. He'd taken the three thousand dollars my uncle had given him and vanished. Had he forgotten me? Gone back east on the railroad to buy a ranch somewhere? I had no idea. I'd been curious enough to send Etta when she first arrived in Sacramento, inquiring at every hotel, steamer and ticket clerk for the Central Pacific. She failed to learn anything about the young Texan. That hurt far more than I expected.

Our last conversation in the Vallejo hotel hallway was clear in my memory. Ace's fury, the gleam in his odd eyes—one blue, one blue-green—matched his determination to win me. But my uncle's insults had enraged him.

Ever since, I'd engaged in daily shouting matches with Uncle Harrison over acting as my guardian. He proved to be a dictator of my clothing and behavior, disregarded my opinion on the Early Bird mine or about social events, parties and dinners he insisted I attend. My resentment grew over being treated like a child. I cherished independence from a young age, since my parents had fostered that. Father had indulged me further after Mother's death. Uncle Harrison wasn't aware of that, however, and his iron-fisted control irritated me.

I sighed aloud and stretched once more. My black skirt and jacket were ruined after the trip to the Early Bird. I'd have to order new mourning attire or else give up my intention to observe the custom. Father would no doubt laugh if he stood here. He'd shake a finger and remind me about his wish to dandle a grandchild on his knee.

The only way to fulfill that was to marry. One man had sparked my interest, yet he was gone. I yearned to hear Ace's drawl, see his face and that boyish grin again. I missed him. We'd spent time together on the train, and several pleasant hours on Mt. Diablo waiting for my uncle's return with the sheriff. My heart quickened at the memory of sharing his hot kisses. And I hadn't protested when his warm hands roamed my neck and shoulders. Or the sly way he'd tugged a few buttons free on my shirtwaist to kiss my bare skin. Along the curve of my bosom above my corset cover, and then . . .

Etta's loud rap at the door scared me witless. She carried in a tray with a silver urn, cups and saucers plus a covered dish. "So you found the letter from San Francisco?"

"Yes. From Kate."

"There's another this morning. I hope you're hungry. You missed dinner last night. Captain Granville told me about that poor man yesterday, who saved your life."

"He did?" Surprised, I glanced up at Etta. She looked wary.

"He's not keen on sending them any money like you suggested, miss."

"I don't understand. He was always generous in the past—"

"To you, maybe, because you're family."

I let out another long breath. As if a little money would help that family anyway. No amount could substitute for a man's life. My resentment increased. I rubbed my forehead and temples, wishing my headache away. The delicious scent of coffee and bacon wafted over me.

"Where's this other letter?"

Etta poured two cups of coffee and handed me one. "I didn't recognize the handwriting on the envelope." She drew it from her apron pocket.

I studied the spidery writing and then used the same hairpin to open the thin envelope. "Hmm. Mrs. Wycliffe says she wrote every word that Aunt Sylvia dictated. It's postmarked from Sacramento, but I thought she was in a San Francisco hospital."

"Could be your uncle brought her here to recover." Etta perched on a chair. "What does it say, miss? If you don't mind me asking."

"Of course not."

I crunched a rasher of bacon, ate the still warm eggs and then wiped my hands on a linen napkin. What did Aunt Sylvia want? She'd warned Uncle Harrison about Ace being a gambler. She'd cursed me, Ace, Uncle Harrison, and every one of the men who rescued her from the ravine that day at Mt. Diablo—worse than a miner—while they carried her on a makeshift litter to the buckboard wagon. Aunt Sylvia hadn't stopped cursing on the journey back to Vallejo. She deserved every bit of rough treatment for what I'd suffered at her hands.

After I flattened the letter, I started reading aloud. " 'The doctors say I have little time to live.' That's doubtful, I bet. 'Gangrene has taken one leg, and another infection is spreading fast.

Come and visit before it is too late. We have much to discuss.' "

"Gangrene is bad, Miss Lily. My father suffered terrible from that before he died. They cut off his leg that summer, but it spread past that point. Maybe you ought to go."

"What could we possibly have to talk about? She hates me."

"True enough," Etta said bitterly, "but she is family. Remember that."

"Father never wanted me to speak her name."

"The colonel's gone to his reward, miss, and is resting in peace. Along with your mother, God rest her soul."

I didn't reply to that, scanning the rest of the letter to myself. The words on the page blurred—words that cut me deep. Words my aunt knew would summon me to her deathbed. My mother's favorite Scripture verse from Luke, and one word stood out.

'. . . *forgive* . . .'

*'Thou shalt guide me with thy counsel . . .'*
*Psalms 73:24*

# Chapter Two

I heard heavy footsteps below and rushed down the steps to the landing. "Uncle? I'm glad you're home. I need to speak to you."

"It's late, child." He handed Etta his overcoat, hat, gloves and cane and took the candle in its holder from her. "I have work to finish tonight. Perhaps tomorrow."

"This is important and cannot wait."

Uncle Harrison trudged into the parlor's adjoining room he used as an office. A far cry from my father's cozy library with shelves of leather-bound books, comfortable sofa and roll-top desk. This room had stark walls, a tile floor that echoed my footsteps and a leather-topped table with a tooled gold edge he used for a desk. That and one carved chair were the lone furnishings. My uncle cared nothing for comfort. Business was all that mattered to him. And his office lacked a second chair for visitors.

I stood by his desk while he pawed through a stack of papers. Uncle Harrison's thin brown hair had streaks of gray, more than I'd noticed when I first arrived in California. His mustache and beard were peppered as well. He met my gaze, his brown eyes shrewd.

"Well? What cannot wait until breakfast?"

"Why didn't you tell me about Aunt Sylvia?" I asked, fidgeting with my wrapper's belt. "She's no longer recovering at a hospital in San Francisco."

"I know. I hired a private nurse to take care of her. Mrs. Wycliffe is experienced in caring for Sylvia's extensive injuries."

"You said she was dead to you after what happened at Mt. Diablo."

He uncorked the bottle of ink. "Lily, what was I supposed to do? Let her rot in some alley or that ranch house in Vallejo? Besides, she did me a favor."

My curiosity increased. "Oh? What was that?"

"She warned me about keeping that no good Texas gambler away from you."

I gripped the table's edge. "Ace Diamond saved my life—"

"That seems to occur too often," he interrupted. "I understand the incident at the Early Bird was not your fault, of course. But trouble follows you."

"That's not fair. I've been cooped up here for weeks, and you convinced me to come along to tour the mine."

"I regret that whim now."

Whim indeed. I clasped my hands together, not wishing to argue along that futile vein. "So you rented a house for Aunt Sylvia and her nurse? She asked me to visit."

Uncle Harrison sat back, pen in hand, looking puzzled. "Why would she want to see you? The last time I saw her, she heaped abuse on your head and blamed you for her injuries."

My heart sank. Was Aunt Sylvia hoping to harangue me further at her bedside? Why would she have quoted that Scripture in her letter? It didn't make sense. Heavier guilt settled over what I'd fought to suppress since Mt. Diablo.

I spoke up after a lengthy pause. "Like you said, she is family."

"Hmph. Bad enough she begged and pleaded for me to hire a lawyer and write up her will. I had to get N. Adam Woodward of San Francisco," my uncle said bitterly. "He works for a friend. Charged me double because of all the paperwork involved with the quicksilver mine, and that ranch land she owns. Leave her in peace, Lily. Now go on upstairs to bed."

Ignoring his curt dismissal, I picked up the ink-stained sheet of blotting paper. "Did you send the money to Henry Matthews' family today? You promised. Two days ago."

He dipped his pen for fresh ink. "All in good time."

That meant if he remembered, given the rest of his business. His pen scratched on the sheet of vellum before him. I planned on reminding him every day, and visiting Mrs. Matthews myself if need be. Now I paced the dim room, my heels clicking on the tile, impatient while he worked. At last Uncle Harrison glanced up again.

"It's late, you ought to be in bed. By the way, I have tickets for a banquet on Tuesday evening. I've ordered you a new gown to wear," he said, "since you cannot wear black."

"And why not? Especially if Aunt Sylvia is dying."

"She'll outlast the two of us. Trust me on that."

"Who is this nurse taking care of her?" I asked. "And where is this rented house?"

"A few blocks away on D Street, the corner of Fifteenth. Mrs. Wycliffe is a former matron from the Central Pacific Railway Hospital." He resumed writing, his head bent, his voice low. "Sylvia won't be dying any time soon. She loves drama. Remember she was an actress. Or perhaps you forgot that when you left Evanston."

I bit back a scathing retort. My uncle wrote a name on an envelope, blotted it with care and folded the letter inside. Then he sealed it with wax. Whether or not he was right, I felt compelled to visit my aunt. I had informed him, as was my duty.

But I didn't have to take his advice.

The following afternoon I spent extra time preparing for my visit. A severe dark maroon skirt and matching peplum jacket would serve well, with black braid trim. I added a veil over my hat. It shrouded my view of Alkali Flats' affluent neighborhood, an unromantic name for these lovely homes. Etta wished to accompany me, but I refused.

Crossing Eleventh and Twelfth Streets, I nodded to the men who tipped their hats at me and the nursemaids steering gauze-covered baby carriages. Before long I caught sight of a small house swarming with deep green ivy, the sole residence at D and Fifteenth Streets, surrounded by a factory, a warehouse and a millinery shop. Dust rose from the street when a carriage and team passed. My veil didn't help one whit. I sneezed hard and groped for my handkerchief. All efforts to wave away the hazy cloud proved futile.

Perhaps I should have sent a message first. Would Aunt Sylvia be up to company? At my knock, a girl in an apron over her sprigged dress opened the door. She retreated once I gave my name. In the hallway, the heady scent of fresh cut roses, crimson blooms wide open, made me dizzy. Inside the wide parlor doors, two plush armchairs flanked an open space. Draperies shut off most of the sunlight from the double set of windows. A creaking sound caught my attention. Dressed in a starched white apron and black dress, the nurse wheeled a high-backed chair into the parlor. The seated figure hunched further, her head lolling to one side.

"You have a visitor, Mrs. Chester. Sit up, dear," the nurse said and straightened her patient. "I am Mrs. Wycliffe. How kind of you to visit."

"Thank you—"

"We had some nice soup for lunch. Didn't we, dear?"

Her patient didn't respond. Stunned, I inched my way toward the wheelchair and fixed my gaze on Aunt Sylvia. Her hair had been combed back beneath a white cap, and her yellow-toned skin stretched taut over cheekbones and jaw. She wore a deep purple silk wrapper. Fine lace trimmed a heavy cotton nightdress that buttoned to her scrawny neck. A pinkish scar ran from her right temple down over her cheek. She slowly raised her head and squinted.

"Is that you, Willy?"

"No, ma'am, it's not your brother," the nurse said and then rolled the chair closer to the windows. "This is your niece, or so she claims to be."

"Lily? Take off that veil, I can't see you," my aunt said in a wavering voice. "So you did come after all. Willy said you wouldn't bother."

Surprised for the second time, I pushed back the gauzy fabric and stammered out a reply. "What— why would he say that? I do hope you're improving, Aunt Sylvia."

Mrs. Wycliffe brought a lap robe and spread it over her charge's lap. "She doesn't eat very well, but we try."

"Ha. You make the most awful porridge and soup. I'm half-blind, I cannot walk, and I'm close to death's door."

That sounded more like Aunt Sylvia. Her grumbling lacked the sharp edge I'd heard on the train, though. "I hope you recover," I said, although my tone sounded insincere. "I had no idea you were recuperating near Uncle Harrison's residence. He never told me."

She hunched again, but her voice grew stronger. "Sit, child, next to me so I can hear you. I am glad you came. We must discuss something important."

I settled on a curved-back Chippendale. The nurse left us alone, sensing our need for privacy. Aunt Sylvia rubbed her claw-like bony fingers. The knuckles bulged. Her right hand had long thin red scars as well. Guilt stabbed me again.

"My younger brother has been good to me," she said with a long sigh. "I don't deserve this treatment. Not after being a fool and believing my husband's stories. He claimed both my brothers had plotted against me. Perhaps I couldn't face the truth."

I didn't respond. What was the use of digging up old wounds? Father was dead and gone, and nothing could bring him back. Pity filled me. This woman didn't resemble the haughty, striking older actress with the booming voice, who'd burst into my life and followed me across the country. After that two-thousand mile journey, we'd both survived close brushes with death. But Aunt Sylvia's words back in Vallejo still haunted me.

*I deserve it all . . .*

How could I forget her hate? She'd resented her family for disowning her, but she'd also made poor choices. Her brothers turned their backs on her after she'd chosen a career on stage. That was unfair, but she'd coveted my inheritance. The house, the money, the Early Bird gold mine—all of it. Aunt Sylvia's greed had bested her. She hadn't considered the consequences or taken responsibility for her actions. Now she was here, barely alive.

She clutched my hand, her voice a croak. "Forgive me," Aunt Sylvia said. "Rupert was a good man when I married him. It's my fault he turned so greedy. He listened to all my ranting about the Early Bird, and my brothers—I blame myself. Not him."

I fought challenging her on that score. Let her believe what she wished. Everyone grieved in their own way. If she wanted to gloss over her husband's faults, then so be it. My aunt shifted in her chair. I grew more uneasy over witnessing her obvious pain.

"I'm naming you my heir for the quicksilver mine," she said, "since the other partner, John

35

William Parker, is dead. He died—before you arrived here. I'm not sure how, but no matter. I will not allow my brother to profit from it—no, let me finish. There's a coal mine nearby, from what my husband said, and we have shares in that too. The ranch near Walnut Creek comes with it. Don't argue with me. The will's been drawn up already."

"But Uncle Harrison is your brother. Shouldn't he inherit?"

"He has enough money, and too much ambition." She coughed. "I've wronged you, Lily. That's why I've chosen to make up for that."

She gripped the arm rests, her knuckles white. My lingering resentment and anger melted at her suffering. Seeing her like this reminded me of Mother on her deathbed, weak and pale, her hacking cough and fingers clinging to Father's until the end. I shut that memory out. Better to remember Mother's kind face, her laugh merry and soft as a healing balm. Aunt Sylvia was no saint, but who was I to withhold a chance at redemption? I clasped her hand in mine.

"I do forgive you, aunt. I'm so sorry for what happened."

"You're a sweet child. Fetch that glass of water," she said and nodded to the table behind me. "Help me drink."

Her hands shook while I held the glass to her lips. She had trouble swallowing and then choked a little. The parlor's heavy drapes and half-drawn shades smothered the air. Perspiration trickled down my neck. I was stunned by her decision to name me heir to the quicksilver claim and ranch. How could I leave too soon without seeming thankless?

"You must listen. I know how stubborn you are, Lily, but hear me out."

I waited, figuring silence was best. Aunt Sylvia eyed me, as if expecting me to reply. She remained quiet until my patience snapped. "What is it you want to tell me, aunt?"

"Good. You've learned to listen." Aunt Sylvia gestured to the glass again and drank when I held it to her lips. "Your uncle—Willy is my only living brother. He's ambitious. He hopes to win a State Congressional office. Are you aware of this?"

"I know he has political ambitions, but not that high."

She drew a ragged breath. "I'm not sure when the State legislature will meet to appoint that position. But Willy hopes to claim it. He's close friends with John Middleton, who's pulling strings right and left. Calling in favors, anything that will work. He'll ask you to support him, by acting as hostess or accompanying him to dinners and the like. Ah. He's already asked you."

"Yes." I hadn't realized the reason for accompanying him to that ball until now. "Would it hurt to agree to what he asks?"

"Oh, yes. It will."

Puzzled, I stared at her. "Why?"

"You have no knowledge of politics, Lily. In order to receive favors from friends and business associates, Willy must reciprocate in kind. Power, child. My brother craves it like a drunkard. He'll do anything to get it."

"It's true he's changed from what I remember—"

"He needs my quicksilver." Aunt Sylvia leaned closer toward me. "He'll speed up production at the Early Bird with it. Willy believes he will inherit the claim upon my death, so he's preparing to reopen it."

"Oh." I swallowed hard. "I'm hoping Uncle Harrison will see reason—"

"He won't listen to you. He's set in his ways, far more than your father was. Willy wants the quicksilver out of my claim so he can strip the Early Bird to its last bit of gold. No matter what the outcome. His friends are counting on him to succeed, so Willy can help fund their own political campaigns."

I felt so stupid. Since my arrival in California, I didn't understand Uncle Harrison's focus on business and politics. Now this development had shocked me. Aunt Sylvia's gift, if that's what it was, would deepen the rift between me and my uncle. He'd be livid to discover the truth. I hoped he was right, that my aunt would outlive us.

I missed my friends back home, and Ace, Kate

and Charles. Even the visit to the Early Bird, and my near drowning in a mud avalanche, had not shaken me from the numbness that weighed on my soul.

"Are you certain Uncle Harrison wants to be a State Congressman?" I asked.

"Yes." My aunt sounded weary. "He needs votes from the California Assembly in order to get that appointment. But there's more involved than that, Lily."

She drew several deep breaths, clutching the chair's arms, sagging further. I realized the cloudiness in the water had been some kind of medicine. Aunt Sylvia reached for my hand and missed. I caught her bony fingers instead.

"You must return to Evanston. Go home, out of his reach."

"But he's my guardian."

"He will force you to marry, Lily."

That stunned me further, and seemed ludicrous. "How would that help Uncle Harrison's political ambitions?"

"Trust me, it will." She started coughing and wheezing, which brought the nurse hurrying back into the room. "Promise me. Promise to go back to Evanston."

"Now, now, Mrs. Chester," Mrs. Wycliffe scolded, "you're upset. You know what the doctor said about overexertion! How can you ever get well?"

"Wait."

Aunt Sylvia reached for the brass drawer pull on a nearby table. She snatched a scrap of brocade wrapped around an object. A pocket watch glinted bright inside the fabric. My breath stopped. I recognized that piece, minus the heavy gold chain that once fastened it to Father's vest pocket. Tears filled my eyes when she pressed the watch into my hands.

"I'm sorry, Lily. So sorry—"

Aunt Sylvia drooped in her chair, her gray head lolling again to one side. Her eyes closed. The nurse wheeled her backward. "It's long past time for her nap, miss. Thank you for visiting, and please come again. Next week, perhaps."

"Yes, I will," I said, my palms clammy. "Goodbye."

Clutching the brocade, I tucked the heavy gold watch into my skirt pocket. Tears trickled down my cheeks when I fled the empty parlor and rushed through the front door. My heels clattered on the porch steps. Halfway down to the street, I swiped my flowing tears. I'd forgotten how she'd pawed through my things at the ranch and stolen the watch. Aunt Sylvia had not given it to Uncle Harrison after all.

Gratitude filled my heart. It meant far more to me than the quicksilver claim.

Slowing my steps, I thought hard about what my aunt had said. The thought of inheriting that ranch near Walnut Creek turned my stomach. Would I be able to set foot there again? Sleep in that upstairs room or in the same house where I'd been held a prisoner? Could Aunt Sylvia's warnings of a forced marriage be true? It seemed so odd.

My uncle had been so loyal to Father throughout the war. He'd treated me like a daughter in those days, sending gifts and money on occasion, and I'd enjoyed his letters and tales from California. Uncle Harrison had offered Father the chance to form a partnership in the Early Bird. He'd revered my mother. Why did my aunt believe I was in danger from him? Her warning sounded like the ramblings of a dying woman.

Uncle Harrison had undertaken a big role in assuring the State Capitol building would be built in Sacramento. That meant the city would become the shining gem of the state. He loved it and California, too. Father had wanted to help improve Evanston, and his efforts spurred others to work harder. I understood that kind of ambition. But I also knew one thing was certain. No matter how hard my uncle persuaded me, I wasn't going to be forced into marriage.

I would make my own way in life. With or without a husband.

*'A feast is made for laughter,*
*and wine maketh merry:*
*but money answereth all things.'*
*Ecclesiastes 10:19*

# Chapter Three

I accepted my uncle's proffered hand and climbed into the open brougham carriage. Drat this silly evening gown, which required a tighter corset. The dragging train caught on a loose nail head. I ought to have shopped for a simpler gown and one paler in color. Uncle Harrison must have thought I was fifteen and entering society as a debutante, given its exorbitant style. Did he plan to foist me onto Sacramento society as if I was the catch of the season?

"My head is pounding, uncle. Perhaps I ought to stay home—"

"No excuses, Lily. You look wonderful in that dress." He leaned back against the opposite seat. Good thing, since the carriage lurched forward and he would have landed in my lap. "You're young. You ought to enjoy life."

"I plan to, following a proper mourning period."

"It doesn't count tonight," Uncle Harrison said.

"Besides, your father would have wanted you to enjoy this banquet. He's with us now in spirit."

I gave up and drew the white lace shawl around my bare shoulders. The cool breeze of autumn was pleasant. Chicago winds could be brutal this time of year. Etta would be brushing and cleaning my wool suits in preparation for winter by now, if we'd returned home. I would have checked on the gardener while he cut back the rosebushes and spread a thick mulch of dead leaves over the flower beds. Another rush of homesickness brought misty tears to my eyes.

Uncle Harrison's insistence that I attend the banquet tonight soured my mood. At least he'd agreed to compensate Mrs. Matthews, the widow of the man who'd saved my life. I'd sent a letter of gratitude to accompany his bank cheque. She had acknowledged receipt of it with a heartfelt reply. It was little comfort, though, in exchange for her husband's presence.

My uncle frowned. "Cheer up, Lily. Tonight will be special, wait and see."

His impatience didn't help, but I wasn't in the mood to explain my worries. Or my lack of interest in attending a dinner with boring speeches given by his businessmen friends—not my idea of a pleasant evening. The bustled taffeta gown slid against the leather seat. I had to dig the toes of my evening slippers into a crack or end up slithering to the carriage's floor. The bright green ruffled overskirt was trimmed with pointed white lace, puffed behind and on either side over a cream underskirt and festooned with ribbons. A fitted bodice pushed up my bosom to the point of indecency. My cleavage was raised like twin plump feather pillows.

"I've arranged for you to meet someone tonight," my uncle said, his tone clipped. "Señor Santiago's family has ties to old California. His grandparents own a huge ranch in Napa Valley. He will be the perfect suitor for you."

Aunt Sylvia's warning clanged like a bell—bringing on a real headache now. "I am not interested in a suitor, uncle."

"You'll change your mind." He smiled as I clenched my gloved hands into my lap. "Think about what this man could offer you, Lily. What else is there but marriage for a young lady with a formidable dowry?"

"I'll pick my own husband, or remain a spinster."

"You, a spinster? Impossible."

I bit back frustration and focused on the gathering dusk past the window. Why argue with him? Years ago Uncle Harrison would have teased me about my opinions on marriage. Things had changed. He wouldn't indulge me like Father. Sadly, Captain William Harrison Granville was a virtual stranger and so different from the beloved uncle I once knew. He had no interest in my ideas about the Early Bird or my plans for the future.

"Courting with a suitor is impossible. I'm returning home to check on Father's headstone at the cemetery. The inscription must be correct."

"That can wait until next year."

"Don't forget I also plan to visit my friends in San Francisco."

"If I give you permission." He turned to me, his eyes hard and dark. "Remember I need a hostess for the necessary dinner parties this month. You'll meet several friends of mine tonight as well as Señor Santiago. You're lucky to be considered unspoiled, given your brazen behavior with that Texan renegade at Mt. Diablo."

"What? I—"

"Don't try to tell me how innocent it was. I saw for myself," he said as if I hadn't interrupted him. "It's time you were married. To a man of my choice."

His tone made it clear that any argument was futile. My curiosity about Santiago led me to question him. "So where is Napa Valley?"

"It's quite a ways north of Vallejo. There's a branch off the main railroad line."

"I suppose this Señor Santiago is wealthy."

"Of course. He owns several businesses and is very ambitious. I wouldn't consider him a worthy enough prospect for you otherwise."

No doubt he was older and had money to match Uncle Harrison, who placed more value on a bank account than anything else. I disagreed. The man I intended to marry would have character and integrity, a loving heart, and strong faith in God. All traits that meant nothing to my uncle. It rankled that he'd never taken the time to ask how I survived the incident at Mount Diablo. Chilled, I drew my shawl close.

"I thought you liked your new jewelry, Lily."

My gloved fingers touched the lumps that lay hidden beneath the lacy fabric. "Yes, I do. Perhaps you were preoccupied at breakfast with the newspaper and your company reports, and didn't hear me when I thanked you."

He shrugged. I sensed the amber droplets set in gold were mere bribes to guarantee my attendance tonight. Mourning etiquette called for dull black jet jewelry, and very little of it during the second six months.

Uncle Harrison cleared his throat. "Tonight is very important, Lily. That's why I want you to look your best."

"It's just another dinner—"

"This banquet honors the most important men in the state." He straightened his white silk bow tie and smiled. "You'll see these same men once I'm appointed to political office."

His self-satisfaction made me uneasy. The carriage had jostled and swerved on the rough road, but now a sharp jolt shot through my backside. I repressed a complaint. Dusk had deepened and the scaffolding that covered buildings rose like shadowy fingers. Soon after arriving at my uncle's house, I'd heard a horrible flood almost a decade ago led to this new project of raising the street grades and repairing old buildings. Dust from the work hung in the air despite the workers having gone home for the day. I brushed my overskirt and shook the folds.

My uncle perused a small black notebook, his top hat on his lap. He often checked a list of tasks before an event. I noted the gray strands on either side of his head, the freshly trimmed mustache and goatee—a new style for him over the past month—his starched collar, shirt cuffs with their heavy gold stud links, low cut white silk waistcoat and his black cutaway coat. His dark hair and sturdy build reminded me of Father at a younger age, but Uncle Harrison's moody temperament and lack of humor detracted from the memory.

"So you visited your aunt last week, Lily. Against my wishes."

I hesitated. "Yes, I did."

He frowned. "You ought to have steered clear of her—"

"I'm not going to be like you and Father, refusing to have anything to do with her for years. That's why Aunt Sylvia became so bitter."

Uncle Harrison snapped his book shut. "She's still a dangerous woman, a viper of the worst sort. You'll be bitten again, Lily. Mark my words."

I bristled at his unkind words. "Whatever the case, she is a blood relative. Christian charity dictates that we must offer aid and comfort. I will visit again in a few days."

He looked displeased. "I'm paying a fortune for that rented house and nurse. She is enough company for Sylvia. Your duty is done."

"Are you forbidding me to visit her?"

"Yes."

"Why?" I waited but my uncle didn't answer. "Aunt Sylvia did not look well, but she may improve with encouragement and a few visits. That's all I wish to do."

"Remember that as your guardian, you need my permission. Stay away from Sylvia, or I'll move her to a private sanitarium."

Silence reigned. My anger grew, since he had no right to dictate terms of what I did or whom I visited. What about my intention to visit Charles and Kate Mason and the Christian Friends Revival in San Francisco? From the first day I'd set foot in my uncle's house, his wishes and commands were set in stone with no chance of negotiation. He was so unlike Father, who listened and often changed his mind with charm and a little persuasion.

This past month had been frustrating, cooped up with Etta for company. The year stretched before me. I'd become a virtual prisoner. Our carriage joined the line of others ahead of us nearing the Golden Eagle Hotel.

"Uncle, I found an engineer who believes his methods are safer for hydraulic mining. He sent me a report a mining magazine had published—"

"I have no interest in reading it." He fumbled in his inner coat pocket and produced the evening's engraved tickets. "Don't argue. The subject is closed."

The carriage halted. I accepted a hotel porter's help in descending to the street. I had to rearrange my hefty bustle, the train and my shawl. Uncle Harrison smoothed his tails and tie, giving me a moment to tug my long gloves past my elbows. I took his arm, aware that the other arriving guests had to be my uncle's age and older. I doubted if there was anyone near mine. Santiago had to be bald and fat with bad teeth, perhaps as old as forty.

The thought depressed me anew.

We walked behind other couples into the wide elegant hotel, which sprawled over the whole block. Ladies wore the latest fashion hues of bright magenta, violet, russet, deep gold and a turquoise shade of blue. The men sported dark cutaway coats and trousers, plus stiff white shirts and ties. My hairpiece, a single white silk orchid, looked puny compared to the overblown feathery aigrettes or vibrant flower headpieces adorning other women's hair. One lady wore a dress that trailed a chain of roses along her elaborate draped overskirt, with a spray of rosebuds in her coiffure. I wished now I'd shopped for my own gown, opting for a simpler style instead of this childish confection. Even the bright green hue seemed inappropriate.

"This way, sir. Miss."

The waiter made a smart bow and led us into the lavish dining hall. "There'll be at least two hundred guests," Uncle Harrison said close to my ear. "The citizens of Sacramento chose this place. They're honoring several Central Pacific railroad officers, including my friends William Ralston and Collis Huntington."

"What about the workers who died in accidents building the railroad?" I asked. "Don't they deserve any credit for all their hard work?"

"Without the men who believed the railroad could be built, and invested in a huge undertaking, those men wouldn't have had a job."

"But—"

"Enough, Lily. Your ideas are far too liberal for someone your age. I see Mr. Huntington has arrived. Come along so I can introduce you."

My uncle hailed Collis Huntington, who was bald with a graying beard and stern visage. The men shared a common enemy, George Hearst. Huntington bowed over my hand.

"I am honored to meet you, Miss Granville. Please enjoy the banquet."

My uncle whisked me away through the crowd to greet his other friends, but the names and faces blurred together. I focused on the sights and sounds in the hall instead. Evergreen boughs lent their fragrance, dotted with shiny fruit, nuts and pinecones, and creamy silk streamers had been looped between the sprays. Small trees, their branches stripped of foliage, shimmered with squat candles in tiny glass votives. I grew warm from the glittering chandeliers hanging above our heads. I hadn't brought a fan, however.

"I believe congratulations are in order regarding the Early Bird mine, Mr. Granville," one portly, dark-haired gentleman said. "So have you found a cheaper source of quicksilver?"

"I'm working on that, Mr. McKay."

"I know of a claim out in Nevada. Transport might be a problem, however."

Uncle Harrison nodded. "Yes, that would be."

A third man joined them to discuss hydraulic prospects in a different county. While they chatted, I suppressed a yawn of boredom. Mr. Ralston arrived along with another gentleman and a lady, widening the circle. The woman's mauve and black gown looked exotic. A black lace mantilla covered her glossy dark coiffure, and her skin had an olive tone. She spoke to the other man beside her in a low voice tinged with a heavy Spanish accent. I almost didn't recognize Pedro Alvarez due to his cutaway coat, white shirt and tie.

What was he doing here? And who was this woman?

Uncle Harrison tugged me out of my reverie. "My niece, Lily Granville," he said and squeezed my wrist tight. I glanced up at a tall, exceedingly handsome young man with warm chocolate brown eyes. A lock of black hair fell over his high forehead. His teeth flashed dazzling white when he smiled. "May I present Señor Esteban de los Reyes Santiago."

This was Señor Santiago? I stammered a greeting, wishing I'd practiced something to say. Santiago had a light touch when he planted his lips against my glove.

"This is indeed a pleasure." His voice was silky smooth, low and enticing. "Captain Granville failed to inform me of your beauty."

"He failed to inform me of yours, Señor Santiago."

He looked amused. "Wit and charm as well. A winning combination."

Heat flared in my cheeks. I glanced between him and my uncle, aware of the unspoken message being exchanged. *Yours for the asking price.* Santiago was close to the same height as my uncle, and his formal evening clothes emphasized broad shoulders and a narrow waist. He appeared to be twenty-five or six, given the depth of experience I sensed in his manner. His eyes had dipped several times to the amber necklace resting above my cleavage. Esteban de los Reyes Santiago. His name alone spoke of old California's Spanish heritage.

Uncle Harrison introduced the exotic-looking woman as Señora Paloma Díaz, a patron of the arts in Sacramento. "Esteban has a promising future," she said and glanced at Santiago. "My nephew is quite taken by you, Miss Granville. He will make any wife proud."

I gritted my teeth in a frozen smile. Santiago rested his fingertips against my lower back above my bustle, as if signaling possession. That irritated me further.

"And how is the powder business?" Uncle Harrison asked. "San Francisco seems a long way from Napa Valley and your family's ranch."

The young man nodded. "My father prefers I keep new and dangerous enterprises at a distance. But the business is growing quite fast." Santiago favored me with a winning smile. "*Por favor*, Miss Granville—allow me to escort you inside."

Before I could say anything, he whirled me into the dining room toward our seats. My resentment lingered. Why would Uncle Harrison believe I'd accept a match with a stranger? Santiago's good looks and wealth didn't matter. Ace Diamond had won my heart. He'd saved my life. Remembering the sweet kisses we shared on the train and far more passionate ones at Mt. Diablo a month ago sent a shiver through my body. Santiago must have noticed. He drew the lace shawl over my shoulders. His fingers on my bare skin didn't move me at all.

"So your aunt is a patron of the arts," I said for lack of anything better to discuss. He nodded. "Anything in particular, like sculpture?"

"Anything to do with beautifying the city," Santiago said and shielded me from the jostling crowd. "*Tiá* Paloma is raising funds now to furnish the new State Capitol with furniture, a gas chandelier, draperies, oil paintings, even a fountain in the gardens outside."

"An ambitious undertaking."

"Yes. She is passionate about her causes."

Several bells tinkled, signaling others to take their seats. Santiago acted the perfect gentleman, pulling out my tall cushioned chair and standing behind until I was settled. My uncle held the chair for Señora Díaz before he took his own. I didn't recognize anyone else at our banquet table. The silverware, crystal and gold-rimmed ivory china sparkled. Crimson roses overflowed bright silver bowls between vine-covered candelabras. The chair on my left remained empty, however. I glanced around the dining room, wondering who else would join us.

"My new business partner will arrive late. He sent word that we are behind schedule," Santiago said. "Far too zealous about factory safety, in my opinion."

"Given the nature of gunpowder, that might be wise," Uncle Harrison said.

"Indeed. He enjoys constant vigilance."

"So who is this partner?" I asked. "He must know the business well."

"He has far more knowledge about the workings than I do. I arrange all the sales and contact our clients—"

The master of ceremonies pounded a gavel on the nearest table. Edgar Mills, the brother of one of the Bank of California founders, introduced himself before booming out a welcome speech to the honorees. Bored, I glanced at the menu printed on creamy silk vellum. It boasted saddle of venison, ham in champagne sauce, beef tenderloin, turkey, quail and other wild game. Mills rambled on about the history of the Central Pacific railroad while waiters brought out oysters on the half shell. My uncle swallowed both his and mine. I'd never liked them. The turtle soup was divine, though, along with stuffed olives and anchovies.

Uncle Harrison lifted his glass of French wine. "To old friends and new."

Santiago nodded, his warm brown eyes hooded, and clinked his crystal rim against mine. "Are you enjoying yourself, Miss Granville? May I call you Lily?" With a mysterious smile, he leaned closer. "I prefer less formality. Stephan is a pet name my family uses for me. I would be honored if you would call me that as well."

I glanced at my uncle, who seemed entranced by Señora Díaz's charms. He hadn't caught any inkling of Santiago's forward request. So much for help from that quarter.

"Only if I may ask a question."

"Stephan," he said with a smile.

"Stephan. What kind of powder business do you own?"

"A very good question, Lily." Santiago paused. A uniformed waiter poured everyone a glass of white wine and set down plates of chicken salad, jellied ham and pâté de foie gras with an array of crackers. "You've studied a great number of books, from what the Captain has told me. And I hear you're a talented artist."

"You didn't answer my question." I watched him slather several crackers with pâté. He held one out in an attempt to feed me, but I refused it. "Stephan."

"Ah, but I never promised to answer," he said and then popped the hors d'oevres into his mouth. Santiago chuckled at my surprise. He offered me the second cracker he'd prepared. "Why so serious? Tonight is for enjoyment."

"Perhaps you were mistaken about my wit and charm."

Santiago burst out laughing. Uncle Harrison and Señora Díaz exchanged pleased smiles, as if they believed we were cementing a bond leading to marriage. My uncle whispered close to the woman's earlobe. I glimpsed her gloved hand snaking below the table—into his lap. I gulped my wine and set the glass down. Some sloshed over the tablecloth.

"Lily, Lily!" Santiago touched my forearm. "You were so pale earlier this evening. Now your cheeks resemble the dawn's first rosy blush. How I would love to share that moment."

Stunned by his words, I flushed hotter. How could this man be bold enough to hint of the bedroom so soon after our first meeting? No doubt he shared sleepless nights and viewed many dawns with other women. And this was a man my uncle considered a suitable candidate for courtship? Then again, most girls my age would swoon over Esteban de los Reyes Santiago's animal magnetism, handsome face and charming words.

I wasn't that gullible.

"The chandeliers—it's a bit warm in here."

"Ah." Santiago raised an eyebrow. "So, Lily. Your uncle tells me you were almost killed in an accident at the Early Bird mine."

"If he would listen to me about the dangers of hydraulic mining, that accident wouldn't have happened," I said, thankful he'd brought up the subject. "Farmers have been complaining for years that their water sources are full of silt and gravel now."

"Yes, I've heard that myself."

"I've been reading about different mining options—"

"I doubt they'll find any better way to get the gold out fast enough. But I do understand your concerns. It takes far more quicksilver than your uncle expected."

"Oh." So that was why Uncle Harrison wanted Aunt Sylvia's quicksilver claim. "Your powder company must help with mining, too."

"If there's a tunnel to dig, yes, or a mountain to blast away. My factory is the only one in the United States with a patent to produce Mr. Alfred Nobel's Safety Powder." Santiago's pride rang loud and clear. "You ought to consider investing in the company. My partner and I have already made large profits on our first deliveries."

"So what is Safety Powder?" I asked, suspicious now.

"Gunpowder, except shaped into a useful form. Some people call it dynamite—yes, you may have read about the explosions in San Francisco." He laughed at my shock.

"Dynamite is anything but safe, from what I've read."

"Handling it does include an element of danger. We are very careful. Like I said before, my partner is the expert when it comes to safety and production. I'm in charge of sales. Finding buyers is easy given the necessity of some projects."

"I suppose the Central Pacific railroad wouldn't have been built if not for dynamite."

"Very true."

But the dangers and possibilities of explosions far outweighed the benefits. I refused to sink any money into his factory and become an investor. My uncle caught my attention and leaned over the table to speak, his voice low.

"The man at the podium is the ex-Governor of California, Leland Stanford. Now he's the President of the Central Pacific Railroad."

Santiago nudged my elbow. "His wife had a son last year after almost twenty years of marriage. Imagine that."

"Children are a blessing." Señora Díaz smiled, her dark brown eyes sparkling. "I am hoping you have many of your own, Esteban. And soon."

"I hope so too, *Tiá* Paloma," he said and caught my gloved hand in a tight squeeze under the table. I pulled away, incensed. "Did you hear the rumor about the Stanfords, who invited their close friends to dinner last year? One of the servants placed a huge platter on the table. Mr. Stanford lifted the cover to reveal their infant son, surrounded by fresh fruits and nuts."

"That's not a rumor," Uncle Harrison said. "Collis Huntington was there and related the story to me. The Stanfords kept the news secret from everyone until that night. His son will grow up to be as prominent and successful a businessman as his father."

"Oh, Enrique. I have always wanted a child of my own," Señora Díaz said with a deep sigh. "Alas, God never granted me that gift."

"Enrique? Who is she talking about?" I whispered to Santiago.

"Your uncle. I believe Enrique—Henry, in English—is the closest she could come to Harrison. Does he not prefer that name over William, or am I mistaken?"

"Yes. I mean, no—he does prefer using his middle name." Flustered, I changed the subject. "I would love to hear more about your business. Can you explain how this safety powder is produced at the factory?"

He shrugged. "I am not certain. You'll have to ask my business partner." Oblivious of my annoyance, Santiago changed the subject yet again. "Did you know my family is one of the first to settle here in California? My grandfather had a rancho of thousands of acres. It stretched from Sonoma to Napa, in fact."

I pushed my plate aside. "Is that west of here, closer to San Francisco?"

"A bit north and east of that city, yes. And General Mariano Vallejo had a fortified adobe right in Sonoma, in fact. He represented the Mexican government."

"Vallejo." I hadn't known that town was named after a Mexican military general. I ought to have studied California's history over the last month. "I visited the town once. It's on the bay north of San Francisco?"

Santiago raised his wine glass. "Yes. What I'm referring to happened a decade before the town was named after General Vallejo. Spain lost governmental control to Mexico. In order to get land, you had to be Mexican or marry a Mexican citizen. And be a Catholic."

"You're Catholic?"

His eyes widened in surprise to match my own. "Of course, and you will—never mind that now." He gestured to a waiter, who brought fresh glasses and an unopened bottle. Santiago waited for him to pop the cork, sniffed it, and then filled two glasses. "So, Lily. Have you heard of the Bear Flag Revolt?"

"No." I pushed aside the wine he offered. "I'm sorry, but I'm feeling a little light-headed. I've had enough for one night."

Ignoring me, he pressed the rim against my lips until I took a sip. The waiter removed my plate of half-finished chicken salad before I could stop him. The next course was fish, glistening salmon, which I disliked, and sole swimming in a butter sauce flecked with dill and parsley.

"You need to eat more to handle all this wine," Santiago said with a bright smile. "I will tell you the story of the Bear Flag Revolt. General Vallejo was enjoying breakfast at home one day in June of forty-six. A group of rowdy Americans showed up to demand surrender. Mountain men and white settlers, for the most part."

"At his adobe?" I asked.

"Yes, in Sonoma. He wore his finest uniform to entertain them. And then the General decided to join the Americans, much to the Mexican government's dismay. They made a flag and raised it over the fortress. It had the words Republic of California on it and a grizzly bear. To tell you the truth, many people thought the animal looked more like a pig."

Señora Díaz, Uncle Harrison and others laughed at that. I hadn't realized they were listening to Santiago's tale. "So what did Mexico do?" I asked.

"Eh, what's a little land between enemies?" Santiago laughed as well and sloshed more wine into my glass. "Mexico and the United States were fighting over Texas by that time. The Americans jailed General Vallejo. They did not trust him. When Captain Frémont and the Army arrived in California, they took down the flag and raised the Stars and Stripes on the Fourth of July. But the Republic had twenty-six days of glory, Lily!"

Confused, I rubbed the bridge of my nose. "The United States is a republic."

"I meant the Republic of California, free from any government's rule."

"So who was in charge?"

Santiago shrugged. "The old families of California lost power and prestige they once held dear. But most agreed that the United States was far better than Mexico, if they had to choose between two governments." He glanced at Uncle Harrison and his aunt, enmeshed in a private conversation. "*Tiá* Paloma looks happy. She deserves happiness after a tragic life."

"Tragic? Why—"

"*¡Perdóneme,*" he said and rose to his feet. Santiago signaled with one hand—the waiter, perhaps, for more wine. Uncle Harrison had smiled at something Señora Díaz said, his gaze fixed on her. Santiago settled on my right once more.

"What is it?"

"I knew my business partner wouldn't miss dinner."

I twisted in my chair, expecting an older man, and then clutched my necklace in stunned silence. Ace Diamond winked at me and took the seat beside mine. He resembled a gentleman from head to toe in his fitted black cutaway coat and stiff white shirt with studs, and a properly folded white silk bow tie. Clean shaven, with trimmed sideburns near his ears, his glossy dark hair had been slicked back with brilliantine. Even his fingernails had been buffed to a shine.

He still had the pinkish scar on his forehead, though, and the white one from his lower lip to his jaw. My uncle stared at him in shock, but Ace nodded to everyone.

"Evenin', folks. Sorry I'm late."

*'. . . abstain from fleshly lusts,
which war against the soul . . .'*
*1 Peter 2:11*

# Chapter Four

I'd almost forgotten that intriguing jagged pattern in Ace's one eye with its greenish-gold hue, a mismatch to his cornflower blue eye. "Y-you—"

"Didn't think I could cut a swell?" Ace rewarded me with a lopsided grin. "I got my Arkansas toothpick handy, though, in case."

"Toothpick? Oh—" I glimpsed the stiletto's leather handle he'd produced and then stuck back inside his polished boot. "You're not wearing shoes like the other gentlemen."

"Nope. One thing's certain. You're the prettiest I ever seen you, Lily."

My cheeks flushed hot. Santiago looked puzzled. "You know Señorita Granville?"

"Sure thing, from a while back. I know a few gents are gettin' some shut-eye with that windbag at the podium right now."

"Senator Edgerton would not appreciate being called a windbag, Mr. Diamond," Uncle Harrison said coldly. Ace shrugged.

"Any beer left, Santiago?"

"Only the best French wines, my friend." He lifted his glass to me with a sultry smile. "Savor them like the sight of a lovely woman."

I met his gaze. " 'Favor is deceitful and beauty is vain.' "

"Ah, but a favorable beauty is a priceless pearl."

Santiago's infectious laughter brought smiles to everyone surrounding us, except for Uncle Harrison. He leaned back in his chair and stared at Ace. Contempt tinged his words.

"So you're this mysterious business partner."

"You never told me you met Señor Granville," Santiago said while Ace cocked his head, gazing at my uncle. "Or his niece."

"I got Lily here in one piece from Omaha to Sacramento. Saved her life, twice. Thought Captain Granville would appreciate that kind of loyalty."

Scowling, Uncle Harrison whispered something to Señora Díaz. Ace unfolded his napkin and laid it across his lap with practiced ease, then chose the correct fork when the waiter brought his fish and a wine glass. Flustered, I fought to regain my composure. When and where had he learned table manners fit for higher society? How and when had he meet Esteban de los Reyes Santiago? I spent the next few minutes pondering while the waiter brought a variety of dishes—chicken medallions, beef tenderloin and veal, all heavily sauced. We all watched as the man spooned servings onto our plates.

"So how did you meet Mr. Diamond?" I asked during a lull between speakers.

"Over a game of poker." Santiago savored a bite of tender beef. "I admired his skill of knowing when to risk and when to play safe. *Que me intrigó*."

"I beg your pardon?"

"He was intrigued," Ace translated. "*Mejor palo para Inglés, mi amigo*."

"Of course." Santiago held up his wine glass. "To *Inglés*."

I blinked. "You met over a card game."

"Yes, and I invited him to Napa and then to San Francisco. I have to say, Ace is a fast learner. He also learned fast when it came to business dealings and handling clients. I'm lucky he has experience in dealing with safety powder, which I do not."

"Oh?" I turned in my seat. "When did you learn that, Mr. Diamond?"

Ace raised an eyebrow. "I ain't no chemist, Lily. But I helped one back in Missouri, mixing up some nitro for a project he had in mind. It's dangerous work. Near blew myself to bits once. Let me tell you, I sure learned that lesson fast."

"This man saved my company." Santiago reached behind me to give Ace's shoulder a playful squeeze. "We had some trouble with our employees at the time, since they had gotten careless with storage. My partner taught them proper techniques. He also had a good amount of cash to invest. He risked his fortune in a poker game. Double or nothing."

"Double or nothing?" I glared at Ace. His face beet red, he gulped wine and then swiped his mouth with his napkin. "And then you invested all of what you won in a dynamite factory. Why does that sound crazy, Mr. Diamond?"

"It's a good investment." Santiago beamed a flashy smile. "In less than one month, he's become as knowledgeable about running a business as any man I have known. *Se encontrará con mucho éxito.*"

I turned to Ace, who didn't get a chance to translate before my uncle addressed Santiago. "Benjamin Franklin once said, 'If you would know the value of money, try to borrow some.' You ought to have come to me when you needed cash."

His face flushed dark. "Forgive me, Captain Granville, but you mentioned several times that you prefer less dangerous investments."

"I'd never risk money in that type of business, no. But I would have loaned you money, no questions asked. You ought to know the reason why."

Santiago fell silent under my uncle's disapproval. Other waiters brought out the game course with duck, veal, quail and sweetbreads. I adored quail, but the tender meat didn't satisfy me. All my attention focused on Santiago's questions to Uncle Harrison about hydraulic mining and the need for quicksilver—they avoided discussing safety powder. Stephan must have picked up on the animosity between his partner and my uncle. When the topic of saltpeter came up, all three men exchanged opinions about chemicals and sulfur. None of it meant anything to me. My ears perked up when I heard something about nitroglycerin.

"—and it soaks up three parts nitro. Then we mold the clay into sticks," Ace said. "Once it's wrapped in paper, the product is very stable. Pure nitro will explode if you look at it wrong, or rattle it even a little. But the clay don't allow that."

"What about storage? It must degrade with age, like the canisters did," my uncle said wryly. "They leaked. That's why they exploded on the San Francisco dock."

"Not a chance with the clay."

Ace rattled off measurements and a list of suppliers, but stopped when Uncle Harrison's fork clattered loud on the delicate china. I pressed a hand against my thumping heart.

"Did you bribe San Francisco's city commissioners to approve your business? Or don't they know you're manufacturing a volatile product?"

"There was no need for bribes," Santiago said in a smooth voice. My uncle did not look satisfied by that answer. "There is far less risk of danger out at Rock Canyon."

"But people live in the area," I said. "Friends of mine."

"Our factory is sheltered. Far away from residents to the north."

Ace grinned. "We're gettin' orders from all over the country. Companies are chomping at the bit to get our dynamite, fast as they can."

"I suppose you'll do what you think is best, Santiago," my uncle said, "but I cannot approve of this dangerous business."

He leaned to hear something Señora Díaz whispered in his ear. The waiter brought the main course—succulent ribs of beef, ham in champagne sauce and stuffed turkey. Ace and Santiago both stuffed themselves. I picked at my plate. Señora Díaz didn't touch hers, although she accepted another glass of wine. Ace finished in record time and then wiped his mouth, while Santiago ate slowly. He dabbed his lips with the napkin and smiled.

"Are you not hungry, Lily?"

"May I have your attention, everyone?" Uncle Harrison had risen from his chair and raised his wine glass. "I would like to announce the engagement of my niece, Lily Rose Delano Granville, to Esteban de los Reyes Santiago—"

I choked on a sip of water from my goblet. Santiago patted my back. "Careful, Lily. All this excitement has been too much for you."

"—and may they enjoy health, wealth and happiness as man and wife."

"Together, they represent old and new California," Señora Díaz said, her eyes shining. "They will unite to bring wonderful changes to our community."

"My beautiful, intelligent future bride," Santiago murmured and lowered his mouth to mine. I failed to dodge his kiss. "Why so shy? Later we'll have more time alone."

He released me and sat back. My stomach clenched, seeing Ace's jealousy and cold fury. Shocked, angry as well, my cheeks flaming, I ignored the clapping all around us and offers of congratulations. How could my uncle do this to me? Aunt Sylvia had been right after all. Santiago must have been aware of my uncle's plan and kept me braced against him. Wine glass in hand, Ace stood and drained the blood red liquid.

"*Felicitaciones*. See you at the factory, *amigo*."

He spat that last word and stalked off in disgust. I half-rose from my seat, desperate to go after him and explain, that Santiago's forced kiss and embrace meant nothing. My so-called fiancé tugged me back into the circle of his arms.

"What has upset you, *mi querida*? We shall be married by early December," he said with a nod to my uncle. "I hope to have a son by next Christmas."

How dare he assume that I'd agree to an arranged marriage? I had no intention of becoming any man's broodmare. Several bells tinkled to announce the dessert course. I broke Santiago's hold and rose, unsteady on my feet.

"If you'll excuse me—"

"We are not finished celebrating, Lily." My uncle signaled Santiago, who pulled me back into my chair. "Your engagement is a joyous occasion."

"Later this week we'll sit for a formal portrait." The young man planted a hot kiss below my ear. "I am looking forward to that."

"And I am planning to visit friends," I said, fuming, but kept my voice low, "so that's not possible. I refuse to be a pawn in my uncle's schemes."

"He assured me you were eager to wed."

"He was wrong."

Santiago clasped my hands between his own. "Then I shall have to convince you to marry. I am quite taken with you, Lily."

Señora Díaz rapped the table with her fan. "Such a wonderful couple you make. I wish you both happiness, good fortune and children to bless your days together."

"Ah, *Tiá* Paloma! You have been like a mother to me."

"And you are like a son to me, Esteban." She

beamed at him. "Lily will make a beautiful bride. Where is the ring I helped you choose for this occasion?"

He fumbled in his pocket. Santiago peeled off my left glove before I could protest and then jammed a tight gold circle onto my first finger. He held out my hand for her approval. A large centered ruby winked in the light, surrounded by alternating pale green peridot gems and blue sapphires. The filigree gold setting reminded me of a railroad track with the stones caught between each bar. I stared at the ring on my finger, repelled by its gaudiness. My attempts to twist it free failed. It wouldn't budge.

"Don't you like it, *mi querida*?"

"Of course she does." Uncle Harrison leaned down to plant a kiss on my right cheek. "Lily has caught the most eligible bachelor in Sacramento."

Hemmed between them, I sagged in my chair. The waiters brought a variety of desserts, Spanish sherry and coffee. Many of the guests had already departed for home. Would Ace ever believe I had nothing to do with this awful announcement? He'd acted as if I betrayed him. Ever since he vowed to become worthy in my uncle's eyes, I imagined how hard he worked. Learning social manners, and then investing all his money into a booming business with hopes of quick success —Ace had risked everything.

All for naught.

Uncle Harrison would never accept any man but Stephan as my husband. How could I escape this unwanted fate? I toyed with my slice of chocolate gateaux, wishing I'd listened to my aunt and returned to Evanston. Santiago enjoyed plum pudding while the pyramid of ice cream in the table's center melted in the candelabras' heat.

The minute my uncle led Señora Díaz toward the hotel's lobby, Santiago pulled me to my feet. "The night is young." He led me out to follow them. "Your uncle reserved a table for us at the Ebner Hotel. For a more intimate engagement party."

"But it's late—"

"We must attend. All my friends are expecting us."

On the street, Santiago stuck two fingers in his mouth and whistled shrilly. A team of black horses drew a carriage forward. After a quick word to the driver, he handed me into the conveyance and then settled on the seat opposite. The horses' hooves clopped on the street while we headed toward the river. A wide yawn escaped me before I could cover my mouth.

"It's been an exciting evening." Santiago adjusted my shawl. I slid out of reach before his fingers brushed my bosom. "So shy, but I shall break you of that habit. The Captain told me that he'd forbidden you from seeing a man you'd met on the train, Lily. I had no idea Ace Diamond was that man until tonight."

"My uncle has no right to dictate—"

"Yes, he does. He is your guardian until you come of age or marry. He also told me how stubborn you could be. No matter. You will come to accept our plans."

That patronizing smile topped everything that had had happened during this nightmare. "You're wrong, Stephan. My uncle wants to use me. Buying votes—"

"Who said anything about votes?" Santiago eyed me, a sly grin on his face. "We will grow in love together, if that's what is worrying you. My parents and *Tiá* Paloma both had arranged marriages. They were very happy for years."

"We're complete strangers," I said. "We just met tonight."

"Your uncle told me everything I need to know about you. As my aunt said, we will unite old and new Sacramento and use our combined wealth to help the city achieve new prosperity." He held up his hand. "No more arguments, *mi querida*. Our friends await inside, and will wish us good fortune tonight."

The carriage jolted to a stop. His friends and Uncle Harrison's perhaps, but not mine. Stephan helped me down from the carriage. I flinched when he kissed my gloved hand and then tucked it into the crook of his elbow.

"What does *mi querida* mean?"

"Sweetheart, darling. Whichever you prefer."

He flashed that dazzling smile, but it lacked warmth now. Lanterns glowed on a passing steamship that surged along the river's current. What if Ace had booked passage on it back to San Francisco? Or perhaps he'd taken the train. He'd looked so different, so handsome, far less boyish, but with that same intriguing hint of danger that I remembered from our first meeting. My heart ached. Jesse Diamond, whose kisses had stirred me into matching passion. I yearned to be safe within his arms again.

Santiago drew me inside the three-story narrow hotel, which was smaller than the Golden Eagle but of similar quarried stone. Uncle Harrison stood in the lobby, pocket watch in hand.

"Come along, you two lovebirds. I was beginning to worry."

Lovebirds? That angered me more than this ridiculous notion of an arranged marriage. "Uncle, I must speak to you in private," I said but he held up a hand.

"No time for that, Lily. You ought to know what's expected of you." He thrust us both in front of him. "Smile. Remember that you're practically married."

One arm tight around my waist, Santiago drew me forward. I caught the stubborn set of his jaw. If I caused a scene, I'd pay for it later—from both him and my uncle. Other hotel guests glanced at us, so I surrendered. For the moment, since I'd had too much wine, not enough to eat, and I was exhausted. Like a broken branch floating down a swollen creek, I walked in a stupor. The laughter of people gathered for late evening supper parties in the dining room buzzed in my ears. Santiago stopped at one round table and introduced me to everyone.

I recognized one man. Pedro Alvarez bowed over my hand. *"Mis felicitaciones a los dos,* Señorita Granville."

"Señor Alvarez is another successful business-man in Napa, Lily. And in San Francisco," Santiago said. "He has also invested in the dynamite factory. In fact, Señor Alvarez was one of the first men who believed in my idea and supported me."

The gentleman nodded. "When a difficult task lies ahead, one must do it no matter what every-one else believes."

*"¡Gracias,* Señor Alvarez. This is Mr. James McKay, another investor in the Colossus Safety Powder Works. He's helped furnish supplies for our production. Mr. McKay owns a newspaper, the *California Enquirer.*"

McKay bowed over my hand, his gaze fixed on my bosom. I drew my shawl closer when he gripped my fingers far too long for social convention. I cringed at the smell of whiskey on the large man's breath. He winked.

"You're a lucky man, Santiago. She's well worthy of Captain Granville's tales."

"What tales?"

They both ignored me and headed to a corner table. Señora Díaz and my uncle waited with several other couples. I lost track of all the names and faces, my eyelids heavy and my mind fuzzier after Santiago forced champagne on me. Plates of food appeared, more questions flew, but very little registered in my brain. Except James McKay's drunken leering, which disgusted me, along with his puffy face and twitching fingers. My uncle's self-satisfaction was annoying. But Santiago's smoky glances alarmed me most of all.

I half listened to more toasts of our upcoming wedding. My face burned hotter after each sip of champagne. I had no interest in eating, since my head pounded, but Santiago held out a piece of rare beef that trickled blood. The sight sickened me. I pushed his arm away, which knocked over my second full glass of champagne.

Uncle Harrison and Señora Díaz jumped to their feet. The liquid had stained her mauve gown. "I'm sorry." I wavered on my feet, dizzy. "Oh, my head."

She mopped the fabric with a napkin, her fury clear. "No matter, Señorita. Perhaps you ought to escort your fiancée home, Stephan."

Santiago embraced me. "Yes. As your uncle said, we are practically married—"

"No." Uncle Harrison clasped my elbow in a tight grip. "It's been too long of an evening for my niece. Please continue the celebration."

Santiago trailed us to the lobby. "I will dream of you every night," he said, his mouth close to my ear, "until we share our marriage bed."

"I'm not—"

"Oh, but you will. I shall steal you away if I must."

He swirled me around in waltz-like fashion. I stumbled when he released me into my uncle's arms, or had I imagined that? The entire scene seemed surreal. I found myself in the carriage, slumped against the seat, and fought a wave of nausea when the wheels rattled over the cobblestones. I'd sipped all the various wines and had not eaten enough at the banquet. My head throbbed, and the champagne had not helped.

"—within the month. Lily, are you even listening?"

"What?" I heard my slurred, thick words and tried to shake the stupor free. I failed. "I'm not feeling very well. Oh, stop. Please. I'm going to be sick."

He rapped on the ceiling with his cane. Before the carriage halted, I leaned over the open window and emptied my stomach. Uncle Harrison handed me a clean handkerchief when I fell back against the opposite seat.

"Once we're home, your maid can assist you."

He rapped again and the carriage jolted forward. "I received bad news earlier. I didn't want to tell you until after the banquet and the party tonight at the Ebner. My sister passed away last night."

"Aunt Sylvia?"

I lurched toward the window again and heaved, but nothing came up from my tortured stomach. My uncle handed me a second linen square. I whispered my thanks.

"Perhaps you're not used to a variety of wine."

I didn't answer. Closing my eyes, I was grateful to escape my uncle's circle of friends. My uncle muttered several choice words about Ace, dynamite and his partnership with Santiago. I dozed off and on. At last we arrived home. Uncle Harrison supported my stumbling gait up to the house and into Etta's arms.

"What happened, sir? Is Miss Granville ill?"

"Too much wine. Can you walk upstairs, Lily?" His words buzzed in my head. The next thing I knew, my uncle laid me on the bed and turned to Etta. "I've arranged everything for my sister's funeral. Neither of us will attend, however."

"I will be there." I struggled to get the words out, although they garbled together and didn't sound right in my ears. I repeated myself, focused on speaking clearly. "I must attend, uncle. I insist."

"Not if you're ill."

"I'll be fine. Tomorrow." I doubted that, since

my head ached as if hammers pounded on every side. "But I will not marry Santiago—"

"I refuse to hear any of this. You will marry him, because he's well-educated, wealthy and family-oriented. Your father would have approved of this man for you, I'm sure of it. Not an unschooled ex-Confederate Rebel." Uncle Harrison shook a finger at me. "If you continue to argue the point, you can remain in seclusion here until you come to your senses."

I closed my eyes, too overwhelmed to listen to his threats. Once he left my room, Etta loosened my corset strings. I breathed deep for the first time that night. She removed my opera gloves and gasped at the ring shimmering in the gaslight.

"What happened, miss? Never mind, you can tell me tomorrow."

"Yes. Please." I sat up, breathing easier, but blinked. My vision didn't clear. "I'm too tired and dizzy."

Etta clucked as she untied my bustle. "All that rich food."

"No."

"Then what?"

"Pressure, I suppose."

Pressure to accept a man like Esteban de los Reyes Santiago. I sagged against the pillow, sick at the thought of what my uncle would do after learning about Aunt Sylvia's will. It might give him further incentive to force this marriage, making sure Santiago controlled any decisions as my husband. Anything to boost production for the Early Bird mine, and profits.

I tugged and pulled at the tight ring until my finger throbbed. At last I managed to free myself from the ring, which flew across the room. It clattered against the wall. Etta searched it out and then set the bauble on my dressing table. It meant nothing to me. An empty promise, from a man who no doubt cared more about business and pleasure than anything else. Santiago's confidence and charm couldn't mask his incredible arrogance and pride. And a stubborn streak that would best my own. Clearly I'd never be considered important. A mere collectible, a woman fit to display his burgeoning wealth with fine silks and jewelry—and produce sons.

Somehow I had to escape this dreadful noose before it was too late.

*'But when they persecute you in this city,*
*flee ye into another . . .'*
Matthew 10:23

# Chapter Five

Two days later, I'd recovered and stood by my uncle's side for Sylvia Granville Chester's burial. A few business friends of Uncle Harrison attended the hurried funeral and then took a horsecar to lunch. I returned from the cemetery on Tenth and J Streets with dread. I knew I'd soon face wrath. But my uncle hadn't mentioned anything about the will. Perhaps he didn't know that I'd inherited the quicksilver mine. I yearned to escape this mess.

I toyed with the cold supper Etta prepared. Uncle Harrison ate with a hearty appetite and didn't notice my lack of one. He patted his mouth with his napkin.

"Your portrait sitting with Santiago will be next week, Lily. You can wear the amber jewelry I gave you. Where is your engagement ring?"

"I'm in double mourning for Father and Aunt Sylvia." I set down my fork. "I'm not wearing any jewelry, as you can see."

"Your grief fails to convince me," he said wryly.

"She is family."

My uncle drummed his fingers on the polished dining room table. "Sylvia dug her own grave, as far as I'm concerned. She deserved her pain and suffering."

"She deserves to be mourned by someone. She had no friends left."

"Not surprising, the way she treated them."

What could I say to that? He sounded as heartless as my aunt back at Walnut Creek. "Everyone deserves a chance for redemption—"

"Sylvia was too far gone." He pushed his plate away. His chair screeched along the floor tiles when he rose to his feet. "She blamed us both for her husband's death. See this?"

He twisted his head and pointed to a long red weal along his neck, half-hidden by his stiff shirt collar. "I never noticed before," I said. "What happened?"

"She clawed me during my last visit. Sylvia disagreed about my plan to serve in public office. It's jealousy on her part, since her husband wanted everything I have and more. Friends in high places, money, influence. I've worked hard. I'll get that appointment before the year is out. But I need your help achieving it, Lily."

I cleared my throat. "What kind of help could I give you?"

"By acting as my hostess on certain occasions until your marriage."

"Then I shall visit my friends in San Francisco this weekend. I'll never get another opportunity if I postpone it. Etta and I will leave tomorrow morning."

Uncle Harrison didn't look pleased. "It's not safe to travel without an escort. I cannot spare the time now from my business affairs, Lily."

"We'll be perfectly safe on the train."

"I suppose that's true since it's a short trip." He picked up his china cup and saucer. "But two women, going alone into a lawless and rowdy town like San Francisco?"

"Remember Charles Mason will meet us, uncle—"

"You don't understand how dangerous it is."

"We'll take all precaution." I stood, although I had to crane my neck to meet his stern gaze. "Can you recommend a hotel in the city?"

"I'll wire the Occidental Hotel on Montgomery Street. A friend of mine owns it. He'll put you and your friends in comfortable rooms for the weekend. The one clerk I can spare from the office is Daniel Johnson, and he'll keep you out of the city's worst areas."

"I've read about the Barbary Coast—"

"Don't you dare visit there out of curiosity, even in broad daylight. One man, or half a dozen for that matter, would never be able to keep you out of trouble if you stray."

"All right," I said and kissed his cheek.

"I'll have Johnson meet you at the train station tomorrow morning." Uncle Harrison led me to the stairs. "I'm meeting the lawyers tomorrow afternoon about Sylvia's will, although that won't concern you. Be back on Sunday night."

Upstairs in my room, I surveyed my wardrobe. Thank heavens Uncle Harrison wouldn't learn the will's details until after my departure tomorrow. And that Etta agreed to accompany me to San Francisco. I quickly stuffed whatever bills and coins I had left from my trip west into my leather pocketbook. Then I packed a larger valise, brown leather with multiple straps, with extra clothing and undergarments, stockings and shoes, a nightdress, my riding skirt and boots. I spent time considering which traveling suit and hat to wear.

The frame holding my parents' photograph still needed to be replaced. I left it with the daguerreotype in the chest of drawers. My father's gold watch, wrapped in the brocade square, fit into my suit's pocket. Guilt over Aunt Sylvia's death had faded to regret. I ought to have read her a few comforting verses from the Bible during my visit. Anything to ease her pain. I'd been so shocked to see her in that condition. At least now she was free from suffering.

I tossed and turned that night, unable to sleep. Nightmares haunted me. I'd experienced an earthquake the week after I'd arrived in California, the furnishings, the floor and walls all trembling after several shocks. I'd never felt anything like it. Tonight a heavy rain drummed on the roof and windows. At last I dozed off and dreamt I'd lost something near the bluff at Mt. Diablo. I kept wandering the ravines and gullies, unable to remember what I misplaced. Ace's voice called to me from a distance. Panicked, I woke to choking fear. I rolled over and punched my pillow in frustration.

Bright moonlight streamed through the sheer curtains. For all I knew, Ace may have severed his partnership in the dynamite factory. But what if he'd left California?

Over the next hour, I dozed off and on. Exhausted, I rose from my bed. After I washed, dressed and pinned up my hair, I was grateful that the switch added fullness to the curls in back. At the last minute, I snatched up a hat with a spray of pink rosebuds and smoothed the gray silk lapels of my navy blue suit. It fit looser, which meant I'd been moping in this house far too long. Etta knocked on my door at five o'clock, her plain black suit adorned with the gold brooch my mother had given her long ago. Seeing it pleased me. After a quick breakfast of eggs, bacon and toast, we hurried outside. Thank goodness Uncle Harrison never rose this early.

"At least the Captain didn't change his mind at the last minute." Etta shooed me along. "This fog is so thick. Oh, there's an omnibus—hurry or we'll miss it."

We rushed to the corner without mishap until I tripped on a tree root. She caught me in time and helped me board the streetcar. I relaxed. "I'm ready for an adventure—"

"Spattered with mud?" Etta clucked her tongue and sat beside me. "We'll be caked from head to foot before we leave the city."

"I've heard they're considering plans for a horseless railway." The gentleman across the aisle tapped a finger on the seat back. "Although it might be a bit of work to lay rails for it. Good thing it's not as hilly here as in San Francisco, though."

Those hills—my excitement grew at seeing the city at last. I remembered Uncle Harrison talking about the various communities clinging to the slopes of Russian and Telegraph hills. Of how Rincon hill was being cut through and leveled, according to his friends. By the time we'd reached the train station near Sacramento's docks, my sense of adventure overcame any dread. A shrill whistle sounded, signaling the crowd to board. I'd soon be back on a train again and heading west. That thrilled me. Smiling, I hurried to the telegraph window.

Etta fidgeted. "Who is this Mr. Johnson your uncle said would escort us? I expected him to be here waiting."

I finished the message to Kate and handed the wire fee to the clerk behind the window grille.

"If he doesn't show up, we'll go without him."

She didn't look pleased. "What could I do to help protect you, miss?"

"Nothing more than what I can do for myself." I didn't want to alarm her by showing the derringer I'd bought and practiced with in secret during my uncle's absences. "Don't worry, we'll be fine. Let's get in line at the other window."

We joined the other passengers, few in number due to the early hour, waiting to buy tickets. Several wrens chased each other, flitting beneath the depot's open side. The white bank of clouds hid the sun and a stiff breeze chilled me.

"Miss Granville?"

I twisted to see a young man holding his derby. "Yes?"

"Good thing the Captain showed me a photograph of you. I'm Daniel Johnson." He was young, and so thin his suit hung loose on his lanky frame, with a shadow of fair hair on his upper lip. He clapped his bowler back on his pale blond head and retrieved tickets from his pocket. "I've already bought first class seats for us."

"Do you have that photograph?" I asked, eyeing him in feigned suspicion. Surprised, Johnson shook his head. "I've never seen you at my uncle's office. How do I know you work as a clerk for him?"

"Uh, well. I-I do," Johnson said, stammering. "For the past six months—"

"What regiment was my uncle in during the War?"

"I don't know, but Captain Granville fought at Shiloh."

"Was he wounded?"

"No, but the Colonel was—your father."

"All right then. I suppose you are who you say you are."

Johnson looked sheepish. "He told me one thing. I'm to keep an eye out for a Mr. Ace Diamond. Dark-haired, same height as me. Dangerous, too."

"I don't expect to see Mr. Diamond on our trip to San Francisco."

"Oh." He sounded disappointed and shifted from one foot to the other. "The dynamite factory is close to Rock Canyon, where the Masons live."

I filed that information away. Perhaps I'd get a chance to meet Ace and explain what happened at the banquet. I hoped Kate would want me to see her home instead of staying in the city during the visit. Meanwhile, Johnson might have information about my uncle's future plans. We'd have plenty of time to chat during the train ride. The young man led the way to seats in first class and stored our valises before settling across from us. Relief flooded my heart at the departing whistle. The train jolted twice and then slowly rolled out of the city.

Etta took out her knitting and settled against

the window. I opened a book but didn't bother to read. Chatter between passengers grew louder than the noisy wheels. The train crossed a bridge that spanned the American River, leaving Sacramento behind, and then headed west between harvest-rich farmland. I studied Daniel Johnson, who didn't look experienced to handle any threatening situation. Did he know Esteban de los Reyes Santiago?

It wouldn't hurt to ask.

"So, Mr. Johnson, you've worked six months in my uncle's office?"

"Yes." His cheeks flushed beet red. "I clerked for Mr. Sawyer, an attorney next door to your uncle's office, before that. For a year."

"Were you born here in California?"

"Yes, in Napa Valley."

"Then you must know the Santiago family," I said with a smile. "I met Esteban, a friend of my uncle's. I'm curious about him."

Daniel Johnson proved to be a mine of information about my fiancé and many Napa Valley families. According to him, Juan José Santiago owned a huge ranch for his winery, plus a grist mill and a sawmill via marriage to Elena de los Reyes. Their only child, Esteban, had been groomed to manage the various businesses. He'd rebelled against staying put in Napa Valley, however, and ignored his father's unhappiness about the Safety Powder factory. No wonder

Stephan needed Ace's money to keep the business afloat, if his father didn't support him with any financial investment.

"Rumor has it," Johnson said in a conspiratorial whisper, "that after fifteen years of marriage, Señora Santiago was barren. All of a sudden, a baby appears, a son! It's rumored Santiago's mistress provided him with an heir. But his wife claimed the boy as her own. Esteban does resemble his father."

How curious that Santiago related the story about Leland Stanford's infant son the night of the banquet, when his parents had been childless. "How old is he? Twenty-four or five?"

"Twenty-nine."

My heart sank. Good heavens, almost a decade older. And due to his superior attitude, my days would be forever ruled by the man's whims. No doubt I'd be criticized about my daily habits, my clothing, social manners and how to raise children. Heaven help me if I produced any daughters. And sons would end up exactly like him. Stephan would want half a dozen, one to handle each of the family businesses—including the dynamite factory.

I shuddered at the thought. "What about his aunt?"

Daniel Johnson blinked. "Uh, his aunt?"

"Yes, Señora Paloma Díaz. A patron of the arts, I believe."

"Ah. She has raises money through her charity balls and fundraising dinners. Your uncle has helped when she hosted the events."

"Oh." I wondered why my uncle needed me to act as his hostess when Señora Díaz was capable of it. Unless it was an excuse to ensure my return. "She's a widow?"

"Yes, indeed." He stuck a finger into his collar, wiggling, as if gaining time before he answered. "Her late husband was very wealthy."

Johnson avoided my gaze. He refused to discuss the man further despite my pressuring questions. Several passengers disembarked at Davisville, a small farming village. The chatter of newcomers who claimed nearby seats didn't die down until well after the train resumed its chugging along the track. Sparks and a cloud of dust invaded the car when someone opened a window, prompting complaints. Thankfully, the gentleman shut it again.

I tapped the young man's knee with my book to gain his attention. "How do you know about the Santiago family?"

"I grew up near their ranch," Johnson said and relaxed against the plush high-backed seat. "George Yount was the first white man there and planted grape vines. My father managed his orchard for years until Yount died, and now manages Señor Santiago's vineyard. My mother is a dressmaker. Both Señora Santiago and

Señora Díaz often requested her services."

"How long ago was Señora Díaz widowed?"

"A decade. Maybe more."

That deepened my curiosity. "When did she meet my uncle?"

"Several years ago, I believe." He steered the subject to my uncle's political hopes. "Sacramento's district congressman is ill, so Captain Granville hopes to be appointed as his replacement. He'll serve in the California State House until the next term election. Then he'll run for a Congressional House seat in Washington after a few years of experience. He's good friends with California's Governor Haight, so that will help."

I guessed Collis Huntington, Leland Stanford plus many other wealthy men I'd met at that banquet would contribute money to my uncle's political campaigns. Señora Díaz shared the same friends. She was no doubt the reason my uncle spent days away from home. Their risqué behavior at the banquet surprised me, though. Then again, no one else had paid attention. Were they having an affair? Perhaps that's why Johnson seemed uneasy about Señora Díaz.

Oh yes. Everything was much clearer.

I shifted in my seat. The train track ran southwest to avoid the higher hills extending north of Vacaville. We had a longer stop in town while passengers disembarked. Johnson filled me in on the history of the California Pacific Railroad, an extension line of the Central Pacific. I'd taken this railroad when I first arrived to meet my uncle, lured by my aunt and poor Charles, into worse danger. But I shoved that bad memory aside.

"Once we arrive in Vallejo, a steamship ferry will take us straight to the San Francisco docks. Quite convenient."

"So there is no actual transcontinental railroad, from New York to San Francisco," Etta said, her knitting needles clacking. She sounded smug.

"Well—er, no." Johnson glanced at me. "But they plan to extend the Western Railroad line from San Jose up to 'Frisco in a year or two."

"Hmph. Promises are often forgotten."

I hid a smile. "It's a wonder anyone can travel so far between the two coasts. I'm not complaining, given the six months it took my uncle to reach California."

"Other railroad lines are being built in the north and southwest," Johnson said, "although it's not safe yet. Apaches are bad in New Mexico and Arizona."

"And perhaps in Texas?" Etta's teasing tone was aimed at me. "I wouldn't know, of course."

She resumed knitting. My cheeks flushed hot, but Johnson didn't seem to notice. He rose to his feet. "Please excuse me, ladies."

He hurried to the men's washroom. Etta lowered

her knitting needles, her gaze shrewd. "He knows a lot more about that Señora Díaz than he told you."

"Perhaps."

Once the young man returned, I pretended to read my book. Etta had laid down her knitting and dozed, slumped against the window. A strand of gray hair had escaped her usual neat bun in back. With the worry lines of her face relaxed, she looked younger—I'd forgotten she was my mother's age, forty or so. I appreciated her loyalty, and hoped she realized how much that meant to me.

Daniel Johnson's restlessness increased. I waited a while longer while he examined his fingernails, straightened his tie, adjusted his collar and shifted positions. I met his bored gaze.

"Aren't you accustomed to periods of inactivity?" I asked. "As a clerk."

"Not really. Your uncle sends me to convey messages several times a day to his colleagues. I also run any errands he needs doing, for any reason. I visit the telegraph office at least twice every day, and the State Capitol."

"That's where Señora Díaz is in charge of coordinating the sculpture and paintings to decorate various rooms."

"Yes, I believe so."

I decided to ask outright. "What is it that bothers you about Señora Díaz? Is there something about her that makes you uncomfortable?"

Johnson cleared his throat. "Uh—"

"Perhaps some gossip about her past? I'm very worried about my uncle, and would hate for anything to ruin his chances for that political appointment."

He glanced around at the other passengers and leaned forward, his voice low. "Did you know Señora Díaz's husband died under—suspicious circumstances?"

Etta nudged me with her knee. I'd suspected she wasn't asleep but continued the pretense. "Suspicious in what way, Mr. Johnson?" I kept my voice to a whisper.

"Poisoned, so they say. No doctor was called, and he hadn't been sick a day in his life. Benito Clemente Díaz had many enemies. His wife buried him and vowed revenge."

"Against whom, I wonder."

Johnson shrugged. "It seemed odd that Pedro Hernandez Alvarez happened to have ready cash to purchase the business when she was forced to sell. Señora Díaz loathes the man, although she has no proof Alvarez was behind the murder. If it was that."

"It does sound odd, on all counts."

The train slowed again on the approach to Fairfield. If Señora Díaz's husband had been murdered, my sympathy grew. But why would Uncle Harrison risk his political ambitions and conduct an affair? That was the real question.

She could wish all she wanted for our happiness, but I would never agree to marry her nephew, Esteban de los Reyes Santiago. I longed for a husband to share my life, on equal terms, who didn't place wealth and power above everything else. Stephan was the last man I'd want. I'd be no different than a plush velvet sofa, a porcelain vase or a Swedish crystal chandelier hanging in his home. Even after I produced his sons.

Was Ace Diamond any better as husband material?

I shared a physical attraction with the Texan. Whether dressed in the familiar fringed buckskin coat, or white tie and tails, his presence alone sent shivers down my spine. I had to admit our behavior at Mt. Diablo skirted the edge of propriety.

But I also knew that Uncle Harrison would never accept him. Ace had vowed to win my hand, no matter what it took. He'd sunk all his hard-won money into a dynamite factory of all things, the riskiest business of all. Was that proof of his devil-may-care lust for adventure, a heady taste for ambition, or love and commitment?

The answer remained elusive.

*'The God of my rock; in him will I trust . . .'*
*2 Samuel 22:3*

# Chapter Six

Within five minutes of our arrival in Vallejo, Etta and I boarded the passenger ferry to San Francisco. Daniel Johnson had disappeared among the crowd.

"He said he wanted to check for any telegrams." Etta craned her neck. "I can't see that far, Miss Lily. The gents all look alike."

Johnson's errand to the telegraph office didn't sit well with me. He was supposed to act as an escort and keep the crowd at bay, yet here we were in a mash of people. I winced when someone's valise banged against my shin. A frantic voice called my name, so I twisted around. The young clerk waved at the back of the crowd with an envelope in hand.

"Miss Granville! Wait!"

The crowd surged up the *Esmeralda*'s gangplank, carrying us along. I lost sight of Daniel Johnson in the sea of faces and hats. The steamer's paddlewheel hummed, revolving slow and then faster, churning up water at the boat's stern.

"Let's get away from the stairs," I said and pulled Etta to one side.

Johnson managed to snake his way through the crush of people and joined us. "Two wires. One from your uncle," he said, panting. "Here, Miss Granville."

"Thank you."

I used a hairpin to slit the first envelope and read the terse message from Uncle Harrison. My stomach dropped to the floor.

*Return immediately, stop. Legal business involving you, stop. W.H.G.*

So he'd learned about Aunt Sylvia's will. Clearly he didn't care if my plans were ruined. Resentment sharpened my determination to continue. Why should I dance to his tune? Uncle Harrison would do anything to get his hands on that quicksilver claim. He'd force me to marry Esteban de los Reyes Santiago the minute I returned. Bought and sold like a commodity, all for the sake of profit. I crushed the paper and its envelope.

Kate had sent the second wire, a brief message to say that she and Charles would wait at San Francisco's docks. Relieved, I turned to my uncle's clerk.

"Please tell my uncle that I will return on Sunday. You don't need to accompany us, Mr. Johnson. We'll be safe on the ferry." I smiled at the young man, since Johnson looked skeptical.

"My friends are meeting us at the San Francisco dock."

He hesitated, glanced at Etta and then the crowd on the ferry. "Captain Granville told me to never let you out of my sight. He doesn't trust Diamond."

"I have no idea why Uncle Harrison is being unreasonable. My friends are missionaries. Mr. Diamond would be the last person to visit a revival tent."

Johnson chuckled. "I'll catch the train back then. Goodbye, Miss Granville, and enjoy your visit."

"Thank you. I intend to do so."

He tipped his hat and squirmed back through the mass of people. Johnson waved from the gangplank's end at the final whistle. I sank onto a bench beside Etta. The steamer churned through a narrow channel between Vallejo's docks and the shipyards on Mare Island. Workers by the dozen stacked brick walls, scurrying like ants between kilns and other workers molding clay. I had no idea what they were building until someone mentioned a new hospital. A clear sign of progress in this small town, and that cheered me.

I relaxed, free to enjoy the rest of the journey.

Vallejo's sloping streets receded. Etta and I enjoyed a cold lunch of meats, cheeses and breads, apple pie and fresh fruit while the ferry sailed far out into San Pablo Bay. I'd forgotten how different water travel on a roomy steamer was compared to the narrow aisle and cramped seats of the train. We lingered at the table and then walked outside to stand by the rail. Refreshed by a salty breeze, I braced myself against the ferry's rolling motion. The blue cloudless sky above, the greenish hills in the distance with smudges of yellow and orange, the churning water below, all gave me a sense of peaceful calm.

Pelicans dove close to shore and ducks frolicked in the marsh grass. Plenty of other ships chugged their way through the bay waters, from steamers to full-rigged ships and small fishing boats. I had my first glimpse of San Francisco in the hazy distance when the ferry passed the tree-covered slopes of Angel Island to the east. A smaller island with few trees and barren rock, jutted from the bay north of the city's shore.

"That's Alcatraz from what I read in a newspaper," I said, although Etta didn't seem impressed. "A camp there was used for military prisoners during the War."

"What a God-forsaken place. We'd better find our baggage, Miss Lily, since we'll soon be at the dock. That wind is stronger."

It did tug at my hat with more force. The warmth of the afternoon had turned cold this close to the open water that led to the deep blue of the Pacific, which I glimpsed between San Francisco's jutting hilly peninsula and the forested heights to the north. I followed her inside and then waited, valise in hand. From the window I saw the approaching docks while the ferry slowed, its revolving paddlewheel cutting the water's surface. We stopped at last. One hill ahead of us held rickety houses perched on the precarious slopes. Shops had been built on stilts close to the dock. The steamer's crew tossed ropes to waiting men, who wound them around the tall pier posts.

My first impression of the city was mud. Muddy streets, muddy water close to the shore, slippery rocks covered with dark slime, along with the stink of dead fish and raucous seagulls swooping from the sky. Etta held me back. Other passengers crushed together in their haste to disembark. At last the crowd thinned. We walked down the gangplank and stood on firm ground once again. Wagons, carriages, surreys and traps loaded with people headed west.

I eyed the myriad of long warehouses mixed with squat houses and tall buildings, the bare rocky slopes and steep unpaved streets. "Heavens. It's nothing like I imagined—"

"Watch your step, Miss Lily! You'll fall in the water if you're not careful." Etta pulled me away from the pier. "Oh, there's Mr. Mason."

I shaded my eyes. Charles wore the same frock coat and trousers I remembered from last month's train trip and the same derby hat. His spectacles glinted in the late afternoon sunlight. And Kate looked as sweet as ever, her blue eyes sparkling, her thick blue-black hair arranged high on her head with a small straw hat perched atop. A wool cape covered most of her rose-hued sprigged dress, and its fullness flapped in the stiff breeze.

"Lily! I'm so glad to see you!" She hugged me with fierce energy. "Look at how pretty you're dressed, too. I was afraid you'd never leave Sacramento."

"I'm glad to be here at last." I hugged her back and then introduced Etta to them both. "Best wishes on your marriage! I'm so happy."

Kate lowered her voice to a whisper. "I wondered if you were jealous after I stole Charles away from you. I've had a heavy load of guilt."

I laughed at her worried smile. "He's a good catch, and I think you're perfect for each other. Maybe I should have told you that back in Salt Lake City."

"Ladies, it's getting late." Red-faced, Charles took our baggage in hand and herded us all toward the horsecar one block away. "It will take over an hour to get home."

"Oh, my uncle reserved rooms for us at the Occidental Hotel."

"We hope you'll stay with us instead," Kate said. "We have a small farm. And the Christian Friends Revival meeting is Sunday. We have to bake and cook tomorrow for over a hundred people."

My mouth fell open. "A hundred?"

"Yes, at least."

"We need a big crowd, and a bigger offering." Charles sounded grim.

"We've been blessed so far," Kate said, chiding him. "Enough to remain faithful."

Once Charles helped us into the horsecar, the team pulled the conveyance away from the docks. I couldn't puzzle out why my neighborhood friend acted so aloof when Kate welcomed us. He sat on the seat opposite and avoided my gaze, silent and glum. We ladies chatted nonstop. Kate demanded to hear every detail about the banquet in Sacramento, the gown I'd worn and the other ladies' fashions, the hotel, its decorations and the elaborate menu. I did not explain about Ace Diamond or Esteban de los Reyes Santiago. Etta, however, had no compunction. She filled in Kate on my two suitors and my uncle's cranky behavior.

"Captain Granville's not at all like the Colonel. He told me flat out I'd better find a new position once Miss Lily married Señor Santiago—"

"What?" Shocked, I reached across Kate and squeezed Etta's hand. "Why didn't you tell me he said that to you?"

"And what good would it do but set off another argument."

I knew the truth in that, but my anger simmered deeper. Somehow I had to escape Uncle

Harrison's control and utter disregard for Etta's loyalty. I eyed a garish saloon on a corner. One young girl stood in a nearby doorway among other women, their cheeks and lips painted, their clothing more revealing than any chorus girl on stage. None of them looked older than my age. Good heavens. The horsecar turned and headed down Montgomery Street's slope.

"This area looks dangerous."

"It is," Charles said, his voice low. "The Barbary Coast, they call it. Some of the women who end up at our mission worked here in the city as soiled doves."

"Some were addicted to opium," Kate said. "When these women come to us, they're usually with child. We help them however we can. Sometimes we have to send the baby to an orphanage if the mother returns to work here in the city."

Etta clucked her tongue. "If the wives of rich men who own the property around here saw what goes on, they'd close 'em down quick. A few in Chicago are trying to do that."

"Let's talk about more cheerful things," Kate said. "Do you like California, Lily?"

"Yes, but I miss the trees back home." I craned my neck to watch the team straining at their harness. "How do they manage the hills when it rains? The streets must get slippery."

"There have been accidents," Charles said.

"Five horses were killed in a recent one this summer. I'm sure someone will come up with an answer, perhaps a special cog railway like they have abroad. At least along the steeper streets."

"So what do you do during this Revival, Kate?" I asked.

"At the Christian Friends' monthly meetings, when several preachers join together in one place, I teach the children."

"How to read, you mean?"

"Yes, learning words from the Bible or other books. Whatever keeps them busy while the parents listen to Charles. He's won many hearts to the Lord," she said with pride, her eyes shining. "So many people in the city live by their wits, collecting rags or junk to sell. Whatever it takes to survive. They look forward to Sunday afternoons, too. I spend Saturdays cooking and baking, like I said. It takes a lot to feed everyone."

"Do you have enough funding?" I asked.

"We make do. People donate food, clothing, money and then help—anyone who wants to set up or cook. I'm hoping Etta will lend a hand, and perhaps you too."

"Of course. I think you're smarter working here than going off to China without knowing the language. It would have taken years to get established there."

"Yes, I agree. Charity begins at home." Kate smiled. "So tell me more about this man Stephan.

Esteban de los Reyes Santiago? An interesting name."

I hesitated too long. Etta sniffed. "He's not that interesting."

"He's not what I expected," I said. "Pompous, arrogant, but handsome."

"You're caught in your uncle's trap, Miss Lily."

"Trap? Do you mean the engagement?" Kate asked. "Why did you agree to it?"

"They barged forward and ignored my protests," I said. "It's complicated. My uncle expects me to return on Sunday and marry Santiago."

Charles spoke up then. "Your father wouldn't have forced you into marriage, Lily. You may have to make a clean break from your uncle, though, to avoid it."

"Stay with us, Lily. You don't have to go back—" Kate tumbled into her husband's arms when the omnibus stopped suddenly, raising a cloud of dust. "Goodness!"

"At least the clerk your uncle sent along as a guard dog didn't accompany us," Etta said.

"What's this about a clerk?" Charles asked.

"Captain Granville wanted him to keep an eye out for—"

"There's the Occidental Hotel," I interrupted, relieved to end the conversation. I climbed down from the streetcar when it stopped at Pine Street. "I'd like to register, in case my uncle wires the hotel to find out if I ever arrived."

"Good idea," Charles said. He helped Kate and Etta down and guided them around fresh manure in the street. "He sounds like a tyrant."

I dodged pedestrians before the hotel's carved wooden doors. The entire block was taken up by the building with its arched windows. Inside the dim lobby, my heels didn't make a sound on the plush Persian carpets until I reached the marble floor by the reception desk. It took a few minutes to sign the register. I opened my pocketbook.

"I'll pay in advance."

"Your rooms are already paid in full, Miss Granville. There's a telegram for you," the clerk said and handed me an envelope. "Will there be a reply?"

I scanned the terse message from Uncle Harrison. He'd repeated his order to return at once to Sacramento. "How about 'arrived safe,' and thank you."

"Yes, miss. Would you like a porter to take your baggage to the room?"

"Not yet. I'm visiting with friends for the time being."

I rejoined Charles, Kate and Etta outside. We walked down Montgomery Street past Bush and Sutter and stopped at the intersection of Post and Market Streets. A carriage and matched team ambled south past lumber yards, warehouses and factories on the opposite side. Tall wooden boards covered with advertising bulletins failed to hide a yawning pit, where hundreds of workers shoveled and dug. Some skeletal buildings remained, sagging sideways.

"Is that where they're cutting through Rincon Hill? My uncle mentioned that."

"Yes," Charles said, hands in his pockets. "John Middleton convinced city and state officials to level it out. Some of the homes slid down the hillside after heavy rains. The city is still trying to clean up the mess."

"But why would they want to level the hills? It's lovely the way it is."

"You're used to flat land, that's why." He grinned. "You might change your mind after a few hikes up and down the steepest slopes in Rock Canyon."

"That looks new." I scanned the four-story hotel with a mansard roof across the street and east of the pit. "It must not be open yet."

"The Grand Hotel was built by William Ralston. He plans to open by Christmas."

"Isn't he President of the Bank of California?" I didn't mention that he was also a good friend of my uncle. Charles nodded.

"Yes, and he built the California Theater also. It opened earlier this year."

"—partner with this Esteban fella," Etta was telling Kate, "in a safety powder factory! Out where you live, from what Miss Lily said. He might blow himself to smithereens. Then where will she be? Men don't think of anyone but themselves."

Charles herded them along the street. "The dynamite factory sells their product to the railroad. We can't see their buildings from the northeast side of Rock Canyon, though. I've talked to Ace, but he never said he was a partner in the business."

"Safety powder, hmph. It doesn't sound so safe to me," Etta muttered.

We climbed onto the next horsecar and headed west on Market Street at an angle away from the city. Kate and Etta kept their heads together. Although my maid had not met either man, she'd made a list of differences between Ace Diamond and Santiago. She had often compared Charles to other suitors back in Evanston. Etta seemed to enjoy how Kate hung on her every word as if starved for gossip. I didn't interrupt. What was the use?

Besides, I wasn't sure what to think about Ace and his partnership with Santiago. Sinking his fortune into the factory seemed utter madness. Could I talk him into backing out and finding another business venture? Somehow I doubted it. He was obstinate about amassing a fortune. Esteban de los Reyes Santiago also didn't strike me as a man willing to return Ace's investment. He matched Uncle Harrison for greed and heart-less ambition. My father wouldn't approve of

Santiago, or the change in his younger brother's focus.

Charles was right. I owed it to Father's memory to refuse this marriage.

Dusk deepened the shadows during the long horsecar drive to Rock Canyon. We'd taken the Market Street cars to a smaller line that followed a plank road, past an old adobe mission church with a tiled roof and cross. I listened to its tolling bell with the others while eating a quick supper of beef wrapped in simple tortillas. Then we walked west in the pleasant evening. Small farms dotted the sand hills with roaming cows and ducks, pens of pigs or chickens, and the usual barnyard smells. I wondered if the Masons lived in an adobe hut like ones I'd seen along the way. What kind of life did my friends lead in this remote area?

And close to a dangerous dynamite factory.

"Here we are at last," Charles said and pointed. "On that rise."

The house resembled the small two-story farmhouses back home. "Isn't it pretty?" Kate threaded her arm through her husband's and grabbed my hand. "Smaller than my parents' house in Indiana. But it's home."

"It's beautiful." I admired the small garden to one side, the wildflowers—red poppies and yellow goldenrod, some type of purple-leafed plants—

111

growing close to the house. "What kind of farm animals do you keep? Cows and chickens?"

"Oh, yes. We need lots of fresh milk and eggs."

"If you go off wandering at any point, keep in mind you may hear explosions. They test nitro in the valley south of here on occasion." Charles loped off toward the outhouse.

Kate smiled at my shock. "It's too far away to do more than rattle the dishes. The canyon is prettiest in the morning. I don't often get to see it, since I'm up at half past five every day and so busy caring for the animals."

"That early? Heavens."

"Charles hasn't mastered milking the cow. I missed my chickens from home so I started a flock. Lily is the golden one, over there. Her feathers reminded me of your hair."

"Lily the chicken?" I laughed. "I'll feel guilty eating her eggs."

"Oh, she's tricky about hiding them," Kate said. "Don't worry."

Etta shook dust from her skirts. "We kept chickens where I grew up. I can help you scout them out, and milk the cow. Anything you need, Mrs. Mason."

I gave her arm a playful pinch. "I didn't know you grew up on a farm."

"A dairy farm in Wisconsin."

"I bet you had to get up earlier than I do now." Kate laughed, that pleasant tinkling sound I'd missed hearing since our shared train journey. "I'll need your help cooking and baking for the Revival on Sunday. What did Ace say to you at the banquet, Lily? I'm curious."

I shrugged. "We didn't have a chance to talk."

"And your uncle still doesn't approve of him?"

"He's biased because Ace served in the Texas cavalry."

"That and a few other reasons." Etta pursed her lips in disapproval. "Taking liberties when he ought to keep his hands to himself—"

"Is that what Uncle Harrison told you?" My face and neck flushed hot.

"That's nothing. I've heard plenty of other gossip."

"What gossip?"

Kate and I both stared at Etta. She looked like a cat with a bowl of cream, waiting until we'd reached the house, and then wouldn't explain until after a tour of the rooms. We admired the tiny parlor with a sofa and two armchairs, the kitchen with an enormous old iron cook stove and a drop-leaf table in the window alcove. Stems of pink and purple sweet pea filled a bowl and added their fragrance. The lace-edge tablecloth and colorful rag rugs must have been items Kate brought from home to start her new life in Cheyenne.

I was so thankful she'd escaped that terrible fate.

Etta and I climbed upstairs to see the attic

bedroom with its wide bed. A colorful quilt lay over the crisp muslin sheets. "It might be a little chilly at night, so here's an extra blanket," Kate said and spread a folded square near the footboard. "You should be warm enough."

"But this is your room."

"You're our guests, Lily. I'll make up a pallet on the floor downstairs. No, don't argue. We often have preachers coming and give them our bed." She turned to Etta once we headed downstairs. "Now tell us what this gossip is about. It must be awful."

"Well." Etta perched on a kitchen chair. "I've been questioning your uncle's housekeeper about things, without prying, hinting here and there. The Captain wasn't pleased about finding you and Ace together on Mt. Diablo. You'd been alone for hours."

"He left without waiting to find out if I survived!"

She hushed me. "Yes, I know that. Mrs. Turner said it's like the pot calling the kettle black, though. Captain Granville had an affair—"

"With Señora Díaz?" I plopped down on a chair. "I doubt that. His friends wouldn't approve, and his political ambitions might be ruined."

"Mrs. Turner said your uncle and Señora Díaz took a trip together several months ago, and then returned as man and wife, but swore her to secrecy," Etta said. "She told me that Captain Granville has spent many nights away from home since then."

"But—"

"Señora Díaz plans to act as hostess at all the dinner parties he's giving for the future political campaign. And she'll plan the menus, the flowers, everything. She must be his wife if Captain Granville wants her so involved."

The fact that my uncle lied about needing a hostess for his dinner parties, when he may have married Paloma Díaz in secret, rankled me. But it made sense, given how they acted the night of the banquet—how Paloma had acted, I corrected myself. Etta nudged me.

"Don't you think they must be married, Miss Lily?"

But Kate spoke before I could. "Perhaps they want you to marry her nephew and keep all the money in the family."

"I'm not going to marry him, no matter what," I said. "I don't want a man like that. He doesn't care about me, or what I want. Only himself."

I didn't want to explain Aunt Sylvia's prediction —that I'd become a pawn in my uncle's schemes. Uncle Harrison was no doubt livid about losing the quicksilver mine. He was desperate to get it. And he needed me to give in to his wishes and cooperate with his well-laid plans. Would my uncle wait for my return?

I hoped he didn't suspect that once I left, I would choose to remain in San Francisco.

*'And when ye see this,
your heart shall rejoice . . .'
Isaiah 66:14*

# Chapter Seven

Despite Etta's snoring, I slept deep. Once I opened my eyes, my fingers inched over the cold empty space beside me. The rattle of stove lids below woke me further. Etta must be downstairs helping Kate already. I rolled out of bed with a heavy dose of guilt, scrubbed my face and hands and then shook out a simple spare dress. I yearned for a bath, but dared not add that inconvenience to Kate's busy day. After getting dressed, I pinned up my hair.

Downstairs, the two women wore full-length aprons over their clothing. Kate's flushed face, her sparkling blue eyes and flour-dusted hands proved she was in her element. Etta too, since she anticipated whatever needed to be done without direction. I gulped down a few stale biscuits with thick crispy bacon. Kate slipped an apron over my head, tied it around my waist, and then put me to work. She showed me how to roll out pie crust to the right thickness before placing the dough into pans and crimping the edges with a thumb.

"The first batch of bread loaves are almost done rising. They'll take up the whole oven, but we need thirty pies," she said. "Can you slice apples without cutting yourself, Lily?"

Etta frowned. "You ought not trust her with a paring knife."

Irked by her lack of confidence, I picked up the tool. "I've watched you peel apples and potatoes for years, Etta. I can try it."

Kate smiled. "Cut out the bad spots, core and slice them. People are so hungry, they'd eat the whole fruit including the stems if I popped them under the crust. Etta, chop the vegetables for the stew and put them in this cold water. We'll boil the ox-tails tomorrow morning for the meat and make a gravy then."

The morning sped by in a blur. We jostled each other in the small stuffy kitchen. My fingers and knuckles stung from tiny cuts, and I gained more respect for Cook back home. For Etta and Kate also, to wake so early at dawn, stand on their feet all day without complaint near a hot stove, serve at table and wash dishes, three times a day or more—goodness. I'd taken such tasks for granted. My feet, shoulders and hands ached after a few hours.

We spent the afternoon making the third and fourth batches of bread and pies, plus washing and sorting navy beans to soak for baking the next morning. I realized that Kate needed a more efficient stove, one that didn't smoke and singe the bread and pie crusts. I waved away hot steam from my face and pulled another sizzling tin from the oven. The apples bubbled beneath the browned knife-slit crust. A spicy scent of cinnamon filled the kitchen, mingling with fresh baked bread. I straightened, one hand on the small of my back.

"Leave it there to cool, Lily, and go outdoors. You look ready to drop."

I didn't protest. Cool air fanned my face when I walked toward a large rock on the slope behind the house. Cows wandered the peaceful canyon. Willows and eucalyptus trees lined the creek that snaked below. It looked so different from home, where the dense forest hid most of the open sky except across Lake Michigan's dark blue expanse. The late afternoon sun dipped to the west. So this was San Francisco's Rock Canyon. Somewhere to the south, Ace might be riding a horse, or working inside the dynamite factory.

Was he still angry over the events at the banquet? He'd stormed off after my engagement announcement, and my stomach tightened at the memory. Loneliness and despair plagued me. Both my parents were dead, and I had no siblings or close relatives beside my uncle. Father had wanted grandchildren. Did I want a husband and family?

Yes—one day. I wanted someone I could trust, to share a future with, a man who loved me and wanted happiness, children and a real home.

Lost in thought, I wandered over a patch of even ground. Charles and two other men fastened the ropes of a canvas tent, then carried several sawhorses and boards to form makeshift tables. They set them on one side. After raising a larger tent, other men set up benches in rows. One brought in a tall wooden post with a slanted piece of wood nailed on top—a crude lectern—and hung a banner of colored squares sewn together that flapped in the wind.

I waved to Charles, who ambled over to meet me. "You look like a farmer in that striped shirt and patches on your trousers."

"Mud-caked boots, not even a clean handkerchief. A far cry from Evanston and how we lived there." He eyed a few birds flying overhead. "I'm glad you came to visit, Lily."

"I'm glad, too. Are you happy with your ministry?" I asked. "Here in California rather than China, I mean."

He met my gaze this time. "Yes. I was fired up to save the heathen after we heard that missionary's testimony, I suppose. Your misgivings proved sound. Kate and I saw so many people walking around San Francisco, barefoot, hungry and without jobs. She convinced me going to China wasn't necessary."

"My father believed that. He was right about me, too. I wouldn't have lasted a few hours doing what Kate does. I don't have enough compassion for service."

"You gave Kate a hundred dollars. That's another way of showing compassion. My sister Adele hasn't sent me a dime. After what I did to you—"

"All is forgiven. I mean that."

Red-faced, he took out his handkerchief and mopped his forehead. Charles removed his spectacles and polished them also. "I'm still ashamed."

"Don't be. Make sure Kate buys a better stove as well as supplies for all the food you cook for the people coming tomorrow." I cheered up to see his excited smile. "What time will they arrive for the revival?"

"Two o'clock, if not before." He donned his spectacles and clasped his hands. "I'm grateful you forgave my cowardice last month. That's what it was, Lily. I'm going to make up for it. No matter what your uncle tries to do, now or later, Kate and I are on your side."

"Thank you."

His sincerity warmed my heart. I trudged back to the house and met Kate, pails in hand, on her way back from milking the cow. We stored the bread loaves and cloth-covered pies in several cupboards, then ate a simple supper of buttered bread, honey, cheese and apple pie. Weary, Etta and I headed for the stairs. Charles worked on his sermon at the kitchen table, hunched over the papers, his ink bottle close at hand. His spectacles reflected the lamp's soft glow. Kate curled beneath a wool blanket on their makeshift pallet, already asleep.

"I'm happy for them," I said and slipped into bed. "They're doing important work. I'm so tired, I could sleep two days straight."

Etta shook my shoulder a few minutes later, or so it seemed. "Miss Lily, it's almost nine! We let you sleep in. You're not used to this work, it's true."

I rubbed my eyes. "Nine o'clock? Good heavens, I'll be down in a minute."

Mortified, I washed, donned a clean dress, brushed out my hair and pinned it up. Kate's hearty breakfast of oatmeal, hash, bacon, fresh bread and pie filled me to bursting. She opened a jar and then helped rub sweet-smelling beeswax salve into my aching hands.

"The visiting women will help today, Lily. Rest your fingers."

"I wish she'd helped me gather the eggs," Etta grumbled. "It's true your chickens hide them well. It took almost an hour to find enough."

"Charles promised to build a proper coop, but he needs help from someone who knows how to do it. Maybe you can tell him."

"Of course. I remember how my father built coops for all the farmers in the area."

"I don't mind helping, though—"

Kate shooed me outside. "You did plenty yesterday. Relax and enjoy the day."

Etta followed her to help other women drape the tables with muslin sheets. I kept out of the way. They ran back and forth, clucking like hens, carrying baskets of sliced bread, pies and crocks of baked beans, stew or soup. Faint church bells tolled in the distance while the crowd waited, patient for a turn to fill plates of food and sit beneath the tents.

Once people finished, women collected soiled dishes and utensils. Charles warmed to his sermon, ignoring the clatter. Clearly he'd learned to use his voice to maximum effect, given his training in the law, and quoted Scripture by heart.

" 'For it is God who worketh in you both to will and to do of his good pleasure.' Trust in the Lord, my friends! Trust in Him, and He will guide you in every path of your life. Does he not provide for the sparrow? God cares for you far more than the beasts of the earth. Peace comes when you trust in Him. Even when your enemies strike you down with evil in their hearts . . ."

His stirring words whipped the crowd into choruses of amen. Kate whispered in my ear. "See that banner? He learned about it from reading Reverend Charles Spurgeon's books," she said.

"Black is for sin, red is for the blood of Christ, and white is for purity after accepting salvation. Charles will baptize people in the creek after the sermon."

"Wonderful. I'm so glad you're helping his mission work here."

"I couldn't be happier, Lily. Why don't you take a walk? See what the area's like."

Kate squeezed my arm and then headed off to wash dishes with the other women. My restless energy grew. I couldn't focus on the message being preached, so I decided to take Kate's advice. A small path led toward the canyon. Several goats bleated atop a rocky outcrop, scaring me. I laughed and drank in the breathtaking view of the city's distant hills. This area was so lovely. Its remoteness added a peaceful atmosphere.

Until I heard a muffled blast.

I half-slid down the embankment in surprise. On Sunday afternoon? Could that have been an explosion from the safety powder factory? Once the echo died, birds began trilling once more. I heard Charles' faint voice rising and falling in the distance.

Blackberry and elderberry bushes grew in small patches along the path. I rounded a curve between two rock piles. After skirting a bit of poison oak, or what looked like it, I fingered the hanging fronds beneath a grove of willows and then emerged onto a sloping hill. A thin stream of water tumbled over some rocks. I followed it, keeping away from the thick grasses and plants which thrived on the moisture. Faded yellow flowers trailed over rocks. I passed an occasional clump of wild scarlet poppies and several trees with gnarled branches.

Shading my eyes from the sun, I faced south. Where was this dynamite factory? Why had Ace invested in a dangerous business? I knew he wanted to trump my uncle in terms of becoming successful, but he oughtn't risk killing himself in the process. Did he expect my full support? Given what we'd shared so far, Ace was more than a friend. My thoughts strayed to him every day. I missed his company, his laugh, his teasing nature. He listened to my opinions—the latter a credit to him as a gentleman compared to Santiago's lack of interest.

I pictured the two of them in cutaway coats, fancy white shirts and ties. But Ace belonged on a horse, dressed in his fringed buckskin coat and slouch hat. Armed with his Colt, his Bowie knife, a rifle, and his Arkansas toothpick, I imagined him flashing that boyish grin and herding wild horses or cattle. Not supervising workers in a stuffy factory.

Perspiration trickled down my neck and back. A crow swooped across the path, cawing aloud, and I jumped back in fright. How silly of me. I followed the trail by the small creek, which bubbled over rocks and meandered around another curve past a twisted sycamore. A crowd of people gathered ahead on the creek bank. More streamed down the slope to line the water's edge. I glimpsed Charles fair hair and heard his booming voice. He stood in the water, knee-deep, and poured water over a woman's head, while people sang *Amazing Grace.*

That had been Mother's favorite hymn. She'd whispered the verses on her deathbed while Father gripped her hands. The sweet notes soothed my raw nerves. Tears blurred my vision. Charles baptized other people, men and women, until I turned and walked back to the willow grove. Halfway, someone grabbed my arm and scared me witless.

"What are you doing here, Lily Granville?"

I stared at Ace's cold gaze, the firm line of his mouth, his clear suspicion, and broke his strong hold. "I came to visit my friends. What are you doing here—oh! Your shirt's wet."

He folded his arms over his chest. "I'm surprised you left your fiancé behind."

"My—I don't have a fiancé," I said, sputtering, and swiped my damp cheeks. "You left that night before I had the chance to explain. I never agreed to marry Santiago, my uncle is trying to force him on me. You of all people ought to understand."

Ace nodded his head, slow and sure. "True. I'm sorry, Lily."

"I am too. That was a nightmare, and I'm glad to be here. Away from my uncle, from Santiago and his aunt." I folded my hands. "I wanted to see you and explain."

"You did?"

"Of course." Shy, I lowered my gaze. "I planned to find you—"

He crushed me against his damp shirt, muscled arms tight around my waist. His slick wet hair felt cool beside my cheek. "Is that right. Thought I'd never see you again, darlin'. It near killed me, the way Santiago kissed you that night."

"Don't remind me! I thought you'd left California for good." I touched the scar on his jaw and leaned back to survey him, his damp shirt and hair. "Did Charles baptize you?"

"Yep. Mason didn't think I was serious. Guess his Bible-thumpin' got to me after all. Plus I figgered it wouldn't hurt to make sure in case my ma forgot. She had her hands full with so many boys when I was born."

Overjoyed, I snaked my arms around his neck and kissed him. Ace kissed me back, long and slow. I pulled away at last. "No one can call you a heathen now."

"I don't feel different." He stole another kiss. "So you never wanted to marry Santiago? Even with all his money."

"No," I said and laid my head into the curve of his shoulder. "That was my uncle's idea. I'm so glad I left Sacramento, because I hoped to find you and explain everything. But Kate never mentioned you'd be here."

"Ha. I've played fiddle and guitar as a favor to the Masons for these revivals. Been doin' that for the past three weeks."

"Fiddle and guitar, as well as the harmonica on the train?" Perhaps I needed to discover more about Ace while I had the chance. "You're full of surprises, Mr. Diamond. What else don't I know about you?"

"Let's find someplace where we can be alone."

Ace drew me further into the willow grove. We sat on a fallen log that stretched toward the creek with its branch tips trailing in the water. I related what happened before the banquet, my shock at meeting Santiago, the engagement party afterward, and how Uncle Harrison had been reluctant to grant permission for this weekend trip to San Francisco.

"I don't like being under his thumb. I'm not returning."

"Then marry me, Lily. You'd be free of him for good."

I shook my head. "I'll never be free of my uncle."

He tugged my hands away from the pebbles I'd gathered and warmed my chilled fingers. "Hear me out. When the Captain stood up that night, tellin' everyone at our table you'd marry

Santiago, it was like a stick of dynamite exploding in my face."

"Yes. I am sorry." His dark hair stirred in the breeze, and I pushed a damp strand from his eyes. "I had no idea he planned to do that."

"I told you how I was set on winning you. Promise you'll marry me."

He pulled me down within the circle of his arms, my back to his chest, his mouth close to my earlobe. More intimate than I'd expected, but I was too happy to protest. Ace stroked my cheek and hair with his fingers. His gentle touch sent a thrill throughout me, and his low murmur against the straw hat brim set my heart racing. A throbbing ache below my belly flared hot.

No other man had affected me like Jesse Diamond. But was marriage the answer?

"Do you think I'd take charge of your money, is that it?" He nuzzled my bare neck with his rough jaw. "I got enough on my plate with that factory, darlin'. We can share the profits and face your uncle together over the Early Bird. He'd think twice about orderin' you around like a little girl if you was my wife."

"True, but I wish you'd invested in a safer business."

"What's safer than safety powder? Business is boomin' for us."

"It's not something to joke about, you know." I hated the prissy tone of my voice but plunged on.

"Tell me how you make these sticks of dynamite."

Ace laughed. "You're like a hound on the trail of a 'possum, Lily. Like I said at the banquet, we take a percentage of nitroglycerin, let it soak into a clay and shape it into sticks. There's a long fuse, too, so it's safe to light. The clay don't leak like the oil canisters neither."

His body's warmth and closeness, the mingling smells of soap and citrus with his musky scent proved too distracting. I forced myself to repeat his words.

"Shaped into sticks. Is the clay sticky to handle?"

"Nah, it's wrapped in paper." He brushed a stray curl from my eyes and turned me to face him. "There. Now I can see the prettiest woman in all California."

"So there's no actual powder," I said, losing the distraction battle. I admired his strong jaw, those intriguing mismatched eyes, the rough bristles he'd missed shaving, the curve of his sensual mouth. "Just nitroglycerin and clay?"

"Yep. We're fixin' to call it something else. Maybe fire sticks, since they offer a bigger explosion than firecrackers. Like I told you before, it's safe to use."

"You sound like my uncle, or Santiago at the banquet—don't worry your pretty little head about it," I said, annoyed. "You doubled the money my uncle gave you, then sunk it into this business. You could lose it all in one single explosion."

"I've trained the workers in storage and handling." Ace nuzzled my neck and ran the tip of his tongue over my ear. I shivered. He pulled me close against his hard chest, closer when he kissed me. "I won't lose my money."

I pulled away, stood and brushed gravel from my dress. "I'm still worried about your partnership with Santiago. I don't trust him."

"Why?" Ace sounded worried now and scrambled to his feet. "Did he try something with you? Tell me, Lily."

He persisted, asking questions, but I couldn't put a finger on what stirred my misgivings. "Please tell him you've changed your mind and get your money back. Try something else, like breeding horses. Didn't you tell me you wanted to do that?"

"All my money's sunk into production," he said and rubbed the bridge of his nose. "We keep getting orders, but Santiago ain't paid me a red cent from profits. He's puttin' me off. Says we'll settle up in another month or so."

"Oh, no. He'll never pay you without a fight."

"Does it matter? No matter what kind of money I ever get in the bank, your uncle ain't gonna accept me. Not even if I was elected Governor of California."

I had to laugh at his half-hearted joke. "I

suppose it's hopeless trying to convince him, not with you being a lowly Texan cowboy."

"Yep, but at least I got me a horse and saddle again." He pulled me into his arms and brushed my cheek with a palm. "Marry me, Lily. I ain't gonna stop askin' until you say yes. Rich or poor, it don't matter to me. Or whatever your uncle thinks."

The fact that he'd never give up warmed my heart. "Being rich doesn't matter to me either, and owning half of the Early Bird gold mine brought trouble on my head." I grasped his hands. "You do realize that—well, that marriage is more than wanting a woman in the physical sense, Jesse. Right?"

Ace met my gaze and held it. "I risked my life for you at Dale Creek. I'm willing to throw in everything I have, everything I want in life, to be with you," he said gruffly. "If you ain't got feelings for me, physical or otherwise, you wouldn't be jawin' here now."

"Yes, but—"

"Tell me you love me. Go on. Say it."

I ducked my head, heat flooding my cheeks. "I think I do."

"You sure about that?" He covered my mouth, his head tilted sideways, pinning me against the tree bole, until I had to catch my breath. "Well now. That proves it."

Shy, I rested my cheek against his and dabbed my misty eyes. Jesse Diamond, the last man I'd expected to be an angel of mercy, had helped me on the journey out west to find my father's killer. Despite our initial clashes, we succeeded. I knew he wanted me. I wanted him too, in the physical sense as well as being his partner in a shared future. I yearned to escape my uncle's trap—marriage to a man I didn't love.

But would I be using Ace, in the same way Uncle Harrison wanted to use me? I didn't want that. But Ace was right. I wouldn't be here in his arms, sharing kisses, if I wasn't in love with him. My thoughts had been haunted by Jesse Diamond since our hours together at Mt. Diablo. And ever since, I'd dreamed about him, yearned to see him and talk to him. I could reject him and return to Sacramento, give in to my uncle's plans, force myself to accept a lesser man and a sheltered life. But that choice was unbearable.

"Yes. I do love you, and I will marry you."

Speechless, surprise clear on his face, Ace picked me up and whirled me around and around until I was dizzy. We laughed, kissed again and then sat down on a nearby rock. This time he drew me onto his lap and nuzzled me breathless.

"Thought you'd turn me down again. I almost gave up hope."

"Never do that. But I wish you'd give up the dynamite business."

"No more dangerous than workin' cattle. I survived being gored by a steer—"

"You did? Where, in your belly?" I asked, half

teasing. He pulled out his shirt and stuck my hand on his warm bare skin. I felt a ridge of scar tissue below his lowest rib, but tugged my hand free when he moved it lower. "None of that, you devil! Were you hurt?"

"Well . . . it's why I'd rather breed horses on a ranch."

"I own a ranch."

Ace raised his eyebrows. "Is that right."

I ran my fingers through his hair when he tightened his arms around my waist. "Aunt Sylvia left it to me in her will when she died, along with a quicksilver claim deed. Yes, Aunt Sylvia. I know, it's difficult to believe. But she did name me as her heir."

"Why'd she do that, after tryin' so hard to kill you?"

"She wanted my forgiveness." I fingered the scar along his jaw and then touched the scar above his eye where he'd needed stitches back in Omaha. "I gave it to her, and it relieved her suffering. Everyone deserves a chance at redemption."

"Do you believe that? I dunno."

"I'm certain of it." I brushed his dark hair away from his eyes. "As for my uncle, he must have met with his lawyers about Aunt Sylvia's will after I left Sacramento. He'll be so angry to find out he won't get his hands on the quicksilver mine."

"So that's why your uncle tried to hook you up with Santiago." Ace's disgust was clear. "He'd hog-tie and brand you if Granville asked him."

"Yes. Stephan is like my uncle, controlling to the point of driving me mad. I'm not surprised Uncle Harrison chose him for my husband."

"Santiago told me Granville took him under his wing on the advice of his aunt."

I laughed. "Did you know she may be my uncle's wife? I haven't verified that yet."

"Whoa. That's news," he said "I wonder why Santiago helped me, then. Taught me how to dress, that kind of thing. Didn't want a cow puncher for a partner."

"Maybe he doesn't know they're married. You looked so handsome in evening dress." I squeezed his hand. "You learned fast, too, about manners and using a napkin, or which fork to begin with at the banquet table."

"Maybe you'll learn fast, too. On our wedding night."

He grinned at my open-mouthed shock, then gave me another brazen kiss. I wouldn't allow him more, although his fingers slid over my backside before I could stop him. I twisted clear from his reach and shook a fist. Ace winked.

"Let's ask Mason to marry us. He's a preacher—"

"My uncle would never consider it a legitimate marriage."

We strolled back until we reached the farm-house. The sun dipped toward the western horizon, ablaze with orange, red and deep purple.

Chickens squawked at a hawk circling high overhead. The crowd had thinned by now, walking home in all directions along the canyon's ridge, their children lagging behind or safe in their parents' arms. Ace kept a firm hand at my waist, as if afraid he'd lose me. We looked east toward the haze that blanketed San Francisco.

"It's so pretty, isn't it?" I breathed in the heady scent of eucalyptus.

The city had reminded me more of Chicago than Sacramento. Except for the sloping hills, of course, but the waterfront's forest of ship masts, the shops, the bustling traffic, the excitement downtown, the tang in the air and the pockets of quiet neighborhoods and even the weather, with the mysterious fogs Kate told me about, all intrigued me.

Somewhere beyond the smudged horizon was Vallejo and the hills near Walnut Creek. Along with the ranch I'd inherited from Aunt Sylvia— and that abandoned quicksilver mine.

"California's prettier than I expected, but I'm going to miss winter."

"There's snow up in Donner Pass."

I pinched him. Together we walked toward the house, where soft lamplight glowed in the downstairs windows. I felt safe. Respected by a better man than Esteban de los Reyes Santiago. And loved by someone I trusted with my life. I put aside worrying about Uncle Harrison.

My future had shifted again onto a new track.

*'. . . with their tongues they
have used deceit . . .'*
*Romans 3:13*

# Chapter Eight

Surprised yet ecstatic about our announcement to marry, Charles and Kate offered to help in any way. Etta was wary of Ace, however, given what my uncle had claimed. He won her over within the hour with jokes and stories. Charles agreed with my plan.

"A justice of the peace is better, since I've never been officially ordained. It's too late to start now, but I suggest we all go into the city tomorrow."

Ace clapped his hat on his head. "Pick a hotel we can meet at, Lily."

"Not the Occidental," I said quickly. "I wish I knew which hotel owners are my uncle's friends so we can avoid them. Like William Ralston, who's building the Grand Hotel."

"We'll register under my name, remember. Not Granville."

"How about the Russ House," Charles said. "It's kitty-corner to the Occidental, and I saw a back entrance once. If Captain Granville sends anyone to look for you, they might think you'd avoid a hotel anywhere close to the Occidental."

"Right under their noses, is that it?" Ace kissed me. "Ten o'clock tomorrow then. Keep her safe, Mason."

He and Charles left the house and headed toward a horse hobbled in a grassy field further west. I hadn't noticed the chestnut gelding before. Kate shooed me from the window.

"A man asked about you during the revival," she said. "I'm glad Etta and I didn't know where you'd gone."

"What did he look like?" My anxiety returned. "Did he give his name?"

"No. Charles didn't answer any of his questions." Kate eyed my dusty green dress. "Let's figure out what you'll wear for the wedding. Something old, something new?"

"I have white ribbon garters," Etta said. Her cheeks turned pink. "They're new."

"I have my navy suit—"

"No, Lily, but I have just the thing. Follow me."

We all hurried upstairs. Kate knelt by the trunk at the bed's foot and drew out a bundle of sky blue fabric. The flowing silk skirt had a layer of gossamer illusion. "Look at the shirred bodice, isn't it pretty? It's a little old-fashioned, and I didn't bring the hoops it requires. Maybe we could pin it up in back over your bustle to fit the style now."

"This dress is similar to one my mother wore," I said, admiring the lace insets beneath the bell-shaped sleeves. "It's lovely. Are you sure you don't mind?"

"Please, I'd be honored if you wore it. Here's the hat."

The tilted straw brim held a spray of delicate dyed blue ostrich feathers. "It's darling! Thank you, Kate." Hot tears stung my eyes. "Are you sure?"

"Of course, don't cry!" Kate sniffled and handed me soft blue-dyed kid gloves. "These are new. I bought them to wear in Cheyenne, but never used them. Now you're all set for tomorrow. I hope Ace can get a marriage license without trouble. Mondays are so busy."

"Can you pack for a few days stay in the city?" I asked. "My treat, dinner and a room at the Russ House. Or do you have to be back for the animals?"

Kate hugged me. "That will be a treat. I'm exhausted, and we can get a neighbor to take care of them for a day or two."

"You worked hard this weekend," Etta said. "Mr. Mason was very pleased at the turnout. He said you had seventy last week, and this time twice that number."

"Then it was worth it."

She laid the dress on the bed and led the way to the stairs. Deep voices below startled me. Charles must have visitors, although I hadn't heard any-

138

one knocking earlier. When we entered the front room, I halted in shock. James McKay sat in one armchair, slouched like at the banquet, his thin hair plastered over his skull, his portly figure and face puffy. A second man, with a thick reddish-brown beard to match his longish hair, jumped to his feet. Charles wearily rose from his chair, clumsy and slower. McKay remained in place as if he owned the house, extracted a cigar from his pocket and clipped it.

"Good evening, ladies. We're here to feature your husband's missionary work in the *California Enquirer*, Mrs. Mason. I own that newspaper. This is my top reporter, Mr. Dodd, who will write the article."

I held my tongue, despite my suspicions. Kate glanced at Charles, who seemed pleased. Dodd had a thin frame and a shabby sack suit. He flipped through a small notebook and glanced at me sideways. McKay posed questions to Charles, puffed on his vile-smelling cigar and then checked with Dodd to make certain the facts were correct.

"You've made a wonderful start in a short time. Congratulations. And Mr. Diamond is also here, helping you? He's a partner in the Colossus Safety Powder Works, I believe."

"Yes, he is," Charles said and glanced at me. "But he's not helping the mission work."

"Oh? Perhaps Miss Granville is, then? Her uncle is charity-minded."

I stepped forward. "Is he? Unless you're referring to his interest in helping Señora Díaz with the Sacramento Court House beautification."

"You mean Señora Granville." He watched me for a reaction. I didn't give McKay that satisfaction, and he seemed disappointed. "I thought perhaps you didn't know about their secret wedding. Seems odd that they want you to marry Santiago—"

"Mr. McKay, tell me why you came here," I interrupted. "It's not to interview the Masons about their mission work, is it? You're here to spy on me."

His cheeks flushed crimson. "I had no idea you were here in Rock Canyon."

"Please leave, Mr. McKay," Charles said, also red-faced. "You misrepresented your intentions and are no longer welcome here."

McKay smiled. "I suppose we have enough information. Good night then."

Dodd closed his notebook and followed his employer out the door. Charles twisted the lock with a heavy sigh and waved a cloud of cigar smoke. Etta slid her arm around my waist. Kate did the same on the other side, as if I needed support.

"Lily, I'm sorry. I had no idea," Charles said.

"It's all right. We'll be gone in the morning, even if they do tell my uncle where I've been. I wonder if they saw Ace at one point, too. Why else would they think he was here helping you? And now I know for certain my uncle married Señora Díaz. He can't hide that from me any longer. And he can't dictate to me who I'll marry, either."

"We need an early start tomorrow morning." Charles checked his watch. "It's almost nine. I'm hoping for a good night's sleep."

"I doubt I'll sleep a wink," Kate said and fretted while she made up the pallet on the floor. "I hope those men don't return."

Etta and I climbed the stairs. At the landing, I saw Charles sitting beside the door. That eased my mind. I wish Ace had stayed behind. He would know what to do if things turned rough— and I dismissed my worries of anything bad happening during his ride to the city. He had experience handling the likes of muleskinners, brawlers or tough sailors out to shanghai him. Etta was already asleep when I slipped beneath the warm bedcovers.

An odd shaking woke me from a dream. Was it another earthquake? Etta snored into the pillow. The house shook again, slightly. I heard low voices downstairs, Charles and Kate no doubt, perhaps getting dressed to milk the cow and feed the chickens. I padded to the window, shivering in my nightdress, and viewed the first glimmer of dawn.

My wedding day.

Nerves hit me and my stomach fluttered. I had

a difficult time imagining myself as Mrs. Jesse Diamond. What did I know about him? Not his family, birthplace, education—or lack of it. That was something to remedy. I'd have to get answers from Ace before we spoke our vows. He owed me that. What little I did know wasn't enough to satisfy my curiosity. If not before our vows, then he'd have to answer before the wedding night.

That would solve any reluctance on his part.

The hired carriage jostled over the ruts on Market Street and then stopped again. What now? Poking my head out of the window, I pushed a stray curl from my eyes. A line of wagons, gigs, drays, men on horseback and several omnibuses congregated at the corner, blocking the way. Etta turned at the row's end and continued her knitting. How could she craft a winter scarf for a family member during all the swaying and jolting? I gritted my teeth, my nerves raw. My sore backside didn't help, along with the rattling, stuffy carriage.

I checked my father's gold watch. "We're late—"

"I'm sure Ace will wait for us," Kate said and folded an old newspaper. "Charles, can't you find out how long we'll be delayed this time? Maybe the driver knows a detour. Have him use a side street instead of this main thoroughfare."

"It's Monday. Everyone has business that's important to get done. I doubt there's any other way, but I will ask."

"See if you can get a current newspaper, too."

Charles rose stiffly and climbed out of the carriage. I breathed in the cooler air in relief. Kate and I stretched our lower limbs and backs, while Etta fetched another skein of yarn from her canvas bag. She laughed at our discomfort.

"There's nothing you can do except get out and walk."

Kate smiled. "True enough. Shall we, Lily?"

We circled the carriage until Charles returned and handed Kate the *Morning Call* edition. The driver cracked his whip, swerving the team, and headed north down a shadowy alley. The crowded tangle of carriages, buggies and wagons on Market Street vanished behind us. Then the driver turned down a side street before the carriage stopped. I glimpsed a small square, although the view out the window was minimal given Etta's bobbing and swaying with the carriage. A rubber curtain blocked the other window. Kate waved a hand before my face.

"Lily? I asked you twice—"

"I'm sorry, what did you say?"

"Did you tell Ace your full name," she repeated. "For the marriage license."

"He won't need to know." Charles yawned. "The Justice of the Peace fills that out after the ceremony. I hope Ace will find one who isn't booked all day already."

That increased my worry. Half past noon—we

ought to have left Rock Canyon before dawn, given all this traffic. Etta continued knitting, Kate pored over the newspaper columns of advertisements while Charles jotted notes for his sermon next week. He grunted whenever the carriage jolted over the rough street.

"What are you looking for?" I asked Kate.

"A stove in the auction listings. That way I can spend more money for supplies."

"I'm pledging a monthly donation to your mission work, so don't worry."

"Oh, Lily, thank you! I can pay off all groceries we've put on credit."

"Yes, that will be the best part," Charles said. "We own the house, thank the Lord for that. I thought we might have to mortgage it to keep our work going."

"Never." Kate flattened the page and resumed reading. "I'd like to find a good deal. And look, here's an auction being advertised—oh!"

We all reeled from a hard impact. The carriage tipped and then crashed onto one side. Charles spilled into Kate. Etta's head cracked against the window frame. Her knitting needle missed my eye by a mere inch, the steel whooshing so close I felt its cool surface on my skin.

Etta slumped over me, stifling my breathing. I gasped, my elbow burning with pain, and wriggled until I could take a deeper breath. Kate moaned aloud, Charles groaned and shifted so that I was crushed again. I pushed harder. Tasted something wet on my lip. Blood. I had no idea if it was mine, or Etta's, but panic hit me. I didn't dare move, so I steeled myself to remain still. Someone yanked the door open above and stared at us through the opening.

"Anyone hurt?"

"Yes! Help us, please." Kate sounded frantic. "Lily, are you all right?"

I couldn't answer, since the weight of three people crushed me against the carriage's side. Charles boosted Kate through the opening, which helped, and then pulled himself up and out. The driver leaned down and grabbed Etta's arms.

"Be careful. She hit her head and lost consciousness." I swiped my bloody lip with a clean handkerchief, then pressed it against the jagged cut on her temple. The scarlet stream tracked down Etta's cheek. "She may have a broken bone, too."

"Yes, miss. I'll try."

With a loud grunt, clearly ignoring my warning, he dragged Etta out of the overturned carriage. Charles poked his head inside but disappeared. Frustrated, worried about Etta, I shifted until I could kneel and then stood through the open doorway. Someone grabbed the carpetbag that held the borrowed wedding dress, and then my valise. Another stranger pulled me to safety. I leaned against a carriage wheel, shaky and

145

trembling. Logs had spilled over the street. Men heaved an overturned wagon away from the driver who lay below it. Two other men held our carriage's team from bolting in fright.

Kate knelt beside Etta, who was prone on the ground with a man's coat rolled beneath her head. "She's waking up. Someone send for a doctor!"

"Are you hurt, miss?" one man asked. I shook my head and stumbled to Etta's side.

My knees wobbled. Every bone ached and dizziness overcame me. "Etta, can you hear me? Move your fingers and toes, please."

"Yes, miss, I'm doin' the best I can," she whispered. "No little bump on the head's going to keep me down for long. I'll be fine."

A doctor soon arrived and examined Etta's cut. "It's deep, you'll need stitches. I can't work on you here in the street."

I squeezed Etta's hand. "Can we take her to the Russ House?"

"Too far," he said. "Better not take that chance."

"You go on ahead, miss," Etta said. "Don't keep your young man waiting."

Charles had directed several onlookers to fashion a makeshift litter. Etta sipped whiskey someone brought from a nearby saloon. Charles held the glass to me and insisted, so I gulped the fiery liquor. And choked. How could men drink this vile stuff? My cheeks and throat burned, and I bent double to regain my senses.

The newspaper that Charles had bought Kate was lying on the ground by the overturned carriage. I snatched it before someone stepped on the front page headline. The words 'Explosion Rocks City' glared in bold letters.

"Look at this, Kate." I read the paragraph below the headline. " 'Early this morning, an explosion disturbed the peace of City Hall at Kearney and Pacific streets. Shattered windows of the buildings all around, too. One man was injured in the blast when a wall fell. They found body parts—ugh! They couldn't identify who was killed.' "

Charles glanced over my shoulder. "Must be anarchists," he said with a wave of his hand. "Such things are becoming common in the city."

"What if Ace was there to get the marriage license? What if he was hurt? Oh, this day is turning into a nightmare!"

Kate jabbed the flimsy paper. "Look at the time reported for the explosion, Lily. Five in the morning. I'm sure City Hall doesn't open for business until eight or nine."

That didn't ease my worries. "Then what if the office is closed all day? We'll never be able to get married without a license—"

"Worry when you come to that bridge." She hurried me over to a horsecar, the carpetbag in hand along with my valise. "Charles will make sure Etta gets to the hotel. Ace may be already there and waiting for us."

Despite my misgivings about leaving them behind, I climbed aboard. We both fretted while the horsecar rumbled along Tyler Street. Once we reached Market, Kate pulled me off to join the crowd waiting in line for the next omnibus downtown. My stomach jitters increased. I'd die if we couldn't find a Justice of the Peace. What if James McKay had sent word to my uncle that I'd been in Rock Canyon with Ace? Uncle Harrison's anger would triple.

If only we hadn't chosen the Russ House, right across from the Occidental. Maybe that was a mistake. Maybe Santiago would come in his place. He'd drag me back to my uncle, wed me and bed me. And not necessarily in that order.

I pulled Kate aside, too impatient to wait for another streetcar. "We're better off walking. There's so many people, we'll never get on. Lucky for us it's not a hot day. Yet."

"But the accident—"

"Walking will help loosen my stiff muscles." I didn't tell her about my aching wrist, nose and elbow, which I'd ignored so far. "You don't mind, do you?"

Kate didn't answer, although she turned cheerful again once we started. We soon passed an area teeming with workers, supplies and piles of sand and dirt where half of a new building stood. The tangle of traffic eased. I darted into a recessed doorway of a building and pulled Kate in with me. I thought I'd caught sight of the reporter, Mr. Dodd, in the crowd ahead, his bowler hat set at a rakish angle. Within a few minutes, James McKay stopped within two feet of our shadowy hiding place. His blustery voice trumpeted above the street's raucous noise.

"The Rock Canyon mission article can go in the back pages."

"I thought that was only an excuse to check on Captain Granville's niece."

"True, but why not use it," McKay said. "I debated sending word last night to Granville. He won't be happy with the news, of course, but he might find it useful . . ."

I missed hearing the rest of his sentence when a buckboard wagon and its team rattled past. Opening the door behind us, I slipped inside. Kate followed. The shop turned out to be a haberdashery. We smiled at the male clerks and rushed out the side door to Powell Street. After walking several blocks to Bush, we headed toward Montgomery.

"Did that horrible man send a wire to your uncle?" Kate asked.

"I suppose so, which means we have to be careful reaching the hotel. I doubt if my uncle would have left Sacramento until this morning, though."

That conjecture didn't soothe my rattled nerves, but once I caught sight of the three-story Russ

House in the distance, I breathed a sigh of relief. A few more blocks. Kate clung to my arm tighter, eyeing every pedestrian, buggy and dray that passed, as if she suspected my uncle would jump out at us. When a gentleman tipped his hat to us, she gasped. Stifling a laugh, I pushed her around the corner and across the street.

"Stop looking like you've seen a ghost."

"I wish Charles was here. He'd protect you."

Kate held me back while another couple strolled past. We walked another three blocks and crossed the street to avoid a group of men who waited outside a saloon. For almost five minutes, we watched a flood of delivery wagons, carriages, several full omnibuses and cabs. At last Kate pulled me out, the space wide enough before the next barrage of traffic.

"It's not too far now. Follow me."

She surged ahead before I could stop her. My feet hurt, my wrist had stiffened and my elbow throbbed. My vision blurred. I put one foot in front of the other, focused on the wooden planks below. I did my best to catch up, but Kate was a good ways ahead and had reached the hotel's wide entrance. A tall man sidled up to her and clamped a hand around her upper arm. She shrieked and fought to break free. I overheard his loud voice.

"Miss Lily Granville?"

"Let go! Help—" Kate gasped when a second

shorter man appeared and grabbed her around the waist. Together the two men dragged her across the wide street toward the Occidental Hotel. The second man dodged when she swung the carpetbag. "Who are you?"

"Pinkerton detectives. Captain Granville is waiting to see you."

Despite her protests, they forced her into the building. I crept after them, keeping my distance, while Kate kicked and howled. The taller detective, his hand scarred from an old burn, retrieved a leather wallet from his pocket and tossed a bill toward the reception clerk.

"We've been hired by Captain Granville to fetch his runaway niece."

"Let go of me," Kate said, although the shorter man dragged her toward the stairs. "The police will hear of this mistreatment!"

I hurried outside and across the street to the Russ House. Uncle Harrison would be furious once they took her upstairs. Would he question Kate about my whereabouts? I hoped not. I wished now we'd arranged to meet Ace far away from the Occidental Hotel. The idea of facing my uncle unnerved me. I wasn't prepared.

My heart jumped into my throat at the sight of two men lurking by the reception desk in the Russ House. They joined another man who entered behind me, shaking hands all around, and then walked to the dining room. A clock in the lobby struck two. I was four hours late. Had Ace waited and then left? Every bone ached from the bruises I'd received in the accident.

Charles appeared at my elbow. "Are you all right? Where's Kate?"

I explained what happened and then begged him to be patient. "They won't harm her, Charles. Kate is smart enough to know what to say. She might spin a yarn about me heading back to Sacramento. Is Etta here?"

"Upstairs—she's resting in our room next to yours. I registered in my name." He paced the hall. "Are you sure Kate will be all right?"

"No, but if you show up they might hurt you to get information out of her. Wait another ten minutes, she might return. I'd rather use the back stairs, if there's one."

He led the way past the reception desk. Off of a narrow hall, one doorway opened into a huge room filled with elegant chandeliers, cloth-covered tables and cushioned chairs. The library held floor to ceiling shelves filled with leather-bound books, carved armchairs, ottomans and velvet draperies. The heavy scent of cigars reminded me of James McKay's visit last night, but he wasn't sitting inside. Several older men held a lively discussion over an ivory chess set in one corner. At last we reached a steep staircase.

"Have you heard from Ace?"

"Yes. The Justice of the Peace had another

appointment, so they'll arrive at six o'clock," Charles said. "Here's your key, I'm going to fetch Kate."

I trudged up the steps, exhausted and sore. Several people walked the long stuffy hallway of the third floor. One man unlocked a door for a woman, who vanished inside before I could catch a glimpse of her face. The door shut behind them. I passed another couple and nodded when the gentleman tipped his hat. Once I inserted the key into the room's door and twisted, it didn't budge. I tried a second time. Nothing.

Someone rattled the door knob from the other side. "Who is it?"

"Is that you, Etta?"

A strange woman flung the door wide. "You have the wrong room! I've been waiting for hours for a maid to bring clean sheets."

Staring at the painted number on the door, I backed away. "I'm so sorry."

Confused, my brain fuzzy, I hurried down the corridor. What had Charles told me? The room's number was engraved on the key. How stupid of me, not checking first. I reached the correct room down the hall. The key turned easily this time.

"Oh, thank goodness."

I staggered inside. Before I could shut the door, Kate bounded past me into the room. Charles set both the valise and carpetbag on the floor, but Kate twirled around, bubbling with laughter. She hugged me tight. Her eyes sparkled with excitement.

"They let me go! I was so afraid the detectives would follow me, but your uncle hadn't finished yelling at them. He was angry they'd brought him the wrong woman."

"What did Uncle Harrison say to you?"

"Nothing, he was too shocked. Remember I never met him back in Sacramento." Kate pushed me toward the four-poster bed. "He reminded me of my father, the way he turned purple. The whole room echoed when he shouted at those men. A nasty temper."

"Yes, he does have that."

"Charles, go keep watch downstairs." She shooed her husband out. "In case."

I sank on the bed's edge once he shut the door. "I hope Ace managed to get a license."

"Wash up and rest, Lily, don't worry about all that now. I'll wake you in time to get dressed. You have a few hours." Kate knelt and removed my shoes despite my protests. "Etta's resting in her room. She made us promise to wake her in time for the wedding. She said she wouldn't miss it for anything."

Exhausted, I scrubbed my face and hands and then stripped to my corset cover and petticoats. Once I crawled onto the soft feather mattress, Kate found an extra blanket in the wardrobe and covered me. I listened to her chatter about my uncle, but the words blurred together. Her figure mingled with a vague dream about shadowy hotel rooms and people who wandered in and out. Then I found myself in a fog-shrouded field filled with rocks.

A loud bang woke me.

I sat up in the dim bedroom. Voices drifted from the hallway, and my stomach grumbled aloud. I couldn't remember where I was until I recalled the accident. Dark bruises along my left arm and the lingering pain in my wrist verified that. I slid off the mattress and drew the chamber pot from beneath the bed. Then I washed up and dabbed at my throbbing nose. It didn't look crooked or broken. I shivered, rubbing goose bumps along my arms to warm up, before a key rattled in the door. Kate poked her head inside while I snatched a towel.

"Oh good, you're awake." She shut the door behind her. "Ace is downstairs. I told him it's bad luck to see the bride before a wedding. He's worried about you."

I yawned. "What time is it?"

"Half past five." Kate sat me on the bed's edge, scattering pins all over when she yanked them from my hair and switch. She rambled from one subject to another while she brushed out my tangled blonde curls. "I wasn't sure Ace would get here at all, but things have worked out for the best. We made reservations for a celebration supper, too. And I found a needle and thread to fix the dress. I had to visit two shops near here."

"How is Etta?" I asked when she caught her breath.

"She has a headache, but she won't skip the wedding," Kate said and tugged harder with the hairbrush. "Oh, sorry. We're not sure it's safe for you to stay here tonight, being so close to the Occidental, but we don't have a choice. Etta will stay in this room tonight. We reserved a different one down the hall for you and Ace with a private bath."

"A bath would be heavenly. Thank you." I flexed my sore shoulders and neck. "Those Pinkerton agents didn't hurt you, did they?"

"No. But let's not talk about that now." Kate rolled up her mother's dress and plopped it over my head. "I figured you might want to soak in a bath before—oh, wait, now your bustle is twisted around, let me straighten everything. Hold still, Lily, please! It's tricky with all this extra fabric. Thank heavens hoopskirts went out of style."

"Mother moved with grace," I said, "although I had trouble learning."

"She put you in hoops, too?"

"Oh yes. We often wore matching outfits."

"How wonderful." Kate sounded wistful. "I was lucky to get a few nicer muslin petticoats handed down from my aunts. Of course, I wore my oldest dress while milking cows and cleaning the chicken coops. You were so lucky."

"You had a big family, and I envy you that." I twisted to watch while she basted some of the fabric to the waistband over my bustle so it would drape in folds. "Don't fuss. I don't want to ruin your mother's dress."

"There, that looks very natural. Now the sleeves."

"Ouch! The bodice will never button—"

"Wait. Hold your breath." Kate pushed me forward to lean against the bed post, pushed aside the layers to reach my corset and then tightened the strings. The buttons held. "I'd never fit into that, goodness! Mother was tiny in the bosom. Don't take a deep breath, Lily."

"I hope I remember that, or the judge will get an eyeful at the wedding."

We both erupted into nervous giggles. I patted the beads of perspiration on my forehead and neck. My jittery stomach added to my nerves. Was I doing the right thing? Could we endure a lifetime of marriage? Did Ace want children? Did I? Where would we live? What about the dynamite factory? All these questions made my head spin.

"Kate, am I making a mistake?"

"Every bride wonders that. I didn't know Charles at all when we married. But we're happy so far, and you will be too."

I stared at my clasped hands. The memory of Ace's fervent kisses and the intimate moments we'd shared at Mt. Diablo bothered me. I ought to marry him by that fact alone. Everything seemed so rushed, though. The one item I had to comfort me was Father's gold watch, so I retrieved it from the borrowed dress's pocket. The intricate scrolls etched on the case were lovely. I held it open against my ear to listen to its rhythmic ticking.

Kate sat me down on the bed's edge. "I forgot to tell you I saw another man in the hotel room—at the Occidental, with your uncle. It must have been that Señor Santiago by Etta's description. Plus a priest, I think. They called him Father something or other."

That information stabbed me like a sharp pin in the backside. So they'd come prepared. My blood boiled. How dare Uncle Harrison track me down like I'd tracked my father's killer, and then attempt to force a marriage with Santiago! I was thankful those detectives mistook Kate for me. If not, I'd be stuck for good without recourse.

My resolve to marry Ace strengthened, chasing all reservations from my mind. He was my choice of a man, someone I loved and wanted.

"Lily?"

Charles stood in the doorway, holding his arm out. Kate jammed several hairpins into my curls to secure fresh rosebuds. "No one will notice I snitched these from the flower arrangement in the hall," she whispered in my ear. "I'm sorry my mother's hat was crushed by the accident. Here, take this handkerchief. I'll fetch Etta and we'll be down as soon as possible."

I grabbed Charles' arm and hurried down the narrow steps to a small parlor. A ladies' parlor, so pretty with its chintz-covered furnishings, wallpaper with tiny rosebuds in between pale pink stripes, fringed lamps and several sofas. Despite his urging to sit and relax, I refused. The bodice buttons strained with every breath, and I dared not sit in case the basting threads in the skirt unraveled. I worried Kate's handkerchief between my fingers until my skin was raw.

When the door opened, a tall stooped man in a rumpled baggy suit entered the room. Ace followed, and his mismatched eyes brightened when he saw me. That boyish smile warmed my heart. He wore a black silk string tie below his stiff collar, plus a dark three-piece suit which fit better than the cutaway he'd worn at the banquet. I relaxed. He seemed uneasy, the way he fiddled with a gold watch chain.

Ace Diamond, nervous? I loved him more for that.

"We need brighter light in here." Charles twisted the valves of the gas sconces around the parlor. "Better, Judge Sanderson?"

"Fine, fine. I understand your uncle was appointed as your guardian, Miss Granville." He smoothed his wrinkled coat. With a grizzled beard and gray-shot dark hair, plus a gruff, no-nonsense tone, he reminded me of Father. "Have you asked Captain Granville for permission to marry his niece, Mr. Diamond?"

"No, sir. He'd sooner shoot first than speak to me."

"I see." Judge Sanderson poked up his wire-rim spectacles. "You look old enough to know your own mind, young lady. I suppose he was appointed to protect any financial assets from being squandered. But once you choose to marry, those assets become your husband's property. Are you certain you wish to marry?"

I met his serious gaze. "Yes, sir."

"We'll be partners, Lily. I ain't gonna take anything away from you—the Early Bird or the ranch," Ace said. "You can trust me on that."

He grasped my cold fingers, rubbed them between his own and then winked. I had to choke back another laugh and faced Judge Sanderson again, who'd been busy examining the marriage license. He cleared his throat.

"First of all, I'm not comfortable with one witness—"

The door creaked open. Etta limped into the room, wrapped in a plaid woolen shawl and supported by Kate. She sank into the nearest chair. My fingers curled between Ace's and he squeezed tight. I was so glad to see Etta. Her pasty skin and obvious pain worried me, but she managed a wan smile and waved a hand. Kate hurried to Charles' side.

"Well then, that's settled. If no one objects, let's begin." Judge Sanderson unfolded a piece of paper. "I'm sure you've witnessed a wedding ceremony at some point."

"Nope, but that don't matter." Ace grinned. "Tell me what to say."

"Repeat the vows after me when the time comes, young man." He glanced at me, as if gauging my readiness or expecting me to change my mind. I smiled. The judge resumed. "We are gathered here today to witness the joining of a man and a woman in marriage. Now, you all may know that marriage is an honored institution, and its vows should not be taken lightly or discarded when inconvenient. I'm appointed in this county to perform legal unions . . ."

My heart thumped in my ears. Ace fidgeted while Judge Sanderson rambled on about past ceremonies and other couples, young and old, before he gazed at us.

"Face each other, join your right hands, and repeat after me."

Ace cleared his throat. "I, Jesse Rawlins Diamond, take you, Lily Granville, to be my wedded wife. I promise to be true to you in good times and bad, in sickness or health, for richer or poorer, and to love and honor you all the days of my life."

I swallowed hard, blinking back tears, awash with mixed emotions. Would Father have approved of Ace? I'd never know. Perhaps. Mother might have recognized his potential and given him a chance. He'd proven his love and devotion to me. I was ready to accept this young Texan ex-Confederate soldier, a penniless wanderer until the day we met, who vowed to be worthy of my love, as my lawful husband.

Judge Sanderson turned to me next. "Repeat after me . . ."

"I, Lily Rose Delano Granville, take you, Jesse Rawlins Diamond—"

The door burst open this time.

*'Let him kiss me with the kisses of his mouth:*
*for thy love is better than wine.'*
Song of Solomon 1:2

# Chapter Nine

"Yes? Who is it?" Judge Sanderson sounded impatient.

The raven-haired woman with large brown eyes stared at us in confusion from the doorway, blinking. My heart had skipped a few beats. I'd fully expected to see Uncle Harrison stride into the room with Esteban de los Reyes Santiago and the priest from Sacramento. When Ace scowled, the woman backed into the corridor.

"Oh! I-I am sorry for the interruption."

Charles had stalked to the door and closed it with a firm hand. I didn't catch sight of who stood behind the woman, but I believed a man dodged out of sight. The woman also had a slight Spanish accent. Dread filled me. The door didn't have a lock.

"Now where were we . . . oh yes. Miss Granville. Let's start over."

I gazed into Ace's eyes, my warmer fingers entwined in his, my voice unsteady due to the swirl of fear and excitement. "I, Lily Rose Delano Granville, take you, Jesse Diamond, as my wedded husband. I promise to be true to you in good times and in bad. In sickness and health, for richer or poorer. And to love and honor you all the days of my life."

"Do you have a ring, Mr. Diamond?"

Charles pulled a slim gold band from his pocket and handed it to Ace. I marveled at its luster when he slipped it over my left hand's third finger. The circle hung a bit loose. I curled my fist and glanced up at my new husband, who beamed at me with pride and love.

Judge Sanderson nodded. "By the power vested in me in the State of California, I now pronounce you husband and wife. If you wish to seal your union with a kiss, you may do so now. You're one lucky fellow, Mr. Diamond. I can say that for certain."

Ace drew me close, his hands cupping my face, and kissed me sweetly on the lips. Then he hugged me tight, lifted me up and whirled me around again. I laughed, his exuberance matching my own. Nothing my uncle did could break our union or undo the vows we'd taken. The judge signed the marriage license plus a second copy, then waved us over to the table. With joy I signed my new name, noting Ace's careful signature inked on the line above, and then handed the pen to Charles. He added his as a witness along with Kate.

Judge Sanderson accepted the gold eagle Ace handed him, folded one document and tucked it within his breast pocket. "I'll register this tomorrow instead of waiting until the next time I visit City Hall. Given what you explained about this business partner, Mr. Diamond, your wife ought to be safe from any shenanigans. And from her uncle's meddling."

The men shook hands all around. "Thank you, sir. Sorry for the delay," Ace said. "Who'd ever guess there'd be trouble with dynamite today, of all days?"

"Good thing you found me after all the hullaballoo this morning." He scratched his beard. "Anarchists. What will people cook up next, I tell you. Heard they arrested one fellow involved. He'd been injured in the blast, and a second man was blown to bits. A third escaped."

"The story's already in the newspapers," Charles said. "They say. . ."

He followed the judge out of the parlor to discuss the details. Kate kissed, hugged me and whispered near my ear. "Dinner's at half past seven, an hour from now. Stay here out of sight and then come to the dining room."

She hurried to help Etta to her feet. I hugged them both and dried my misty eyes, while Ace dragged a heavy armchair from the corner. Once they departed, he braced it under the brass door-knob. My husband turned to me with an easy grin.

"You're lookin' mighty fine, Mrs. Diamond."

"I wish I felt better—"

"What? Whoa, Lily." He caught me when I wavered on my feet and then pulled me toward the horsehair sofa. "They never said you was hurt in that accident."

"Bruised, mostly." I touched the flowers pinned in my hair once he sat beside me. My gold ring glinted in the lamplight. "Everyone landed on top of me when the carriage tipped over. Etta suffered that cut on her head and concussion. My shoulder and arm are a bit sore."

"You're all lucky you weren't killed. Here, let me." His warm hands kneaded the areas and relieved the ache within a few minutes. "Better?"

"Yes. Thank you—"

"You're my wife, Lily. No need to thank me for anything."

I still thanked him with a lingering kiss. His hand swept a stray curl from my forehead. We both twisted at the doorknob's loud rattling. Someone knocked several times, but we ignored the noise. I smiled at my husband.

"So it's official, Mr. Diamond."

"Yep. Hitched for good, and no goin' back."

"We're not going anywhere for an hour or so. I could read a book—"

"Ha." Ace pulled me onto his lap. "Feel any different now that you're married?"

"No. I suppose that might change after tonight,"

I said, deliberately coy. "This wasn't what I expected for a wedding ceremony. But I wouldn't trade it for the world."

"Me neither."

His fingers roved over my bodice's buttons, but I captured them tight. "I have some questions you need to answer first."

"Oh?" One hot kiss left me shivering with need. "What about?"

"Well. I'd like to learn more about the man I married. We haven't known each other for very long." My fingers stroked his smooth jaw, so different from the scruffy growth of beard. "Where were you born, what were your parents' names? Now that we're married, I'd like to know the family I married into—even if you and your brother are the only ones left."

Ace raised an eyebrow. "You need to know that now?"

I pushed his other hand away from my bosom. "Yes. Didn't you say your mother was raised in Natchez? Where is that?"

"On the Mississippi River." He leaned back against the sofa and loosened his tie. "A ways north from New Orleans."

His drawling intonation, the way he pronounced the city's name as Nawlins intrigued me all over again. "What was her name, and didn't you say your father was a lawyer? Were you born in Texas or Mississippi?"

He drew me against his chest and planted a kiss on my cheek. "Texas, born and raised. My father was Ned Diamond. He studied law under Sam Houston, or so he told us. But he also worked as a drummer or a carpenter, even a sawbones. Whatever he got paid to do. Plenty of times he didn't work at all, from what little I remember."

"So he wasn't often home?"

"Nope. Off fightin' the war with the Mexicans, and then travelin' to find work after Ma died." Ace rubbed his forehead. I noticed the long sweep of his eyelashes when he blinked. "He took to whiskey as comfort. Royce worked two jobs to keep us all from starvin'."

I almost fell off Ace's knee at the furious rapping on the door. A man's voice gave a command. "Whoever's in there, open up! Hello?"

The door itself shook, as if someone rammed their shoulder against it. Thank goodness the chair didn't budge. A woman voiced unhappy complaints, but I couldn't discern the words exchanged between them. At last I rested my head in the hollow of Ace's shoulder when the voices and muffled footsteps died away.

"How did your parents meet?" I whispered.

He let out a long breath. "No idea. Pa met Juliana Layne in Natchez and then talked her into running away with him."

"I suppose her family wasn't happy about that."

"Nope. They searched for her, but didn't know

Pa had taken her to his folks down in Louisiana. Ended up in Texas. He built a dog-leg shack north of a town called Henderson. Patch of garden, a few cows and chickens. They had five sons— Royce, Travis, Owen, me and Layne. All pretty wild. Ma tried to teach us some manners, but we never listened."

"I thought you were the youngest."

"Born in April, and Layne came the next year in early March. Almost twins, or so Ma said. I was six or seven when she died. Plumb worn out."

Touched by his mother's tragic death, and hardscrabble childhood, I felt blessed in comparison. Ace seemed melancholy, lost in thought. He breathed deep and then rested his cheek against my hair.

"So you had no chance of going to school," I said, tracing a finger along his collar.

"No schoolteacher. A few kids around learned to read out of their family Bible. We never had time for it. Wasn't easy fightin' for enough to eat most days. I ended up doin' Travis and Owen's chores at home so they could work for a blacksmith. They still walloped me."

"Is that what happened to your eye? Changing color like it did."

"That was an accident. Sort of." He grinned. "Royce threw a punch at Travis, but I got in the way. My whole face puffed up like I was snake bit. Ma had a fit, wouldn't speak to either of 'em for a few days. I must've been three or four, I guess. It healed up quick. Why don't you tell me more about your folks? Probably had a happier time growin' up."

"I wish I could show you the daguerreotype of my parents, but I left it in Sacramento. Do you have any of your family?"

"No money for that kind of thing." Ace sounded cheerful. "I'm gettin' used to having a bit of jingle in my pockets now. I might get spoiled. Ma grew up with money, of course. She never complained about losing it all, though."

"Juliana, what a beautiful name. Maybe if we have a daughter, we'll name her that."

"Sure thing." Ace nuzzled my ear, his hands roving, and this time I didn't stop him. "I'm fixin' to give you one tonight. Or right now, if you're ready."

"And ruin our wedding night—oh!"

I buried my face against his chest at more loud pounding on the door. My heart echoed after every solid thump. This time I sensed my uncle's hired detectives were in the hallway with the hotel manager, although I didn't dare suggest finding out. And held Ace back when he half-rose from the sofa. He shifted, tense with anger, and then settled back with his arms around me again. I took a deep breath and then clapped a hand over my bodice buttons. They'd strained to the breaking point. Heavens.

"I'm glad this parlor doesn't have a window."

"If I wasn't so hungry, I'd suggest heading

upstairs now," he said and kissed my ear.

"I don't want to disappoint Kate and Charles. Remember they're newly married, too, and have helped us so much."

"All right, but it ain't easy to wait."

"You may have to, since I didn't have time for a bath this afternoon." I bolted upright at another thought. "Oh, I don't have a clean nightdress—"

"You won't need one, darlin'."

After sharing a passionate kiss, I breathed in his scent of musk, bay rum and soap. He tasted salty, too. "Remember you said how you lost your cutter? Your horse, right?"

"Yep. Good old Reb."

"Reb?" I laughed. "For Rebel, I suppose. That seems to fit."

Ace snorted. "Best gelding I ever had. A bay roan, and his coat turned darker in winter. Reb knew which way a steer would run, a few seconds before it moved. He was more intelligent than most people I ever met in my life."

"So what happened? How did you lose him?"

"Broke his leg in a gopher hole, and had to put him down," he said, eyes downcast. "Worst day of my life, too. Kept my brother company from Fort Riley, Kansas, up to Nebraska. He was headin' west to his next assignment. I started back but never made it."

"And then—"

"Ended up in Omaha. No horse, sold my saddle

for a room and a few meals. No jobs till that boardinghouse landlady took pity on me."

"We'd never have met if not for your horse," I whispered in his ear. "I'm sorry you lost the cutter, though. How did you learn to speak Spanish?"

He ran his tongue around my earlobe, his breath hot, making me shiver. "Told ya that me and Layne worked to round up mossy horns down in Texas. A few men never learned English, so we picked up Spanish pretty quick. Is that important?"

"No, but I remember something else you told me on the train."

"Mm? What's that?"

"That I'd never get a chance to see your scars."

Ace flashed a mischievous smile and leaned back, arms held out wide. "Go ahead and search for 'em. What, are you too scared? I dare you."

"It wouldn't be proper," I said, my cheeks burning.

"I'm all yours, Lily Diamond. Whenever and wherever you want me."

"Is that so?"

"Yep."

I slid one hand over his chest. "After supper and a bath."

"Maybe I'll change your mind." He came close to succeeding until I tugged his vest chain free, but there was no pocket watch attached. Ace looked sheepish. "Never got me one for this fancy getup.

172

Haven't had a free minute since I arrived in 'Frisco."

"Then I have a wedding present for you." I drew out the heavy gold watch from my skirt pocket. "It's all I have left of my father. This means the world to me, and I'm giving it to you. Wear it on this chain. Think of me whenever you open it."

Speechless, Ace eyed my movements when I fastened the timepiece to the chain's end. He hugged me tight. "I ain't ever had a gift like this before, Lily. I didn't think about findin' a wedding present for you—"

"Buy me a horse so we can ride together one day. On our ranch."

I ran my fingers through his thick hair, admiring the coppery sheen in the gaslight, the variety of brown and red hues. Awash with delicious yearnings, I leaned forward. He had too, though —and his hard head smacked into my nose. Stabbing pain shocked me. My eyes watered and I hunched over, waiting until I could think straight. I held my palms over my throbbing nose. Maybe it was broken now. Tears leaked from beneath my lashes.

"You hurt?" he whispered. "Lily, I'm sorry. Don't cry."

"I'm not, it just—hurts." I sat up, embarrassed, and then smeared blood on my sleeve. "Oh no, this is Kate's mother's dress! It'll stain if I don't sponge it right away."

Ace clapped a linen handkerchief against my nose and tilted my head back. "Not until this bleeding stops. Hold still."

More tears trickled down my face. I felt foolish, ruining the few minutes we had left to ourselves. "How can I go to supper—there's a few drops on the bodice too."

"All right, don't cry. Want me to fetch some cold water?"

I sniffed, my head dizzy, and stared at the ceiling. "Yes. Thank you."

"We could go up to our room," Ace said, but I shook my head.

"I know better than to tempt you like that. If I sponge the blood off, I won't have to change my dress before supper."

"Why not change? You could wear what you had on last night."

"That old thing? Oh—never mind. Fetch the water. Please."

Puzzled, he headed toward the door and tugged the chair free. Ace glanced back once before the door closed. I dried my tears, my cheeks still warm, and checked for more blood on the dress. I wasn't about to explain how unseemly it would be, appearing at supper in not-so-fresh clothing. As if we'd been so eager to share intimacy that we couldn't wait for our wedding night! I fanned myself. A man had appetites, of course. Mother never had the chance to explain what happened between a husband and wife in a marriage bed, but I wasn't naïve.

I hadn't expected to feel wonderful wicked pleasure beyond a wife's duty, though.

Two ladies entered the room and looked surprised. "I'm sorry to disturb you, ma'am. Are you injured? Perhaps we ought to call a doctor."

"No, thank you. I'm fine. My husband will be back soon."

Ace pushed past them with a shallow ceramic bowl of water. The ladies left us alone. "Saw Charles in the dining room with Kate, so we'd better join 'em soon."

"Yes, of course." I folded his blood-smeared handkerchief and watched him stuff it in his pocket. "Did Kate tell you about the Pinkerton agents? My uncle hired them."

Ace scratched under his tight collar. "Ain't surprised he'd do that."

"It wasn't a coincidence that he announced my engagement to Santiago right after you showed up at the banquet," I said, sponging the bodice front. "I hope he changes his mind one day about you. He ought to give you a chance."

"I got other things on my mind—"

He kissed my neck, distracting me while I scrubbed the spots on the sleeve. Once I'd finished, Ace drew me into his arms. I pushed against his chest.

"We're already late for dinner—"

175

"Lily? Ace?" Kate poked her head inside. "Are you ready?"

"Do I look all right?" I smoothed my hair and straightened my skirts.

Ace grinned. "You look like a bride with an impatient husband. Come on."

The three of us joined Charles in the dining room. I noticed several guests staring when we passed, including the two women who'd interrupted a short time ago. Thank goodness we had a table in a private alcove. After the waiter poured champagne into narrow crystal flutes and took our dinner orders, Charles raised his glass for a toast.

"May God bless your marriage with health, wealth and happiness you both deserve."

Ace lifted his again after we sipped. "To the gospel mill."

"Gospel mill?" I laughed and clinked my flute against Kate's. "To the mission's new cook stove. May it never burn anything."

"New stove? What are y'all talkin' about?"

I turned to Ace. "A monthly donation to the mission, because Kate cooks meals every week for so many people. I forgot to mention that."

"From what I hear, the wife's supposed to spend her husband's money like wildfire," he said with a wink. "But it's your money anyway."

"Ours. We're in this together."

We all drank again. Giddy from the sweet bubbly wine, I sampled the consommé and broiled trout, but preferred the tender roast lamb with mint sauce. Golden baked squash, mashed potatoes along with pickled vegetables and fresh rolls arrived. The waiter brought a Damson tart with custard. We finished supper with coffee, dates and sugared almonds and walnuts.

"So what about your partnership with Santiago?" Charles asked.

"Nothing's changed." Ace leaned back and folded his hands over his vest. "He might be a bit steamed about Lily when he finds out. But he don't seem the type to hold a grudge. Least as far as I've known him."

"Which has been what, a few weeks?" I asked. "Or a month?"

He shrugged. "I don't expect trouble now we're married. If your uncle wants to produce quicksilver, he'll have to bargain with you to reopen that claim."

"With us." I glanced up in surprise when the waiter brought a small white frosted cake topped with a posy of orange blossoms, plus a sweet dessert wine. "A wedding cake!"

Kate clasped her hands in delight. "To celebrate both of our marriages. I asked the chef to make something special, but I didn't expect it to look so pretty."

"What a lovely surprise." I raised my refilled wine glass. "To our lasting friendship and success here in San Francisco."

While we enjoyed generous slices of cake, Kate and I planned visiting some of the shops in the city before she left for home. Ace and Charles discussed the explosion at city hall and other news in the papers. I didn't follow until Charles mentioned familiar names.

"Who would trust Gould and Fisk with anything?" He set his silver fork down with a clatter. "It's going to reflect on the President before long. Hard to believe, but politicians seem to have weaker morals now."

"Jay Gould and James Fisk? What's all that about?"

"The scandal over a run on the gold market, from what he's heard," Ace said. "I don't know a thing about stocks and all that."

Charles laughed. "Neither do I. We'll never have enough money to invest."

"So where do you plan to live?" Kate asked. Ace answered before I had a chance.

"On that ranch Lily inherited. Breedin' horses might be a safer business than dynamite production," he said and squeezed my hand under the table. I smiled.

"Yes, but we'll tear down that house. I have bad memories of that place."

"You could rent it out," Charles said, "and build a new one in a better spot."

"I'd rather live in San Francisco," I said. "Or out your way with a view of the city. That would

178

be nice. How's Etta? I'm so worried about her."

"I woke her several times this afternoon while she napped like the doctor said. We ought to check on her, though." Kate folded her napkin and nudged Charles' arm. "Time to retire for the night. I'm sure it's late."

"Half-past nine." Ace held out the open gold watch with pride and closed it with a snap. He returned it to his vest pocket. "I feel like a real gent now."

"You signed your name on the marriage license, too," I said, clinging to his arm, "so you must have learned penmanship this past month."

"A little. Still can't read, so Santiago handles all the contracts—"

"I'd like to see them and make sure he hasn't cheated you."

I rose to my feet, reluctant to end the party. "Did you want me to return your mother's dress tonight or tomorrow?"

Kate leaned close to whisper. "You'll be busy, don't worry."

My face flooded with heat. She pushed me toward Ace so hard, I stumbled. Perhaps I'd indulged in too much champagne, plus the dessert wine and rich food. My husband escorted me up the stairs, his arm firm around my waist. Once he unlocked our door, Ace swept me off my feet with a laugh.

"I'm not that tired—"

"Tradition, Mrs. Diamond. I'll carry you over the threshold again once we build that new house," he said and kicked the door shut behind us. "Or anywhere we live."

"Even if we move to Chicago?"

I laughed at his sour face. After sharing a long, deep kiss, Ace carried me to the four-poster bed and deposited me on the soft feather mattress, then shucked his coat and tie. I blinked. He unfastened his tight collar and tossed it toward a chair.

"You missed."

I'd pulled off my French-heeled shoes, dropped them over the bed's side and curled my feet beneath me. Ace removed his stiletto, tugged off one boot and then the other, peeled each sock and stripped off his vest. I laughed behind my hand while he undid his shirt buttons.

"What? Haven't you seen a man get undressed?"

"No, I can truthfully say I have not. If you don't count the Pullman palace car," I said, stretching back against the pillow. "But I was careful not to look at anyone preparing for the night. Have you forgotten I wanted a bath first?"

His fingers halted. "You're serious?"

"I'll be quick. I promise."

Ace sank onto the bed's edge with a groan. "Lily, darlin'. How about we take a bath together after—well, afterward."

"You didn't listen to Charles' preaching last night, did you? He talked about the virtues of Christianity. Kindness, meekness, honesty and patience."

"Patience ain't my strongest suit."

"Then maybe you ought to learn that lesson—"

I rolled out of his reach, too quick for his grabbing hands, and raced to the tiny adjoining bathroom. The washstand held a generous amount of towels. I leaned over the claw-foot tub and turned the brass spigot. Warm water, not hot, gushed forth. Steam soon engulfed the narrow room. A shaving strop hung beside the mirror. The idea of watching my husband lather his face and scrape his jaw and neck smooth sent a delicious thrill through my veins.

Ace hooked an arm around me from behind. He hefted me up and whirled me around, laughed when I thrashed about in pretense, then carried me back to the bedroom and pressed me against a wall. He trailed kisses along my neck.

"Mm. You smell nice. I'd say that bath could wait."

"I disagree. And I can tell you need one too. Oh! You pinched me—"

"You pinched me last night, remember."

We stopped laughing at a heavy thumping sound on the wall's other side. "Keep it down, will ya?" The man's voice sounded sleepy, and a woman scolded him when he cursed.

Eyebrows raised, Ace held a finger up to his lips. I'd doubled over, one hand over my mouth to suppress my laughter, but it bubbled over until my throat ached. He snatched a hairpin and then another, chasing me around the bed. He soon held my switch in his hands.

"Oh no!"

"Don't get all mad now. Kate told me you'd cut your hair—"

"She did?" Embarrassed, I grabbed the curly hairpiece from him, marched back to the damp bathroom and turned off the tub's spigots. "The whole story?"

"You cut it after your pa died. Right?" He caressed my neck where my loosened curls spread over my shoulders, and then slid his arms around me. "It don't matter. I love your hair, short or long. It's soft as silk."

"This water's getting cold."

I faced him, my bodice already unbuttoned by his fast fingers, and raised my arms so he could lift the dress over my head. Ace squinted in dismay at my corset cover's tiny pearl buttons. I finished unbuttoning his shirt and pushed his suspenders aside. My hands roved over his warm shoulders, admiring the sculpted muscles, and noticed the raised scar running from his ribs into his trousers' waistband. I'd glimpsed his chest once in the dim light of the Pullman Palace car, with its dark thatch of hair. While he struggled with the pearl buttons, I slid my fingers around to explore his smooth back. Another scar ridge marked one shoulder.

"What's this from?"

"Long story. No time for it now."

"You're not serious about taking a bath with me," I said after another heady kiss. "We both won't fit in this tub."

Ace groaned in frustration at my corset's hooks. "We'll manage."

"Where there's a will, there's a way?"

"Mm, sounds about right."

He tossed the item over his shoulder, kicked aside my petticoats that dropped to the floor. Somehow my drawers and stockings disappeared while he kissed me again, deeper, hands roaming beneath my chemise. He lifted me to perch on the tub's narrow edge, his breath warm against my ear. My arms slid around his neck. I squirmed.

"Oh, don't let me slide off."

"I won't, promise." Ace pressed me against his hips, his hands on my backside. "You sure you want that bath?"

"Hmm?"

"You heard me."

I jabbed his taut stomach. "Yes, I want that bath—"

With a smirk, Ace tipped me backwards. Water splashed everywhere. I sputtered in shock, sitting up in the tub and gasping for air, then coughed hard. I'd swallowed some of the hot water. I shook my head and rubbed my streaming eyes. He stood above me and unbuttoned his trousers with a wicked grin.

At that moment I screamed.

*'It is not good that the man should be alone;*
*I will make him an help meet for him.'*
Genesis 2:18

# Chapter Ten

"What the—"

"Behind you, look!"

I crouched, hiding myself the way my soaking wet muslin chemise clung to my skin. Clutching his trousers together, Ace shoved the man who stood in the doorway. He didn't budge. Several inches taller, with massive shoulders, the man had silvery dark hair, pale eyes and a chiseled jaw. He stared at me and then back at Ace.

"Who the devil are you?"

"San Francisco Police Department." The man pulled a badge from his coat pocket, shaped as a seven-pointed star, with a raised number in gold between his rank as Detective Sergeant. "We're conducting an investigation. You are registered as Mr. and Mrs. Diamond in this hotel. Is that correct, sir?"

"Yeah. Hold your horses so I can help my wife."

The policeman avoided looking at me again, thankfully. Ace buttoned his trousers, shucked up his suspenders and then lifted me from the tub. He wrapped a towel around my shoulders. Water streamed into my eyes from my wet hair. I dared not wipe it away in case I lost my grip on the extra towel I'd snatched to cover my hips. Speechless from shock, I stared at the man's pale gray suit and bowler hat, his thick handlebar mustache and sideburns.

"Did my uncle send you?"

"And who might that be?" the man asked.

"Captain William Harrison Granville. Of Sacramento."

"Never heard of him." He stood aside to let us pass. "It's a bit cramped in here. I suggest we move to the bedroom for our little chat."

Furious by the sarcasm in his voice, I gathered my dignity and walked out of the bathroom. Two other policemen stood by the bed, smirking at each other.

"Found a sweet pig-sticker, Detective," one man said and held up the stiletto. "Derringer in the lady's bag, too."

"Leave 'em." The policeman circled the room. "No other weapons, Diamond? Man like you would have at least a pistol on hand, or a knife."

Ace scowled. "This is our wedding night."

My cheeks grew hot, my gaze caught by the shoes and clothing strewn about. Ace drew me against his bare chest, clearly furious by his tense body. How dare these men invade our privacy?

Hadn't the door locked behind us? I couldn't remember.

Water dripped from my wet hair and spotted the carpet at my feet. I shivered. But I kept my gaze on the other men until they looked elsewhere. That gave me a chance to wrap myself in the bed's nubby white cotton coverlet. Ace eyed the taller policeman.

"So what's this all about, Detective—what's your name again?"

"Detective Sergeant Roy Crocker. I hear you're a partner in the Colossus Safety Powder Works, Mr. Diamond. Is that true?"

"Yeah. So?"

"We're investigating the explosion this morning at City Hall. Your company's products were used by the anarchists. We've questioned your partner, Mr. Santiago. He gave us several bills of sale to examine."

"That should prove we don't sell fire sticks to anarchists."

Crocker gave a benevolent smile. "Where were you this morning? Between the hours of four and seven?"

"Asleep."

"Where was this?"

Ace ran a hand through his mussed dark hair. "In a bed."

"You were seen at City Hall this morning," he said and flipped open a notebook.

"Yeah, at nine o'clock to get our marriage license. That's when I found out the clerks wouldn't open until noon because of the explosion."

"And where were you before that, Mr. Diamond?"

"Having breakfast."

"With your anarchist friends, perhaps?"

My husband closed the gap between us, one arm around me. "I don't know nothin' about any anarchists. You can't barge in here on our wedding night—"

Crocker motioned to the other policemen. They grabbed Ace's arms and pulled him away from me, fighting to keep him in check. He succeeded in breaking free, but one sucker-punched him in the stomach. Ace doubled over in pain. I cried out, rushing forward, but Crocker tripped me. I lost my grip on the bedspread covering. Ace cursed, kicked and bit, earning him more punches. The other men managed to get him under control between them.

"Where was this hotel, Mr. Diamond?" Crocker asked. "We can continue down at the jail unless you cooperate with us."

"Battery Street." Ace sounded winded. "Corner of Washington."

"Ah, and close to the site of the explosion. What did they pay you for the dynamite, Mr. Diamond? We have that bill of sale."

"I don't deal with that side of the business!"

"So you say. Now tell us the truth, how much did they pay you?" The detective waited, impatient, and then signaled the men. "Loosen him up again, boys."

Crocker caught my arms and prevented my interference. Blood streamed from Ace's nose and mouth already, but they hammered him further. Frightened and confused, I twisted to break Crocker's strong grip but failed.

"Please, don't hurt him! He isn't involved with criminals—"

"Leave that for us to decide, miss. Ma'am, that is." He signaled to his men and stared at my husband's battered face. "What time did you arrive at the livery stable last night?"

Ace spat blood. "Midnight. Maybe a little before."

"You must have noted the time."

"He didn't have a watch until today. I gave him my father's as a wedding present," I said. "I can show you—"

The detective smirked. "How convenient."

I ducked out of his loosened hold and fumbled for the watch and marriage license. It unfolded from my hand when I shook it free. "Here, this is proof I'm telling the truth. Judge Sanderson officiated at the ceremony this afternoon."

Crocker held out a hand. "Sanderson, eh? Let me see that." He scanned the paper. "So, little lady, maybe you accompanied your husband to city hall? Kept a lookout for him?"

Ace still fought against the men's tight grasp. "You leave my wife outta this!"

"Do you know a man named Jacob Fuller, Mr. Diamond?"

"No." He spat a second time, closer to the detective's shoes, and swiped his bloody mouth on his bare forearm. That didn't stop the bright red flow. "Never heard of him."

"Odd, because he claims to know you." Crocker smirked when I held out my hand for the marriage license, but tossed it my way. "How about Billy Bauer?"

Ace shook his head. "No."

"He told us he bought the crate of dynamite from you last week."

"I don't handle sales!"

"We'll have to get to the bottom of who's lying, then." When Crocker motioned to the others, they dragged Ace toward the door. "We'll take his shirt and boots, ma'am. Until we get the truth out of him, he's staying in jail."

I grabbed the closest policeman's coat sleeve. "My husband is innocent—"

"If he is, then we'll release him."

Ace kicked and bit, fighting every inch. Crocker drew a heavy revolver and slammed the butt against his temple, dropping Ace like a stone. Stunned, I watched them drag his limp body into the hallway. The door banged my elbow, but I ignored the sharp stinging pain and followed them. Crocker stopped me with a stern look.

"Get your husband a lawyer tomorrow, ma'am. That's my advice."

They descended the stairs. I watched until they disappeared. Several shocked hotel guests peeked out of their doors. I hitched up the bedspread and then stumbled back to the room. Once the door shut, I tripped, scrambled to my feet and tossed aside the coverlet. I almost stepped on Ace's stiletto, but picked it up by the handle and hid the weapon in my valise. Touching it felt vile. It brought the events of Mt. Diablo rushing back.

I shook those thoughts away. Ace needed my help. Where was my corset? I rushed to find my scattered clothing. My fingers fumbled with every hook and button. I wanted to use a few curses I'd learned from Ace. My shoes—I knelt on the damp carpet.

The door banged open again. I glanced up, still on hands and knees, one arm stretched under the bed. Uncle Harrison sauntered into the room.

"Did you lose something, Lily?"

The two Pinkerton agents followed him inside. One of them picked up the unfolded marriage license and scanned it. "Her husband, I'd say."

"What? Give me that."

My uncle snatched the paper from him, eyes narrowed, his face purple with rage while he read in silence. I sank onto the ottoman by the armchair, jammed my foot into the slipper I'd found and forced myself to stay calm. The matching shoe lay near the washstand. Stretching out, I closed my hand over the silk-clad toe and dragged it closer.

"I'll get this annulled in the morning—"

"No, you will not." I rose to my feet and brushed off my skirts. Once I straightened my shoulders, I met his steely gaze without flinching. "I shan't allow it."

"I am your guardian."

"No longer, according to that document. I am Mrs. Jesse Diamond."

Uncle Harrison's chest expanded and his hard eyes never strayed. "All my careful plans are ruined now! You stupid girl. Santiago will be a better husband."

"It's too late—"

"Looks like she's tellin' the truth, Captain Granville." The second Pinkerton agent pulled the blood-stained handkerchief from Ace's coat pocket. "Guess they were in that back parlor long enough after all."

My uncle signaled the men outside. He glared at me, one hand raised, as if ready to slap my face. I refused to cower. "That Texan dog doesn't deserve you."

"Jesse Diamond is a gentleman, and my husband. I love him, and he loves me."

"The police dragged him out of here! Your reputation is ruined, and this will affect my good name, too. Everything I've worked hard for, that political appointment, the quicksilver, the alliance with Santiago's father!"

I folded my arms over my chest. "All you care about is how it affects you. Your plans, not mine. You never asked me if I wanted any part of them."

He stared at me, his graying brown hair and beard so familiar, but his shrewd brown eyes glittered with hard anger. "So this is how you repay me, after all I've done for you since you arrived here? Betraying me for that no-good cowboy."

His bitterness enraged me in turn. "I haven't betrayed you! Aunt Sylvia betrayed me when she lied to you about Ace," I said. "He saved my life twice, remember. At Dale Creek and on Mt. Diablo. You never gave him an ounce of respect, for that or his loyalty. And he deserved every penny of that reward money you begrudged him."

"Diamond's a criminal. If you're blind to it, you've no one to blame but yourself." Uncle Harrison pushed me aside. "He's involved in that anarchist plot."

"How do you know that?"

"I spoke with the detective who carried him out now."

I glared at him. "Ace never met those men who set off the explosion."

"The truth will come out soon enough."

"So are you ready to admit you married Paloma Díaz? Perhaps you wanted to keep that a secret, since my marriage to her nephew might seem odd to your society friends—"

"That's not true." Uncle Harrison yanked the door open. "As for you, you made your bed. Don't expect any assistance from me, financial or otherwise, when you end up a widow."

He stalked out of the room, his face darker than the dried blood on Ace's handkerchief. Why had my uncle given up on the annulment? I retrieved the square of linen from the floor. Perhaps they believed I was no longer . . . oh. I swallowed a lump in my throat. Now I realized what that Pinkerton detective meant. Ace and I had yet to share the intimacy of a marriage bed, but no one else knew that. I would die before admitting the truth.

This talk of murder, and hanging, terrified me. Why did the police believe Ace had ties to anarchists who dared to blow up city hall? The man I loved would never take part in a deadly scheme. Somehow I had to prove him innocent.

My blood ran cold at the thought of being a widow before a true wife.

Moonlight streamed through the glass between the lace curtains. I stopped pacing the room.

Once more I was alone in a strange place without any idea of what to do or how to escape. Frozen with fear, I hoped and prayed that my husband would return. Perhaps any minute Ace might stroll back into the room. We'd both laugh at how the police had been mistaken.

But the truth was hard to face. Hours had passed. Ace was in deep trouble. He had no patience, and didn't understand how to rely on God through faith. To be still in prayer and listen for heavenly guidance through instinct—or take action. I stripped off my clothes, aware that I'd missed several buttons in my haste to dress, and then rushed to the bath tub. Some water remained. After I scrubbed and dried myself, I dressed with care this time, brushed out my hair and twisted it up without bothering to attach my switch. Room key in hand, I tiptoed down the empty darkened hallway. Once I reached my friends' room, I rapped my knuckles on the door, softly. I ought to have checked the time.

I knocked harder, then banged with my fist. "Kate, it's Lily! Please, help—"

"What in the world?"

Charles stood in the doorway, his nightshirt stuffed into trousers. Two other guests had opened their doors out of curiosity, one of whom grumbled about the noise. Charles drew me inside. Kate wrapped a shawl around her flimsy nightdress, her long dark braid falling over one shoulder to her waist, and hurried to my side. Her voice soothed my jangled nerves.

"What happened, Lily? Where's Ace?"

I clasped my hands together. "In jail." They both stared at me in stunned silence. "The police arrived and took him away for questioning. About that explosion—"

Sinking on the ladder-back chair by the door, my words rushed together when I explained the whole story. Twice they slowed me down. Kate slid an arm around my shoulders. Charles paced now, back and forth before me, while he fired questions. He forced me to repeat every word of the exchange between the policemen and Ace.

"I'm supposed to find a lawyer. I don't know where to look here in the city."

"We can't find anyone until morning, Lily." He rubbed the bridge of his nose. "It's half past two. Try and get some sleep."

"How can she possibly sleep?" Kate asked, horrified. "If you'd been beaten by the police and hauled away, I'd be just as upset!"

"I said try," Charles repeated, stubborn. "Tomorrow we'll search out a lawyer. The front desk clerk is sure to have a business directory to the city."

"Oh, wait, Uncle Harrison hired one. What was his name again?"

My head spun. Kate grabbed an extra blanket and handed it to her husband. "Well, one thing is certain. Lily can't go back to that room alone. She'll stay here with us."

"Why can't she sleep in Etta's room?"

"Charles Mason, I've spent every half hour waking her like the doctor ordered me, to make sure Etta's concussion doesn't worsen. Now that I know she'll be all right, I'd rather let her sleep in peace. Lily will stay here. They won't release Ace until morning."

"I'll be fine in my own room—"

"You're shaking like a leaf, and you look ready to faint." Kate pulled me to my feet. "Come on now, no arguments. From either one of you."

Charles settled into the armchair, grumpy, and thumped the pillow behind his head. Kate spread the plaid wool over him, kissed his cheek and pulled me toward the bed. I stretched out on top of the covers. Lying on one side, my back to them, my silent tears flowed into the pillow. How had the police known where to find Ace? Detective Crocker had mentioned that the room was registered to us as a married couple, but it remained a puzzle.

Their reason for questioning him didn't make sense either. Thank goodness they hadn't interrupted us in bed. I replayed the sequence of events over and over in my mind. Why hadn't the police interrupted us at dinner? And why had Uncle Harrison arrived on the heels of the police? That wasn't a coincidence. He seemed to know far more about Ace being dragged away for questioning than he first let on. Was he behind the scheme?

Further guilt settled over me. I hated putting more problems on my friends' shoulders. They'd already taken care of Etta, although she was my maid and therefore my responsibility. Now Kate had shoved her husband out of bed for my sake. It wasn't fair. But I dared not sneak back to my room. That would wake them again. Charles snored so loud, he sounded like a sawmill's blade. I blocked my ears and shut my eyes tight.

A name popped in my head. Woodward . . . N. Adam Woodward. I had no idea what the initial N stood for, nor if it would be easy to find his office. My head ached. The dried traces of my tears itched and I rubbed my face with a sleeve.

At last I gave up trying to sleep and tiptoed to the window. From this angle, I had a clear view of the Occidental Hotel's entrance. At dawn, people hurried out with their baggage. Cabs, horse-drawn carriages and wagons soon filled the surrounding streets. I opened Father's gold watch —no, it belonged to my husband now. I would keep it safe for Ace until he was released. Tucked in my pocket, the bulk of it gave me a boost of confidence.

I braced myself before the washstand and mirror, poured a trickle of water into the bowl and then splashed my face. Puffy redness marked the skin under my eyes. My hands shook. I couldn't rest until I'd contacted Mr. Woodward. Even though he dealt with wills and estate law, he might know another lawyer who could help me. And if Uncle Harrison had taken part in this scheme to get rid of Ace for good, I'd sever all ties to him.

"Lily? Didn't you sleep at all?" Kate stretched and yawned wide. "What time is it?"

"Not quite six."

"Goodness, I'm freezing even under the covers."

"Could you and Charles stay more than a few days here?" I asked. "Oh, but you have the farm animals to care for—I forgot."

"The neighbors agreed to take care of them, remember. Perhaps one more day might help Etta recover faster." She sat up when I opened the door. "Where are you going?"

"Off to find a lawyer. Get Charles into bed with you where he belongs. Sleep in, enjoy a good breakfast. I'll be back as soon as possible."

Ignoring her protest, I hurried out the door and down the corridor to my room. This task was mine, mine alone. I was a married woman. The gold ring on my finger proved that. I owed Jesse Diamond my life. Now was my chance to repay him, to extract him from this mess. We were in this together. Once I'd fetched my hat and gloves, I rushed down the stairs and rang the bell at the front desk.

A clerk hurried out from the back, straightening his collar and cuffs. "Good morning. Do you have a city business directory?" I asked.

"Yes, miss—"

"Mrs. Diamond."

I smiled and accepted the printed book. In the lobby's armchair, I flipped through the pages. Would Mr. Woodward be listed? Impatient, I searched until I found his name, memorized the address and returned the book. Then I headed outside and walked north on Montgomery. It wasn't too far. The autumn air had a crisp chill despite the morning's wan sunshine. I managed to find Belden Place at last, which turned out to be a narrow lane off DuPont Street. The shop buildings looked weather-beaten and old, the windows grimy. Mr. Woodward's squat building seemed out of place, the frame walls painted white, the windows sparkling in the sunshine. The brass knocker on the door resembled a wolf's head.

A bell jangled overhead when I entered the office. "Hello? Mr. Woodward?"

"Be with you in a moment," a voice called from the back.

I glanced around the large front room. Several polished oak tables had neat piles of stacked papers beside ink wells and writing instruments. Glassed-in cabinets lining two walls held scores of leather bound books, and other cabinets with drawers filled one wall. A worn but clean carpet covered most of the slanted wooden floor. A rotund man of around fifty entered the room, dressed in a rumpled black suit and crooked tie. His hands resembled huge paws, soft and fat-fingered. He seemed agile when he hurried to greet me.

"Good morning." His resonant voice echoed to the room's rafters despite the heavy furnishings. "Can I help you today?"

I nodded. "Are you Mr. Woodward, the attorney?"

"N. Adam Woodward at your service. Call me Adam, if you wish, or Woodward."

"What does the N stand for, if I may ask?"

"Noble. Most people don't believe lawyers have that trait, so I don't use it."

He took a proud stance beside a desk that held a gilt-edged blotter. Bushy grayish hair surrounded his shiny bald head, from one side around the back to the other, spilling over his collar, with a bit of fuzz inside each ear. His goatee looked whiter, trimmed neat compared to his hair, and balanced his bulbous nose. Woodward pulled out a chair for me.

"May I ask your name, miss?"

"Mrs. Diamond."

"Please sit down, ma'am."

I perched on the wooden seat, uneasy. This man had ties to my uncle. For all I knew, the Pinkerton agents may have visited him with Uncle

Harrison. They might show up at any minute. I wavered, wondering if it was too late to make an excuse and leave. But something about Mr. Woodward kept me in place. Curiosity, I suppose.

"How can I help you, Mrs. Diamond?" Woodward eyed me in a questioning manner, as if he expected me to turn tail and run. "You have half an hour to explain what you require. I have no pressing appointment until nine o'clock."

"I understand your practice deals with last wills and testaments."

"That is true. You seem a bit young to require a will, however—"

"Oh, no. I need advice about a different matter. A crime, in fact."

"Ah. I have taken criminal cases from time to time."

I took stock of his kind manner. He walked toward the window and closed the shutters to relieve my painful blinking. Woodward had a restless energy despite his advanced age. He patted his pockets, checked his desk and then searched the tables. At last he held up a pipe, cherry wood with a long stem and well worn. The lawyer continued scouting around the papers and books as if he'd misplaced something more valuable. I took a deep breath and spoke.

"Will you promise to keep everything I tell you in the strictest confidence?"

"My dear lady, I have never yet betrayed a

client's trust." Woodward raised his eyebrows and then snatched up a leather pouch with delight. He settled into the chair before the desk, a few feet distant from me, and filled his pipe. "First of all, while you may be Mrs. Diamond in truth, you may also be called something else entirely. And I prefer not taking any case founded on deception. You look the honest type, however. I am rarely in the wrong about people."

"I am Mrs. Jesse Diamond."

Woodward nodded. "All right, that's a start. What type of crime?"

Something about the man's perception, his frankness, his manner of speaking his mind without hesitation, or perhaps it was a genuine confidence, won me over. I plunged ahead.

"The anarchist explosion."

"I beg your pardon?"

"My husband was accused of being involved in the anarchist explosion," I said, "and I need help to prove his innocence. He is innocent, too."

"A natural assumption, being his wife."

"Yes. We were married yesterday at the Russ House by Judge Sanderson. My full name is Lily Granville Diamond."

*'He shall be driven from light*
*unto darkness . . .'*
*Job 18:18*

# Chapter Eleven

Startled by my announcement, Woodward caught
his pipe before it clattered to the floor. He
brushed bits of tobacco from his trousers and set
the pouch aside, along with the pipe. Then he
folded his hands over his rounded paunch. The
attorney studied me.

"You're Captain Granville's niece?"

"Yes."

"Ah." He exhaled a long breath. "So you're the
slip of a girl who inherited Mrs. Chester's
property. That has not set well with your uncle.
Not by any means."

"Then you understand my situation is a delicate
one."

"An understatement, Mrs. Diamond."

His wry assessment and half-snort sounded
odd. Woodward snorted again and then let out a
deep laugh. He seemed genuinely amused, which
both relieved and intrigued me. I relaxed in the
wooden chair.

"Shall I assume my uncle made his displeasure known to you?"

"Yes. A stack of telegrams arrived yesterday. The last arrived around midnight. I'm expecting him at nine." He waved me back into my chair when I stood in alarm. "Do not fear, young lady. I'd already decided that no matter what Captain Granville required today, I would be unavailable. I haven't yet recovered from an accusation of cheating him."

"Cheating him?"

"By writing up Mrs. Chester's will as she dictated. He accused me of not persuading her to benefit him instead of you."

I'd kept one ear alert for any sounds of a carriage. Woodward noticed my alarm and glanced out the window once rattling wheels stopped in the street outside. The attorney led me through the narrow doorway into a back room, part kitchen with a cast iron cook stove, with a narrow bed nestled in the alcove opposite. He pulled a chair away from the scarred wooden table over, sat me down and hushed my protests.

"Wait here. You and I have more to discuss."

Uneasy, I shifted in the chair and eyed the door beside the iron stove. It must lead to the alley. I could slip out and then—what? Return to the Russ House, and lose the chance to gain advice about Ace's situation? I had to wait.

Loud voices, one of them my uncle's, drifted

through the thin wall. "I'm offering you good money in advance, Woodward. How dare you turn me down?"

"I said you better retain another lawyer."

"Before I explain what I need? Don't forget you cheated me, too."

"Your sister made her wishes known, I transcribed them. The papers have been filed already with the Probate court, by the way."

Silence followed Woodward's announcement, and then cursing. I had never heard my uncle use vile words. My face and neck flushed hot. Their fiery exchange continued for several minutes while I shuffled through a stack of letters from various businessmen. Robert Woodward of Napa Valley. Pedro Alvarez. And numerous thin sheets, telegrams, all written in my uncle's usual style. With a twinge of remorse for snooping, I read them all. *'Delay filing probate, stop. Vital importance—'* Another contained a warning that any expenses accrued would not be repaid if Woodward defied his orders. My uncle had also written a letter last week, with an odd paragraph in the brief message.

*A minor change, here or there, and compensation for the trouble . . .*

I stacked the papers in order again. Anger seethed inside my chest. Uncle Harrison had no right to thwart my legitimate claim to an inheritance. Ought I go out there and face him? Tell him I was aware of his attempt to cheat me?

But if I confronted my uncle, what would that prove? He'd heap more abuse on my head, claim once more that I'd ruined his chances for securing the votes he needed to get that political appointment. He'd wanted free access to Aunt Sylvia's quicksilver, knowing Esteban de los Reyes Santiago as my husband would allow it. Uncle Harrison wanted and expected to get his own way. Clearly I'd underestimated his greed and ambition. Aunt Sylvia had been right.

The voices died away after the front door slammed, which had rocked the small building. I waited at my post. Twice I checked Ace's pocket watch and snapped it shut. Five minutes dragged into fifteen. Then twenty. I stood. Woodward met me in the hallway.

"Forgive me for making you wait, Mrs. Diamond, but I noticed a man lingering across the street after your uncle's departure." He led me to the front room again. "No need to worry, he's gone now. I've never seen him before."

"Is he tall?" I asked. "Thin, with scars on his hand as if he'd been burned? He's a Pinkerton agent, hired by Uncle Harrison."

"Yes, he did have a burn scar." Woodward lowered himself into the desk chair and plucked up his pipe. "Perhaps he once worked as a Pinkerton, but no longer. I don't appreciate being spied on, by anyone, for any reason."

I peeked out the window and then sat. "My uncle sent you several telegrams."

He tamped tobacco into the pipe's bowl with his thumb. "Quite illuminating, aren't they? Captain Granville must realize that my hands are tied. I refused to alter his sister's will as he hinted in a letter. I spent considerable time and my own money traveling to Sacramento to meet with your aunt. She kept me hopping, mind you! She gave me strict instructions to keep the will secret from her brother until after her death."

"They didn't trust each other."

"True enough. It wasn't easy acting as a liaison between two stubborn siblings." He struck a match. "So, you need me to represent your husband?"

"Yes," I said. "Within minutes after the police took my husband away for questioning, my uncle arrived at our hotel. I don't believe it was a coincidence."

Woodward straightened up in his chair, eyebrows raised. "This is far more complicated than I expected." He struck a match and puffed on his pipe, eyes closed as if savoring the taste. "All right. Why do the police believe your husband is involved?"

"I guess because—"

"No guessing, please. The facts as we know them. You said you were married yesterday? Against your uncle's wishes, perhaps?"

I exhaled slowly. "Yes. He forbid me to ever see Ace. That's a nickname. His Christian name is Jesse Diamond. My uncle hated him, too."

"Hm. I wonder." He scratched his bald head. "Captain Granville is a difficult man. Difficult to please, difficult to persuade he may not be right. As well you know."

"He wasn't always that way," I said. "Uncle Harrison was wonderful to me when I was a child, and I adored him."

"People change." He waved his pipe in the air. "You're aware he had his heart set on the Mt. Diablo quicksilver claim."

"Yes. He accused me of betraying him, too."

"I'm sorry to say he's the type of man to blame me, you, his sister, your father, the stars above for upsetting his grandiose plans. Captain Granville would no doubt blame John Sutter for building his mill, where gold was first discovered in California."

I suppressed a laugh. "Do you think my uncle played a part in what happened last night? For the police taking my husband away."

"You'd better start at the beginning, Mrs. Diamond. Tell me everything."

"It's a long story, going back to when my father was murdered."

"Take your time." Woodward glanced at the ticking clock above my head. "I have no other appointments today. I'd rather hear all the details and not be surprised later by discovering something you missed by chance."

I explained what happened since that horrible September night back in Evanston. The long journey west, my reliance on Ace, Charles and Kate for help and support in finding my father's killer, the events at Mt. Diablo and the aftermath of being packed off to Uncle Harrison's house in Sacramento. Woodward fetched a pitcher of water and two glasses and brought sliced bread with butter and honey, which helped settle my growling stomach. He listened with few questions while I related my visit with Aunt Sylvia and her warnings, the sumptuous banquet, meeting Santiago, Ace's surprise arrival, and the sudden announcement of my engagement.

"And this man Santiago is your husband's partner in the dynamite factory."

"Yes."

"Another interesting development. Go on, please."

Woodward watched me with intensity when I recounted the recent events over the past weekend. He brushed aside the wedding and dinner, focusing only on the questions Crocker had asked Ace last night, and made me repeat the details.

"What have you heard about these anarchists, Mrs. Diamond?"

"I read a brief article in the newspaper yesterday."

"Tell me the men's names the police mentioned, if you remember."

The attorney jotted the information in a notebook. He asked other questions about how many times the police hit Ace, where the blows landed, and whether Crocker manhandled me while preventing me from interfering. Then I gulped a full glass of water, grateful for a respite. Woodward nodded.

"You did very well keeping your story straight. If your husband is arrested and charged, you may be cross-examined on the witness stand. Now, let's return to your uncle. Captain Granville disapproved of your husband after you arrived in California, then banned you two from ever associating together. And once he discovered this partnership between Santiago and Mr. Diamond, he announced your betrothal to his choice of a husband."

"Yes. Against my wishes."

"So you chose to leave Sacramento, met Jesse Diamond and married him. Suddenly your husband is charged as a conspirator in the City Hall explosion."

"It sounds unbelievable—"

"It is a puzzle, Mrs. Diamond," Woodward said. "Study the pattern, rearrange the pieces to see how they fit together. Is your uncle a good friend of Santiago's family?"

I rubbed my aching arm. "I believe so. Do you think he's behind this scheme to involve my husband in the anarchist plot?"

"I'm a firm believer in calling a mule a mule despite what a horse trader might say." Woodward tapped his pencil against the notebook. "It might be coincidence, however. What we need is more information before we can prove he's been framed."

"The police believe Ace sold dynamite to the anarchists."

"That's hearsay, so far." Woodward struck a wooden match, sending an acrid odor of phosphorus into the now warm room, and lit the tobacco in his pipe. "We must work together, and fast, before they find evidence against your husband."

"My friends might help," I said, but he shook his head.

"The Masons ought not risk their reputation. It's better they return to Rock Canyon. We shall rely on other methods and means of acquiring knowledge."

"Perhaps hiring our own spies?"

"Perhaps."

Woodward rose from his chair and raised the window higher. The breeze stirred a few papers on one table, so he moved a heavy glass paperweight to secure them. Then he returned to his chair. He smoothed his bald head, eyes bright, pipe clenched between his teeth.

"Captain Granville hates being thwarted. He once told me a story about his feud with George Hearst, and what happened long ago in Nevada. But I'd heard of their disagreement from several different sources. Your uncle's version missed a few important details that I picked up from Hearst. There's two sides to every story."

I nodded. "My uncle didn't want Hearst acquiring the Early Bird."

"Among other ventures. And now, this feud with your husband along with the police visiting last night—that would give anyone with half a brain suspicion." He snorted again. "Shall I read the contents of your aunt's will to you?"

"Yes, please."

Woodward held up a thick folder and rattled at least five minutes of legal jargon before getting to the heart of what the estate included. " ' . . . a coal mine on Mt. Diablo, in production, plus a quicksilver mine, non-productive at this point in time, one hundred and eighty five acres of land and its buildings, all left to Lily Rose Delano Granville. Any estate debts are to be settled by Captain William Harrison Granville.' "

Confused, I blinked. "Estate debts?"

"A minor amount, which your uncle has already paid out of funds his sister had in her bank account. That included the monetary settlement upon the nurse for her services, and the cost of interment for her husband's remains."

"In Sacramento?"

"Yes. She wanted him to rest beside her."

I sent a prayer of thanks heavenward. That temporary grave at the ranch would no longer haunt me. "When can we visit my husband in the jail?"

"After I consult with a colleague. His office is close," Woodward said and returned the folder to its stack. He tapped out the ashes from his pipe's bowl, stored it in his pocket along with the leather pouch, and beckoned to me. "I dare say we could ask Martin to spy for us. He might find out a few useful facts to benefit you."

Once outside, he guided me toward Kearney Street and across, walking east along Union for several blocks. The exercise helped. I couldn't have asked for a more beautiful morning, sunny and bright, with puffy white clouds overhead.

After sitting so long, I enjoyed the salty tang in the air, the sloping hills and occasional glimpse of the sea-green bay dotted with ships. Gulls squawked and wheeled overhead. My back and feet ached by the time we reached a narrow brick building with bay windows thrusting one atop the other. I counted five steps up to the stoop and noticed the door to the left with the name Dr. Hanson painted in gold. A dark, damp stairway led to the second floor.

"Who is this man you believe will help us?"

"A good friend. He's always aware of the latest

events in the city," Woodward said and followed me up the steep steps. "Martin is an invaluable resource."

He opened an unmarked door at the top and shooed me into a dim room filled with cigar smoke. Ugh. I waved a hand in front of my face. Half a sandwich lay on a dirty plate on one table by the door, the bread spotted with mold. I averted my eyes. Three men were present in the room, two at the far end comparing notes among a stack of notebooks and papers. The third glanced up from his cluttered desk and then jumped to his feet. I'd recognized him by his thick reddish-brown beard, thin build and shabby clothing.

Martin Dodd rolled down his shirt sleeves and donned his coat. He also must have visited a barber to trim his hair, and its short length emphasized his large square forehead and long nose. He squinted down at us both.

Woodward began introductions. "This is Mr. Martin Dodd—"

"Yes, he works for Mr. McKay's *California Enquirer*. We've met."

Woodward seemed puzzled by my cold tone. "Oh?"

Dodd gave a sheepish grin. "My boss is friends with her uncle. McKay took me out to Rock Canyon this past weekend, where she visiting friends."

"You old devil. So you could write an article

about the history of farming in the area, is that it?" The lawyer perched on the desk's edge. "Front page news."

"Well, no."

"That was a pretense for spying on me," I said, folding my arms over my chest. "Either Mr. Dodd or Mr. McKay sent a wire to my uncle, telling him I'd been with Ace Diamond. That's why he took the next train from Sacramento and caused trouble for me."

The younger man shrugged. "I followed my boss's orders."

"Charles Mason believed your ruse, so it was a dirty trick."

"I wrote about the mission work he's doing," Dodd said, his tone defensive. "It's going in tomorrow's paper."

"Never mind that now, Martin. We've come to ask what you've learned so far about this anarchist plot."

"Not much I can tell you, really."

"I beg to differ. I'm proficient in reading upside down, remember."

Dodd flipped his notebook over with a scowl. After I perched on a chair beside the desk, Adam Woodward settled his bulk in a corner armchair. The other two men grabbed their bowler hats and headed toward the door, grinning at Dodd.

"A shame you work for the wrong news-paper, Marty," one said. The other laughed. "We all caught a big story before you for a change."

The door slammed shut behind them. Dodd muttered something and shuffled the papers on his desk. I surveyed the small room, a disaster given its jumble of books, files, dirty cups, saucers and other flotsam covering every table, desk and shelf surface. If Adam Woodward was meticulous in his rooms on Belden Place, Martin Dodd and his friends seemed the extreme opposite. The newspaper reporter sprawled into his chair. He twisted the ink pen between his fingers and stared at the ceiling above Woodward's head.

"McKay wants me to back off," Dodd said, "so I'm missing out on one of the biggest scandals of the year." He tossed the pen down. "The Colossus Safety Powder Works is involved, and McKay is friends with the owner. You heard those other reporters. An aide to Governor Haight was hurt bad, so it's a big story."

"Why would anarchists target the Governor?"

"Seems he planned to visit Police Chief Crawley, except he sent his aide instead. Lucky for him, and lucky for the state of California."

Woodward drummed his fingertips together. "How serious was the aide hurt?"

"Not expected to live. The explosion killed one of the anarchists—they found parts of him all over. An arm, part of his leg."

Sickened, I posed a question of my own. "How do the police know the dynamite came from that factory? Couldn't the anarchists have obtained it from a mining company employee? Or maybe some other company who uses dynamite."

Dodd cocked his head. "They got the bill of sale as evidence."

"But my husband doesn't handle sales."

"I guess he did this time, because it's signed by Jesse Diamond."

"Is that so?" Woodward glanced at me. "How convenient."

"You didn't hear that from me," Dodd said with a scowl. "The police questioned that wounded anarchist up and down. He told 'em where they bought the fire sticks."

"Fire sticks." I winced at the memory. Ace had called them that at the banquet when he explained their production. "You mean sticks of dynamite."

"Pretty powerful stuff. Blew out the building's windows on the west side's floors—used to be the Jenny Lind theater, remember. Collapsed part of a wall," Dodd said. "That's what fell on the governor's aide. Good thing Henry Haight wasn't there himself, or Chief Crowley for that matter. There'd be a worse ruckus if they'd been blown to bits."

Woodward nodded. "Remember when the first dynamite factory had to move due to an explosion at the docks. I believe this Santiago fellow owned the business then. Or am I mistaken on that fact?"

"That's correct, from what little I know."

"So what kind of hard proof do the police have that Mr. Diamond is involved?"

"You mean besides the paperwork? That's it."

"There must be other information you've learned, Martin."

Dodd shrugged. "There are several witnesses."

"Witnesses?"

Woodward and I had both echoed his words. I stared at the newspaper reporter, dread filling me. "Witnesses to the actual bombing?" the attorney asked.

"Someone saw three men with a crate at the theater, half an hour before the explosion," Dodd said. "When this man heard the noise, he reported the incident to the police. Said the anarchists had covered half of their faces with bandannas, like cowhands."

I sucked in my lower lip, fretting over that tidbit. Another deliberate nod to my husband, who'd worked on the range in his past. Ace mentioned how Santiago didn't want a cowhand as a partner. That meant he'd been open about the various jobs he'd held. And it was possible these men planned to point the finger at Ace by wearing such western gear.

Woodward folded his hands. "Who is the other witness then?"

"The wounded anarchist? The police questioned him pretty hard. He swears that Ace Diamond set the bomb to go off at five o'clock that morning."

*'For your hands are defiled with blood . . .*
*your lips have spoken lies . . . '*
*Isaiah 59:3*

# Chapter Twelve

"He's lying! My husband wouldn't do that." I'd jumped to my feet, although Woodward guided me toward the door. "It's not true!"

"Husband? She's married to him?" Dodd gaped at me, his eyes wide. "When?"

"Last night—but don't spread that bit to your friends," the attorney said. "Have you heard the names Jacob Fuller and Billy Bauer?"

I watched the man's eyes widen before he feigned disinterest. "Maybe."

"Spill, Martin. We're not leaving until you tell us."

"Bauer was the unlucky one. Fuller survived and told them who was involved." Dodd eyed me with interest. "Now what's this about you marrying Diamond?"

"But if my husband is innocent, then who could the third anarchist be?" I asked, ignoring his question. "Ace swore he never heard of those men before."

Dodd glanced at Woodward and then back at me. "You'll have to ask the police what else they got on Diamond to keep him in custody."

"That is our next move, yes." Woodward led me by my elbow toward the door. "If you hear anything more, Martin, we would be forever in your debt."

"I will say this." The reporter cleared his throat. "This Santiago fella, who owns the safety powder company. When he first started here in the city, he had a partner."

"Yes. What about it?"

"Seems he committed suicide after embezzling funds. Then Santiago moved out to Rock Canyon with a second partner, and built the factory complex. Within six months, that man was hauled off to jail. Tried and convicted. It was a big scandal, because a young woman accused him of ruining her. He was already married, too."

"Hm. It seems Mr. Santiago can't keep a partner to save his soul." Woodward shook Martin Dodd's hand. "Thank you, and let me know of any other information you learn about these anarchists. Or about the police investigation."

"I'm looking into it, even though McKay might not be happy about it. Now what about her marriage to Diamond—"

The attorney drew me down the stairs before Dodd finished his question. Woodward led me toward a streetcar. "I shall investigate Mr.

Santiago's past misfortunes," he said, "but your husband's defense comes first."

"It's clear to me Santiago wants to be rid of him."

"We need evidence to prove that."

My worries tripled during the tedious journey to City Hall. The jangling harness, jolting wheels and the driver's sing-song patter of calling out street names interrupted my thoughts. My heart ached. Ace was in worse trouble than I'd thought, given the two major forces working against him —my uncle and Esteban de los Reyes Santiago. All that reward money, sunk into a dynamite factory, with no chance of getting it back. And a possible prison term, if not a trip to the gallows. I banished that horrid thought before it took hold.

"You must allow me to do the talking." Woodward helped me alight from the horsecar. "Focus on cheering your husband's spirits. I'll question the detectives about their case and any evidence. If I need your help, I'll ask."

"All right."

I eyed the large brick building that rose before us, five stories with long narrow windows. A gang of men worked to repair the fallen wall, close to City Hall's back side and the police station's entrance. Woodward opened the door and followed me inside. At the massive front desk, a police sergeant argued with a heavyset man. His son had been dragged in during the night as well, but the man's pleas fell on deaf ears. A second policeman behind the desk crooked a finger, signaling other men who tossed the visitor out the door. Wary, I waited for Woodward to address the sergeant. Thank goodness I hadn't come here on my own.

"My client, Mr. Diamond, was brought in last night," Woodward said and then waited while the policeman consulted the ledger before him. "Mr. Jesse Diamond. I'm here to consult with him on his case."

The gray-suited man glanced at me once and then jotted something on a slip of paper. "Stairs to the basement down the hall. Give this to the guard."

Woodward led me down the twisting corridor past a maze of other halls with closed doors. Once we descended the narrow stairs, the musty smell changed to a rank odor of unwashed bodies, urine and other awful smells. The tiny windows in every door were far above my head, but the inmates must have heard my swishing skirts. At their whistles and a few lewd comments, my face burned. The guard shouted a warning. Another guard peered at the note and then shuffled off with his keys. Woodward turned to me.

"This is already unpleasant, Mrs. Diamond. Are you prepared for worse?"

I glanced up at his impassive face. What did he mean? "Yes."

We waited at least ten agonizing minutes in the hallway until another policeman led us into a windowless room. He took a post by the door. A table stood against the wall, with flakes of peeling paint scattered on its surface. Woodward fetched a wooden chair for me.

"Better sit down. It may be another long wait."

I sank on the chair's hard edge. He blocked my sight of the door. The room closed in on me, but I refused to lose hope. Soon I'd see Ace. What had he endured since the police brought him to this hellish place? My throat was parched. I checked his watch often, noting each span of twenty or thirty minutes. Prayer didn't help, but I closed my eyes and recited as many scripture verses and hymns that I'd learned during childhood.

At last heavy footsteps sounded in the hall outside. I held my breath. The door swung open and my stomach twisted when the guard spoke.

"Fifteen minutes."

Woodward cleared his throat once the door slammed shut. A key clattered in the lock. "Mr. Diamond? I am your attorney—"

"Let me by, please!" I stared in horror, one hand over my mouth, and darted around to my husband's side. "Oh, Jesse! What have they done to you?"

He gripped my forearms, squinting through the one puffed eye that hadn't swelled shut, but kept me at a distance. "I'm all right, darlin'. I been worse."

Woodward tried to pry me away, but I resisted. "We are only allowed fifteen minutes, Mrs. Diamond. I need every precious minute to question your husband. Please, sit down."

Ace nodded. "Better do as he says, Lily."

"No. I've been sitting enough today, but you need to sit down."

He slumped into the chair, avoiding my gaze, hunched in pain. I couldn't bear to look at his swollen mouth, crusted with blood, the red welts and scrapes on his temple, cheeks, nose and jaw, the bruises turning purple. His trousers were filthy, his shirt torn at the shoulders and sleeves. Had he slept at all? Ace and Woodward took stock of each other, aloof and wary.

"Why did they beat you so badly?"

He flinched at my touch. "Didn't give 'em the right answers."

"And what answers did they expect, Mr. Diamond?" Woodward asked.

"A confession. That I set up the dynamite at City Hall and lit the fuses." Ace took a few short breaths. "Feels like a cracked rib."

"I will arrange for a doctor—no arguments, Mr. Diamond. You ought to be checked. I am meeting with Detective Sergeant Crocker after we're done here," he said, "and I will insist on medical attention. So you believe you're being framed?"

"Never met any of them anarchists, never sold 'em any dynamite. They don't believe me, of course. And I sure as hel—uh. I wouldn't send a man back to check on a fuse."

Woodward cocked his head. "I'm sorry, you'd better explain."

Ace flexed one shoulder and captured my hand when I reached for him. "Guess that fella who was injured, someone named Jacob Fuller, claims I sent his friend Billy Bauer to make sure the fuse was burnin' proper. That's plumb crazy. Once a fuse is lit, you keep well clear of it."

"So the police questioned you?"

"More than that." Ace breathed hard. "They drug me to a room this morning, lined me up with half a dozen others. Next thing I knew, they arrested me."

"I'll check whether they scheduled a bond hearing." Woodward explained the events, of how Governor Haight had been targeted, his aide injured instead with one anarchist, and the other man's sadder fate. "Tell me about this bill of sale. Did you ever sign any papers?"

"A few supply orders. That's all."

From his downcast eyes, I knew his pride was wounded. Woodward was an educated man, a lawyer. He might not understand Ace's humble background, his fight to survive during and after the War, his rock-bottom job in Omaha and how he'd risen far and fast to become a real businessman. Now Ace had landed back in the dregs of despair and misery.

"Somehow Santiago tricked you," I said. "He either altered that supply order, or forged your name to the bill of sale. He had two other partners who came to bad ends. One is dead, the other's in prison. Now he's trying to get rid of you."

Ace clenched his fists. "That son-of-a—he done cheated me out of six thousand dollars! If I ever get my hands on him, he'll regret ever meetin' me at that poker game."

"I didn't hear that, Mr. Diamond," Woodward said sternly. "Beware voicing your thoughts in this place. Leave it to us to discover the truth about your business partner. We must have evidence in order to build a case and prove your innocence."

"We will, too." I slid an arm around his shoulders and bent close to his ear. "I'm praying, and you must have faith that everything will work out, Ace."

We all heard the key in the lock before the door swung open. The guard motioned to us. "Time's up, both of you. Leave now."

Woodward balked. "This is a complicated case. I need more time to consult with my client before I meet Detective Sergeant Crocker."

"Ask him for more time then. Out, you and the lady."

"Don't worry about me, Lily." Ace stood, his voice low, and caressed my cheek. "You be careful dealin' with that snake Santiago."

"Yes, of course." His fingers were cold, his knuckles bruised and filthy, but I pressed his palm against my cheek. "I know you're innocent, Jesse. I'll prove it, too."

"I ain't never faced a rope before." He gave a shaky laugh.

My heart ached. "You won't die on the gallows. I refuse to become a widow—"

Woodward pulled me away. "Come along, Mrs. Diamond. We must go."

I lost my chance for a quick kiss and found myself in the hallway. "A pretty pickle indeed," the attorney muttered as we walked. "It won't be easy. A visit to your uncle might be warranted, Mrs. Diamond. I'd like to hear what he has to say for himself."

Numb, I followed him through the maze of halls to the front desk. Woodward spent another half hour demanding to see Detective Sergeant Crocker. We waited at length, watching other men brought in by policemen—some in ragged clothing, others dressed in fine wool three-piece suits and gold watches, and several Chinamen with long black pigtails and odd collarless tunics and trousers. The police had battered them worst of all, given their bloody faces. They also ignored their foreign jabbering, shoving and pushing them to the basement stairs.

Helpless myself, I failed to banish the sight of Ace's swollen and bruised face, his pain and dejection. His new faith was being sorely tested, indeed. Mine as well.

At last a man led us up two flights of stairs to an office. Detective Sergeant Crocker stood when my attorney and I entered the room. He didn't look so imposing against Woodward's bulk, but his pale gray eyes hardened.

"What can I do for you today?"

"You arrested my client, Mr. Diamond, this morning. What are the charges?"

"Attempted murder, murder and conspiracy." He smoothed the lapels of his gray suit. "Assaulting a policeman too, if we need it."

Woodward sat down without invitation, so I did the same. "I'm sending a doctor to see to Mr. Diamond's injuries. It's apparent you used brute force despite his cooperation."

"Cooperation? He fought us tooth and nail." Crocker sank into his own chair. "That little lady, who claims she's his wife, was a witness to that. We also have witnesses to his involvement in the dynamite explosion at City Hall."

"Physical evidence, or hearsay?"

The policeman's thick mustache twitched. "Fuller claims Diamond set the dynamite and asked Bauer to check the fuse. Another man saw all three men loitering that morning."

"At five in the morning?" I asked. "When it was dark—and even though these men wore bandanna coverings over their faces."

"We got that bill of sale. And a witness from the Colossus factory who saw Diamond handing over the crate."

"He saw the contents of the crate?" Woodward asked, but Crocker didn't reply. "And what might his name be? I'd like to interview this witness."

"Alvarez, I think."

"Pedro Alvarez?" I asked, stunned. The detective shook his head.

"Emilio Alvarez."

"Thank you, Detective. Don't forget I'm sending a physician to examine my client and tend his injuries." Woodward rose to his feet. "I trust there will not be any further ill treatment of Mr. Diamond, correct? Thank you."

The attorney ushered me out of the office. He hushed me from speaking until we reached the outside steps. "We cannot do more for your husband. Not without further information."

"I wonder if Emilio Alvarez is related to Pedro Hernandez Alvarez," I said. "He may be involved in framing Ace. Alvarez is my uncle's business associate."

"Yes. He's a landowner in Sonoma, but I haven't heard if he ever had any children. That's something else to look into," Woodward said with a scowl. "Alvarez is a common name in California. And in the city, so we'd better confirm that as fact."

My hands shook. "What else can we do?"

"I will send someone out to Rock Canyon and ask about this Alvarez fellow. I wonder if Martin might be interested in writing an article about the Colossus Safety Powder Works." Woodward scratched his beard. "Not a bad idea."

"I wish to accompany Mr. Dodd," I said, "and question Emilio Alvarez."

"That would be far too dangerous, Mrs. Diamond. I'll hire a photographer on the ruse of documenting the factory. That would legitimize Martin's visit."

I followed him to the street at a slower pace. His quick response irked me. Woodward seemed to consider women too delicate and more of a nuisance—as did my uncle and Santiago. An old-fashioned perspective, and one I fought against for years. I knew the attorney would never accept my help. Unless he had no choice.

We traversed the narrow alley to reach Kearney Street. "Speak of the devil," I murmured and nudged Woodward's arm. "Esteban de los Reyes Santiago."

A carriage had disgorged the dapper business-man. He wore a tan coat and a flat straw hat. Knee-high polished brown boots flashed in the sun, along with his winning smile.

"Lily! So the lost lamb is found. We have all been worried about you, *mi querida*. But why are you here, of all places?"

"I am not your sweetheart or your fiancée any

longer." I drew off my left glove. The gold band on my finger glinted. "I'm a married woman now. May I introduce my attorney, Mr. Adam Woodward. This is Señor Santiago, my husband's business partner."

"Your husband?" Santiago sounded puzzled, although I sensed he'd already heard the news by the dark flash of anger in his eyes. "When did this take place?"

"Last night. Surely my uncle informed you. Plus how the police dragged Ace off to jail. He's being accused unjustly, and I will prove his innocence."

"I did hear a rumor about his troubles. It must be a simple mistake, Lily."

"Not since they arrested him."

Woodward's tone held a hint of accusation. I held my breath while Santiago hesitated, as if trying to come up with another bit of feigned reassurance. He shrugged.

"Ace is a valuable asset to the company's success. I'd trust him with my life. And I will vouch for his character if the need arises."

"Since you're so willing to help my husband," I said, "tell me how his signature ended up on a bill of sale the police believe is evidence. You're in charge of sales at the dynamite factory. You admitted that the night of the banquet."

"A bill of sale, Lily? I will inquire into the matter, but you are correct," he said. "Ace does not handle sales. A piece of evidence like that is most alarming."

"Unbelievable is the word I would use," Woodward said.

Santiago eyed him with interest. "Surely the police would know if it's genuine."

"I doubt the police know anything yet," I said. "Is there a man named Emilio Alvarez working for your company?"

"The name is familiar," he said, although he avoided my gaze. I sensed he was lying. "Ace hires and trains the workers. He knows more about production, storage of the dynamite, how to set the fuses."

"My husband would never risk his investment with a criminal act."

"I cannot answer that, Lily, but you must know that Ace does enjoy risk. I witnessed his excitement during the poker game when we first met."

Santiago stepped back to allow several people into the building, and tipped his hat to a pretty young woman. His wink and a murmured compliment of her beauty sickened me. He'd tried that ploy to win my affections. I wanted to scream and rake my fingernails across his face, certain he must be behind the plot to frame Ace.

"Where are you staying in the city, Señor Santiago?" Woodward asked. "I'd like to ask you a few questions about my client if you're free."

"I'm willing to help Ace in any way, but my schedule is full for the next few days." He smiled at me. "You see, Lily, my reputation is also at stake along with the Colossus factory. We have had past troubles. I wish for this matter to be resolved, and quickly."

He sounded worried, but that didn't fool me. "Past troubles including your business partners, who happened to end up dead or in jail?" I ignored Woodward's tighter grip on my arm. "Can you explain that pattern, Señor Santiago?"

"Pattern?" His voice held an edge. "Coincidence, perhaps."

"Hardly, since you profited from their misfortunes—"

"I cannot be blamed for the actions of my partners," he cut in. "I chose to trust the wrong men. *Felicitaciones por su matrimonio*, Lily. *¡Buenas dias* to you both."

Once Santiago disappeared inside City Hall, Woodward released a long breath and pulled me toward the street car. "Mrs. Diamond, you may have tipped him off by mentioning his former partners. I'd hoped to question him tomorrow and gain more information. He may be unwilling to meet me now."

"Oh. I'm sorry."

"Take my advice and return to your hotel. Please," he said. "Don't do anything more, or say anything to anyone until you hear from me."

Men! They were impossible. I restrained the impulse to stamp my foot. "When will that be? Tomorrow, or next week? I'm supposed to sit around, embroidering or reading a book, while my husband rots in jail?"

"Patience, Mrs. Diamond."

I shook his hand from my arm. "You can't stop me from visiting Ace."

He sighed. "No, I cannot. But I pray you will not go alone."

"I want to make certain they allow a doctor to see him. Weren't you planning on meeting my uncle and asking him questions?"

Woodward shook his head. "I've changed my mind. I shall ask Martin to learn about this dynamite factory and Mr. Santiago first. Let me know if Captain Granville shows up, too. He may have said he wants nothing more from you, but he won't let go that easy."

"Why do you say that?"

"Because those two former Pinkerton agents are following us. Don't turn around, Mrs. Diamond. Return to your hotel and stay there." Woodward tipped his hat. "For now."

He headed back in the direction of Martin Dodd's office. My instinct was to ignore his advice, but what good would that do? I couldn't visit Ace by myself. I wanted to wrap his injured ribs myself and tend his cuts and bruises as any wife would, but I recalled the lewd comments and whistles with a shudder. Instead I boarded the streetcar heading south on Kearney. The two ex-Pinkerton agents hopped on the back platform.

I faced forward. What was the use of worrying about them following me? Uncle Harrison had the same trait of stubbornness I did—or as Ace termed it, a hound on the trail of a possum. If he wanted to pay men to follow me like bloodhounds, so be it. A waste of money, in my opinion. But it wouldn't be easy waiting for news.

Here I was, in a large city, not confined like Ace in a jail cell. Or a Pullman Palace car, for that matter, yet my hands were tied. I hated feeling helpless without any control over events. I'd chided Ace for a lack of patience, but I shared that failing. My raw anger at the events last night and a wrenching need to act proved it.

I descended from the horsecar near the Russ House and blindly made my way inside. The desk clerk handed over my key and two messages—one from Kate, the other sealed in a small envelope. No writing marked the front. Out of the corner of my eye, I saw the two hired men slip behind a pillar. I scanned Kate's message first. She and Charles had returned home, since Etta complained about the city's noise. Kate offered to return if I sent for her. She begged us to come out to Rock Canyon once things resolved for Ace. I wrote out a quick reply and handed it to the clerk with a delivery fee.

Woodward was right. The Masons needed to be outside the city, away from any chance of jeopardizing their mission work. And Etta needed to recover.

The second message was a handwritten, polite invitation to lunch tomorrow at noon—signed by Uncle Harrison. I couldn't remember if I'd eaten anything today. My stomach rumbled so I returned to the desk and ordered a tray sent to my room. The clock in the lobby chimed six times. I could wash up, eat and then what? Read or twiddle my thumbs. Worry myself to death, pacing the carpet. That would fill my hours through the long evening and night.

And what about lunch tomorrow? Adam Woodward had suspected that my uncle would contact me again. Perhaps after lunch, I'd drag Uncle Harrison to his office. Woodward could question him, and update me on any progress. If any progress was being made.

Upstairs in my room, I removed my hat, dusty skirt and jacket. Cool water in the pitcher refreshed me. I rubbed myself dry with a clean cotton towel and surveyed the tidy room. The bed was straightened, the room cleaned and aired. My valise sat beside the armchair. Ace's coat and vest had been folded neatly on the seat. Seeing his clothes, abandoned, stung me. I walked over and plucked up his vest. Held its satin lining against my cheek. Breathed in Ace's musky scent and fought tears. I had to be strong.

I thought back to last night. Our wedding, my joy afterward, the wonderful dinner with friends, our brief time spent together before the police burst upon us. Hadn't I suffered enough in the past few months? I'd failed my father—his murder turned my world upside down. Somehow I'd survived multiple attempts on my life, with Ace's help. Fallen in love with him and married him. And then ended up alone on our wedding night. It was all too much.

Maybe Woodward was right. I needed time to regain perspective.

I fetched the gold watch and opened the case. Father's engraved initials marked the inside cover. I'd hire a jeweler to add the letters JRD beneath, but I couldn't bear to part with the watch yet. His awed words returned.

*I ain't ever had a gift like this before . . .*

I crawled onto the bed and wiped my wet face with the back of my hand. Weeping would not help me now, or Ace. The watch's steady tick, tick, tick soothed my nerves. It also measured out uncertainty. How long would our forced separation be? Days? Weeks? A month or more? One day married, and I was still not a proper wife.

A haunting memory rose from the past, a year after the War, when Father and I saw two condemned men standing on a gallows. The crowd seemed eager to witness the execution.

One man sold apple tarts, another hawked snake oil. Boys had swarmed up an oak tree's branches for a better view. The preacher read from a worn Bible. Each man was given a chance to say a few last words, but both declined.

When the hangman tugged black hoods over their heads, I chose not to watch. Father had reminded me that convicted criminals deserved their sad fate. Would my husband be convicted, when he was innocent? Whatever it took, I had to find proof.

I refused to fail him.

*'Deceit is in the heart of them
that imagine evil . . .'*
*Proverbs 12:20*

# Chapter Thirteen

"You've been very quiet, Lily," Uncle Harrison said and set aside his soup bowl. "I know we may have disagreed on some things lately—"

"Disagreed? Is that the correct word for it?"

"We are family. Remember that."

"You said you washed your hands of me. Or have you forgotten?" I kept my voice low due to the proximity of others enjoying their lunches. "You never told me about your secret marriage to Paloma Díaz. You forced me into an engagement with her nephew. Then you hired two men to kidnap me. If you trusted me, you'd have been honest from the start."

"It's not a matter of trust."

"Then what would you term it, uncle?" I gazed out the window at the traffic passing on the street. "Business? You're afraid I'm going to sell my share of the Early Bird, or the deed to the quicksilver claim. Isn't that the truth?"

Uncle Harrison scowled. "I'm worried about

your future welfare. I have been since you arrived in California, and I saw you in the arms of that scheming Texan cowboy."

He fell silent. The waiter had brought our plates with braised lamb chops, potato chunks sprinkled with dill and glazed carrots. My stomach growled at the heavenly aroma. I ate with less than ladylike manners, famished since I'd missed breakfast. Last night I'd lain awake for hours, worrying and fretting, before sleep came at dawn. Then I slept until the maid woke me an hour ago. She'd brought a message from my uncle, that lunch would be at half past one after a vital business meeting. After washing up, I'd changed into clean underclothes and my navy suit. It needed pressing and sponging, but I hadn't bothered. Uncle Harrison wouldn't notice.

"Lily? You haven't heard a word I've said." He pushed his plate aside and took a sip of wine. "Are you serious about selling your share of the Early Bird?"

"Give me a good reason why I should keep it." I laid down my fork. "I don't agree with your method of hydraulic mining, since it's damaging to the farmland in the valley. I'd rather look into some other way—"

"The engineers believe it's safe. You've been under a strain, I understand that. And I am sorry for what happened the other night. Seeing your husband dragged off to jail, I mean."

"I suppose you're sorry I chose to marry Jesse Diamond."

"Yes. You ought to be, too, since you'll be widowed before the year is out." His eyes darkened. "Why not consider an annulment?"

I stared him down until he glanced aside. "Never."

"Listen to reason. The men I hired have checked out the evidence against Diamond. It's a solid case. Why not be free of all this? You have the rest of your life ahead of you."

"I'll prove his innocence."

"Impossible. He'll be hanged, and you—"

"Who is Pedro Alvarez?" I interrupted, weary of his pressure. "I saw him that day we visited the Early Bird, when Hank Matthews was killed. Alvarez attended the banquet at the Golden Eagle hotel, too. Why was he invited?"

"He's an important businessman in Sonoma." Uncle Harrison waved the waiter away, declining dessert. "Alvarez knows the land around the Early Bird better than anyone, so I trust his judgment. His family farmed there before California became a state. They lost it when land grants were given to Americans, for some odd reason. He never explained why."

"So you are friends then."

"Business associates."

"Does he have a son employed at the Colossus Safety Powder Works? Or a nephew? Any close relative by the name of Emilio Alvarez?"

"You'd have to ask Stephan."

I sloshed coffee when my cup clattered on its saucer. "I'm asking you, uncle. You must know if Emilio Alvarez works at the factory. He told the police that he witnessed Ace selling dynamite to these anarchists. I wonder now if you had a hand in his arrest."

Uncle Harrison stared at me, shocked. "Why would I do that?"

"Because Ace is Santiago's partner. Framing him for murder would make certain I'd never see him again."

"No, Lily. I had nothing to do with it, I swear." This time my uncle held my gaze, his brown eyes steady. "You must believe me."

"What about his aunt? She is your legal wife, correct?"

"Yes, but Paloma preferred keeping it secret until after my appointment. Although now that may not happen." He pushed aside his empty coffee cup. "I wanted the best for you, Lily, given your father's standards. I considered Santiago's good breeding and education, his family connections, his fortunes. Diamond has nothing except the money I gave him."

"He has my heart and my loyalty." I rose to my feet. "As for my half of the Early Bird and the quicksilver, I intend to contact George Hearst this week."

"Lily, wait! Please." Uncle Harrison caught my elbow. "This has all been a huge misunderstanding. I didn't arrange for Ace to be arrested. If anyone wanted to be rid of him, it was Santiago. Let's find a more private place to discuss the matter. Come along, and I'll tell you everything I know. I promise."

Too curious to reject his offer, I followed him out of the crowded dining room. Five steps past the library, I noticed a tall man shadowing us—the former Pinkerton agent. He slipped out of sight around a corner, however. Uncle Harrison opened the door of the same ladies' parlor where I'd married Ace. I hesitated. I didn't want to spoil the memories, but my uncle shooed me inside without noticing my discomfort.

A faint scent of lavender and roses tickled my nose. No doubt toilette water from a few previous visitors, ladies who might have enjoyed the cozy room's ambience and windowless privacy. I sat, arranged my skirts and waited for him to speak. Uncle Harrison remained on his feet. The silence stretched to my breaking point so I spoke first.

"So, is Emilio related to Pedro Alvarez?"

"Yes, his youngest son."

"Then he followed Santiago's orders and lied about that bill of sale."

"It's possible—"

"You promised you would tell me what you know," I said with impatience. "I'm wasting my time, when I could be visiting my lawyer."

"Half a minute, Lily. Give me time to think this all through."

He paced the room while I rubbed my chilled fingers. How much did Uncle Harrison know about the Colossus Safety Powder Works? Why was he debating what to tell me? What did he know about Santiago's role in this anarchist plan? Had he taken steps to stop it?

"I believe Stephan wanted to get rid of Ace, and he might have set up the explosion at City Hall," I said at last. "He's had other business partners who ended up in trouble. The timing seems too convenient. What do you know, uncle?"

"Stephan was unhappy that you balked at marrying him. You hurt his pride. Women flocked to him before, begging him to court or marry them. Your disinterest cut him deep. Paloma was upset too when she found out you left Sacramento. She accompanied me on this trip and plans to visit family here in the city."

"Why should she be upset? Stephan can choose anyone to marry."

"The fact that you knew Diamond, and preferred him, stuck in Stephan's craw. It may have pushed their rivalry too far."

"So he framed Ace for murder."

"I doubt that, but their business relationship was already strained to the breaking point. They disagreed over safety conditions at the factory. Santiago admitted that."

244

"They seemed to get along well at the banquet, until the engagement announcement. Did Paloma push you into doing that?" I asked, curious.

"Yes, I suppose she did. I hadn't planned to announce it until the private dinner later that night. But I wasn't aware of problems between Diamond and Santiago until Paloma explained. Buyers wanted their dynamite faster than the company could provide. Diamond's stubbornness about following safety rules slowed production. Things got ugly fast over profits, too."

"So Stephan didn't care if the workers took risks? Like at the Early Bird, when Mr. Matthews was killed in the mudslide."

"Mining is far different. Besides, Santiago doesn't understand production. He's impatient because few companies are producing dynamite in the country."

I folded my hands. "All right. We need proof that Emilio Alvarez lied about Ace giving the crates to the anarchists, do you agree? And we need to know who set up the dynamite at City Hall that morning. If you sent those former Pinkerton agents out to the Colossus today, perhaps they could help clear Ace's name."

He exhaled a long breath. "Perhaps."

"That's your answer? Perhaps," I said with skepticism. "Perhaps I'll contact George Hearst today and set up a meeting."

"Lily. You must be patient in times like these."

I rose to my feet, furious. "You promised to tell

me what you knew. Perhaps you're going to say that you didn't send James McKay to spy on me at Rock Canyon either."

"He sent me a telegram about you being there, I won't deny that. But it wasn't my plan to spy on you." Uncle Harrison twisted to face me. "McKay wants help to fund his newspaper. He thought by doing me a favor, I'd agree. I turned him down flat. I'm not interested in another investment. And his newspaper isn't consistent in quality."

"I don't care about anything but proving my husband's innocence. Thank you for lunch, Uncle Harrison, but I have other important things to do today."

He drew out his pocket watch and opened it. "It's past four already. You realize it's late to pay a call on anyone."

"Next you'll tell me I cannot hire a carriage and go alone to see my lawyer—"

"I would advise against it."

"In broad daylight, why not? I'm a married woman." I gritted my teeth. "I went to Adam Woodward's office yesterday without an escort. I was perfectly safe."

"Lily, you're unaware of dangers to all women, married or single, in this city. Please. At least allow me to accompany you."

"On one condition. Send your hired men out to the dynamite factory."

Uncle Harrison sighed. "I suppose you won't

rest until I do. I doubt they will learn anything at the Rock Canyon factory."

"They won't learn anything if you don't send them."

"I'll do what I can."

"Send them as soon as possible, uncle. Have them interview Emilio Alvarez and a few other workers, in case they have a different story about Ace."

"I will, if you agree to put off seeing your lawyer until tomorrow." He pocketed his watch. "First we will meet for breakfast in the dining room. I shan't miss my coffee, bacon and eggs. Nine o'clock sharp, my dear niece. Enjoy your evening."

I didn't reply, given my husband's absence. But I enjoyed triumph. Uncle Harrison had washed his hands of me a short time ago. Now I'd convinced him to take action on Ace's behalf. His hired men would question Emilio Alvarez and trip him up in lies. Ace would be proven innocent and set free. The sooner, the better.

The following morning I prayed that Woodward had news. Any news. Uncle Harrison knocked at the attorney's office—more of a cottage, unlike the row house with bay windows where Martin Dodd worked. Oddly enough, the bearded newspaper journalist answered before my uncle rapped a second time.

"Captain Granville. Miss—er, how can I help you?"

"My niece has business with Mr. Woodward. Is he busy right now?"

"He was called away to City Hall. Please come in."

Dodd stood aside. He wore the same wrinkled sack suit, and the ink staining his fingers looked fainter. We strolled into the front room. Everything was in the same tidy order, except for a cup and saucer on the desk, and a spoon on the blotter next to a piece of paper. I peeked inside the delicate porcelain. It held a pale brown liquid, no doubt tea given the swirl of damp dregs in the bottom. I chose the chair closest to the desk.

"When do you expect Mr. Woodward to return?"

"I don't know. He's gone to see Mr.—" Dodd hesitated.

"Mr. Diamond. Captain Granville is aware of my recent marriage," I said.

"I see."

"Mr. Dodd accompanied Mr. McKay to spy on me last Friday, uncle."

"We didn't—well, that wasn't the only reason we visited." Dodd licked his lips. "And we published that article on the Masons' missionary work. In today's edition."

"I saw it, on the back page while my uncle read the front page headlines. I wonder why the *California Enquirer* failed to mention the anarchist bombing at all. Every other newspaper had the story on the front page."

"Is that true, Mr. Dodd?" Uncle Harrison set his hat and gloves on a side table, although he kept hold of his silver-knobbed walking cane. "When Governor Haight was the target of these crazed anarchists? McKay failed the newspaper's loyal readers."

The young man cleared his throat. I rearranged my skirts, my elbow jarring against a short bookcase by accident, which shot pain up my arm and shoulder. I gritted my teeth. At last Dodd answered, although he didn't sound pleased.

"I believe he wanted to protect the Colossus Safety Powder Works. Along with your husband's partner, Mr. Santiago."

"I suppose McKay wanted to protect Santiago because he's an investor," Uncle Harrison said, "although from what I observed, they're not close friends at all."

"When has that stopped anyone? McKay often talked about Santiago and the Colossus factory, since he invested in it. They've met for dinner every week. I'd say my boss knew very well what Santiago planned. It would kill two birds with one stone—getting rid of his partner, Mr. Diamond, and also further their political cause. A pretty neat trick."

"What political cause?" I asked, curious.

"Their group planned to kill Governor Haight. Didn't work, though."

Uncle Harrison shook his head in disbelief. "Stephan is not involved in a political group. Nor with crazy anarchists."

Dodd laced his fingers together. "Perhaps you've never heard of *Oso Español*. It's a secret group formed to establish a republic separate from the government. Santiago is a member of that group along with my boss, James McKay. I'm sure they paid those men to pull off that explosion. I don't have proof, though. Not yet."

"But what does their name mean?"

"'Spanish Bear,' Mrs. Diamond. Very few people know about the history of the revolt. It happened back in nineteen forty-six when the Americans took over Sonoma."

"Stephan said the Rebels raised a flag, with an animal that resembled a pig instead of a grizzly bear. He told that story at the banquet." My excitement increased, and I continued on despite my uncle's clear displeasure. "He said Mexico and the United States were at war, over Texas. I remember that since Ace was born in Texas. And the Mexican General Vallejo switched sides to support the Americans. But they jailed him."

"That's part of it," Dodd said. "The members of *Oso Español* are either related to the old Spanish families that settled around Sonoma, or have ties to them. There was bad blood between the leader of the American rebels and Vallejo. The general was imprisoned and mistreated too. Señora Díaz is a niece of his."

Uncle Harrison shook his head. "She may be related to General Vallejo, but you're wrong.

Stephan isn't a member of any crazy political group."

"You wanted Mrs. Diamond to marry him. That would have given Santiago a hefty source of money he could use for *Oso Español*, with his aunt's blessing."

"Paloma is a society matron. She'd never approve of funding anarchist plots."

Dodd leaned back in his chair, his pose relaxed, a wide grin plastered on his bearded face. They acted wary of each other, but the journalist jabbed my uncle with further information as a child might poke a snake with a stick. I didn't feel sorry for him.

"Did you know that James McKay handles the treasury funds and donations for *Oso Español*? He admitted that to me, and that Paloma Díaz groomed her nephew to take over as head of the group. After they gained control of the government, of course."

"Poppycock," Uncle Harrison said. "Besides, the dynamite explosion failed. Governor Haight never even arrived from Sacramento."

"Perhaps the group has more explosions planned."

He stared at me as if I'd sprouted devil horns. "You cannot believe this rot! Paloma is above politics. She's a gracious lady, charitable to people, kind and compassionate."

"Everyone harbors secrets," I said. "I learned that on the way to California."

"She's never shown an interest in politics."

"Perhaps she doesn't want you to know the truth."

Dodd pulled out a slip of paper and unfolded it. "This is the letter from Pedro Hernando Alvarez to James McKay. He mentions Señora Díaz, too."

"Why would Pedro Alvarez speak of her?" I asked. "Didn't he have a hand in her husband's death? I thought I heard that—"

"It's not true." My uncle thumped his walking stick against the floor. "Alvarez wanted to buy her husband's business after she was widowed. She doesn't hate him, but there's no love between them. A cool indifference, if anything."

"May I read the letter, Mr. Dodd?" I held out a hand. "Pedro Alvarez's son is involved in this plot to implicate my husband. I'd like to know more about this political group."

"It's written in Spanish. A friend translated the contents, but I didn't write it out by hand in English. Now he's out of town for a month." Dodd handed me the thin onionskin sheet. "I've come across other letters, too."

"How did you manage that?" I examined the crabbed handwriting.

"I stole them." He didn't sound a bit ashamed. "McKay left them in plain sight, and my curiosity got the better of me. Can you read Spanish?"

"No, but I recognize the words California and

Capitan Frémont. Ace knows Spanish. If I sound out the words to him, maybe he could translate. Are the other letters similar?"

"Yes. Let's fetch them at my office, and then head straight to City Hall. Woodward may be at the jail," Dodd said and scribbled something. "I'm leaving a note in case he returns."

Excited, I hurried after Martin Dodd. These letters might be proof of Ace's innocence. My uncle tagged after us with obvious reluctance. Despite his defense of his wife, my opinion of Paloma Díaz Granville was mixed. She'd taken advantage of his friendship and their secret marriage. Would she be hurt, along with her cause of beautifying the State Capitol, if people suspected Stephan of framing Ace for murder? No doubt my ex-fiancé would worm his way out of any censure. Stephan had plenty of charm and resilience.

We crossed Kearney Street and headed east along Union. For some reason, pedestrians swarmed around his office building. Our efforts to push a way through the thick crowd earned muttered complaints and a few curses on our heads. Several gray-suited policemen held back more curious onlookers from the entrance.

"What is it? What's happened?" I asked someone.

A man twisted to answer. "This ain't no place for a lady, ma'am."

"He's right, Lily," Uncle Harrison said. "There's been trouble of some kind."

Ignoring him, I slithered sideways and jostled my way to the front. "Oh, I beg your pardon, sir. I didn't see you."

"My apologies." The gentleman touched his hat brim and shook a medical bag at the crowd blocking him. "I am Dr. Hanson, and that is my office. Please, stand aside!"

Martin Dodd and Uncle Harrison fought their way through the crush of people further behind. Instead of waiting, I plunged after Dr. Hanson and managed to reach the doorway where a policeman stood guard. He grabbed two boys who'd squeezed past people, so I slipped inside. My relentless curiosity pushed me forward.

The stairs had the same mildew stench I remembered, as if the roof leaked. A wide crack in the outer wall allowed in a sliver of light, and moisture when it rained. A fly crawled through and buzzed near my cheek. I swatted it away and hurried up the steps. By the time I reached the top, Dr. Hanson had disappeared. What if the police recognized me from my visit yesterday to City Hall? Perhaps it was too late for second thoughts.

I entered the office. The jumbled disarray looked far worse than my previous visit. Papers had been trampled underfoot, wooden shelves turned over and books strewn across the muddy floor. Chairs had been smashed. Splashes of rusty brown marked the far wall. My finger touched a trail of those spots across papers on a desk. It wasn't ink or paint. My nose wrinkled at the faint coppery scent in the air, reminding me of Father's library. On the night I'd found his body.

"Is this blood?"

"Yes. How did you get in here, miss?" A policeman in a gray suit stared at me, bowler hat in hand. "Unless you can help identify the dead man—"

"Yesterday I met the journalists who work here."

"All right, ma'am. This way."

Triumphant, I allowed the policeman to guide me forward through the maze of desks and scattered books, papers and other items. My elation proved short-lived. Dr. Hanson knelt beside a man sprawled on his stomach. I stared in alarm at his dark hair, one arm outstretched, his pale beefy hand and buffed nails. It wasn't one of the journalists after all. My ex-fiancé, Esteban de los Reyes Santiago, lay on the floor with a knife protruding from his back.

"Mrs. Diamond is here to identify the victim, Dr. Hanson."

I swallowed hard. Stephan's shirt had been soaked with blood, dried now, with some staining the floor beneath him. The doctor rolled the body onto one side. We all gasped at the deep crimson slash across the throat. Cut from ear to ear.

I fell senseless into a swirling black void.

*'. . . the revenger of blood shall slay
the murderer . . .'*
*Numbers 35:21*

# Chapter Fourteen

"Lily, wake up and drink this."

I blinked several times and then straightened in the chair, groggy. "What—"

Uncle Harrison pressed a silver flask on me. I gulped down a mouthful of brandy in gratitude. The fiery liquid burned all the way, but helped steady my nerves.

"I know this has been an awful shock, of course, to all of us. Are you feeling stronger now, my dear?"

"No." I pushed him away and struggled to sit up. "Where is—"

"They took the body away."

The horrible shock of seeing Esteban de los Reyes Santiago, his dark eyes lifeless and staring, his face ashen, washed over me once more. Who would have done this? And why? I bent forward, eyes closed, and yet failed to wipe that gruesome sight from my mind. His slashed throat, the blood staining his shirt, the creamy rectangle of muslin beneath him, with a stripe of crimson silk along the side. It also had a hulking painted image of a grizzly bear, plus the words *Oso Español* in crude letters.

"What was Stephan doing here?"

My uncle shook his head. "I don't know, Lily."

I gripped the chair's arms, staring at the policemen who huddled in a group where the body—Stephan—had lain. The last person I'd expected to see. Brutally murdered. A memory surfaced, of a large knife in Ace's hands on the Pullman Palace car. Would he have taken his revenge on Stephan for cheating him?

Impossible. That couldn't be his Bowie knife. Ace was safe in jail. He was incapable of cold-blooded murder—and this murder was no accident. Whoever killed Stephan made sure he wouldn't survive.

I glanced around the room. "Where is Mr. Dodd?"

"Being questioned by the police," my uncle said. "He knows who else works in this office, and if any of them had links to Santiago. So far, Martin Dodd is the only one."

"Because he was investigating this political group, I suppose."

My shoulder throbbed. I must have fallen on it during the fainting spell. I hated losing control, and had never acquired the habit of swooning like Adele Mason and other friends back home.

But in two episodes, within two months, I had succumbed after viewing murder victims—my father and now my ex-fiancé. Both times the rooms had been searched. In Father's library, his safe, papers and books had been scattered after he'd been shot. Here, the mess suggested that Santiago had been ransacking the office until the killer interrupted him.

"That flag. Did they take it away, too?"

"Yes." Uncle Harrison scratched his goatee. "It's possible Dodd killed Stephan and then rushed to Woodward's office. He needed an alibi."

I shivered in silence. Had the journalist done this horrible thing, then fled the scene? Somehow I didn't see Dodd as a killer.

"I find that hard to believe—"

"What, that he could sit there in Woodward's office talking to us about this political group? It's all hogwash anyway. Let's get you back to the hotel. You've had a shock. Don't argue, Lily! I'm as upset as you. Stephan was like a son to me. God only knows how Paloma will take the news, too."

My uncle helped me to stand and guided me to the stairs. A policeman halted us before we reached it and blocked the doorway.

"Sorry, sir. We might have a few questions for the lady. Please wait."

That set Uncle Harrison off on another tirade. The gray-suited policeman folded his arms and refused to budge. I listened with one ear, my mind whirling. Had Stephan suspected Martin Dodd of getting too close to the truth? Perhaps James McKay had discovered the letters were missing and sent Stephan. Why else would he search this office? But I had no idea where the flag had come from, and why it was lying beneath him. What an odd puzzle.

That huge knife was also a mystery. I couldn't deny my husband had the best motive. *If I ever get my hands on him . . .*

Those words echoed in my head. Ace wouldn't have slit a rival's throat with his Bowie knife. Stabbed him, yes—but not in the back. More likely he'd have shot Stephan with his Colt, face to face, in self-defense. But this scene didn't look like self-defense at all.

"Well, I'm glad that's over." Martin Dodd's voice broke into my thoughts. He mopped his damp forehead with a handkerchief, although beads of sweat still ran down to his collar. "To think a murder could happen here."

"What did you tell the police about your whereabouts?" Uncle Harrison asked without preamble. "Or did you make up a story to avoid suspicion?"

Dodd stiffened. "I didn't kill Santiago, Captain Granville. I never come to the office before noon. I keep late hours, working on deadlines. My landlady can testify that I left the boardinghouse this morning at my usual time, and stopped by

Woodward's office first. Minutes before you and Mrs. Diamond arrived."

"I'm sure the police can find a hole in that alibi."

"Did Stephan find the letters?" I asked, ignoring my uncle's snide remark.

"No, he never reached that shelf before—before he was killed. They should be right here." Dodd selected a bound volume of *Little Women* from a nearby shelf, cracked open the spine and removed the thin envelopes. "This is my sister's book. I figured it would be the last place anyone would look. Especially a man."

I gave a shaky laugh. "Indeed."

"Did you have that flag here or did Santiago bring it?" Uncle Harrison asked. "Seems odd he would, given it was a secret political group."

"I didn't know one existed."

"Then the killer left it," I said. "But why? Unless he wanted to draw attention to the group. It doesn't make sense otherwise."

Dodd shrugged. "It doesn't to me either. I'd like to know who's going to lead the *Oso Español* group now that Santiago's dead."

"Who else are members besides McKay and Alvarez?" my uncle asked.

"Several of the Vallejos, plus Ruíz, Vacas, and a slew of others I can't name," the journalist said. "Señora Díaz and one of her Vallejo cousins started the group. I know, there's no proof of that. But you could ask her if it's true."

Uncle Harrison's cheeks had reddened when his wife's name was mentioned. "I'll tell you for the last time, Señora Díaz is not part of this group. And why would they blow up City Hall in order to kill Governor Haight? That would have brought the police down on their heads faster than an assassination attempt."

"I wish I could tell—"

The journalist jumped in surprise when Woodward clapped him on the shoulder. The attorney looked grim. Detective Sergeant Crocker had also entered the office but joined the knot of gray-suited policemen on the room's other side.

"What the devil happened here?" Woodward asked. "I found your note, Martin, but didn't hear anything about a murder until I was out in the street."

Dodd hesitated, as if waiting for us to reply first. "Santiago's throat was slit with a Bowie knife. The police found a flag under his body— with *Oso Español* on it. And a grizzly."

"A grizzly?"

"Yes, painted on it. Isn't that right, Mrs. Diamond?"

"I didn't get a close enough look at it, but yes. I think so."

Detective Crocker joined us. "So, we have a murder on our hands this time."

"Was it a random killing?" Woodward asked.

"A throat injury like that isn't what I'd term random." Detective Crocker eyed me in suspicion. "Odd that Diamond and Santiago argued every day, from what I've heard. And your husband is known for his prowess with a knife."

Startled, I fought for words to reply. "Who informed you of that?"

"Emilio Alvarez. We questioned him yesterday about Diamond. Seems he often used that knife of his to cut ropes around the factory. And Santiago was first engaged to you. All of a sudden you up and marry his rival—money and a woman. Classic motives for murder."

"My husband isn't a murderer."

"Wouldn't Señor Santiago be the one blamed for killing Mr. Diamond?" Woodward asked. "That seems more logical, if they were rivals."

"Could be they fought, which is why the room is a mess. Then Diamond drew his big Bowie knife and took care of things," Crocker said. "Ruthless, but all Texans are."

Speechless, I fought boiling anger. Uncle Harrison jumped to my defense before I found my tongue. "Motive without evidence won't get a conviction in court, Detective."

"We got that knife. We'll show it to the factory workers, see if they recognize it as Diamond's. More than likely it is."

"Plenty of men must own a knife like that."

"It's also true there's bad blood between the

Santiago and Alvarez families," Woodward said. "You ought to consider that before you jump to conclusions."

Crocker shrugged. "We ain't done investigating. We'll stir up the ant's nest and see what pops out. Witnesses, maybe. Someone must've seen the killer leaving this building."

"I'm sure you'll find people willing to say they did—"

"Whoa there! Are you suggesting we bribe people into false testimony?" The detective spat on the floor. "The San Francisco police ain't corrupt, and you know it."

Uncle Harrison stepped forward. "My niece is exhausted. She's had a big shock, and I'm escorting her back to our hotel. You may contact us there if you need us further."

Crocker waved a hand in dismissal. The memory of Stephan's poor body, blood-soaked shirt and that flag returned. The bear resembled an illustration I once saw in a book. I had never seen that creature in my life, and hoped I never would. Who had brought it here on purpose? Someone who knew of Stephan's involvement— not my husband. I hadn't the chance to tell him anything about *Oso Español* or my uncle's secret marriage, and now this murder.

Woodward accompanied us to the stairs. "A Bowie knife, eh? I suppose a gunshot would have made too much noise and brought attention to the crime."

"That knife had a leather handle and a metal guard. A long blade, too," Martin Dodd said. "Similar to a butcher knife, about ten to twelve inches. Spanish, I'd say."

"Double-edged, too, from what I saw," my uncle said.

"Yes, it is—" I kicked myself for adding fuel to the fire. "I mean it's possible."

"I planned to give you good news, although this business has changed its nature," the attorney said. "I talked to the judge and prosecutor about Mr. Diamond's case—"

"Did you see Ace today at the jail?" I interrupted. "Is he all right?"

"That's the problem, Mrs. Diamond. Your husband was released this morning."

Adam Woodward and Uncle Harrison talked in low voices while I picked at my dinner. After leaving Dodd's office, we'd returned for a late afternoon meal at the Russ House. I wasn't in the least bit hungry. A few other hotel guests lingered over conversation. The waiter hovered behind my uncle, as if waiting for a signal, and then brought coffee and a platter of fruit, cheeses, nuts and tarts. He whisked my plate away. Worried, I gnawed on a few apple slices.

Where was Ace? Why hadn't he come here to find me? Surely he'd have sent word—if not a message, then some kind of signal. Then again, he'd probably left jail without money and in the same filthy clothing. Would he have gone to that hotel, near the livery stable? I tried to recall those streets. My uncle's voice caught my attention.

"—will hang him for certain now, once they find him."

I bristled. "How could Ace have known where Stephan was?"

Woodward nodded. "True enough. I inquired at the desk, Mrs. Diamond, but the clerk has not seen your husband. I'm surprised he didn't come to change clothes. He also strikes me as a man who wouldn't be without his weapons. He must own a pistol."

"Perhaps," I said, aware that his assessment was on the mark, "but it's a huge coincidence that he might see Stephan. And he wouldn't kill him."

"It's unfortunate that he stayed at a hotel on Battery and Washington. A few blocks from Martin Dodd's office, and City Hall where the explosion occurred."

"Hardly a coincidence," my uncle said.

"Circumstance. There's no proof that Ace went there this morning," I said hotly. "And I won't believe it even if the police find a witness to lie for them. He wouldn't kill Stephan. Fight him, maybe. Ace wanted his money back, and killing him wouldn't have accomplished that."

Woodward nodded. "Detective Crocker seems to prefer the easiest answer."

"It's not fair. I think that third anarchist was someone in the *Oso Español*."

"Emilio Alvarez, most likely." The attorney drained his wine glass. "As for fairness, most people believe that justice includes it. That's not always the case, Mrs. Diamond. Bias comes into play. And deep-seated prejudice."

"But judges have to be fair in their dealings."

"They rule on the law, which is in itself not fair depending on a person's point of view," Woodward said. "Take for example the issue of slavery in Kansas. I left that mess behind when people on both sides believed they were right and would not compromise. It was eye for an eye, tooth for a tooth. Killings back and forth, with little fairness or justice."

"Kansas was a hotbed indeed." Uncle Harrison fingered his goatee. "Quantrill was a bas—a murderer and a thief. Some believe he was a hero. That's not justice in my book."

"But the War is over, uncle."

"I don't need a lecture. I fought at Shiloh, remember."

"Ace lost all his brothers but one at Shiloh, but he doesn't hold that against you or any other Union veteran."

"He's young and resilient," Woodward said. "Men of our age tend to dwell on wrongs of the past. It's not easy giving up lost dreams, Mrs. Diamond, as age creeps on us."

"What type of dream have you lost, Mr. Woodward?" I asked.

" 'All that we see or seem, is but a dream within a dream.' Written by Edgar Allen Poe, whose tragic life was far more difficult than my own. I have no reason to complain."

"Do all lawyers learn how to dodge direct questions early on?"

He smiled. "Indeed. It's the foundation of our practice."

Uncle Harrison cleared his throat and tossed his napkin aside. "You'd better prepare yourself for tragedy, Lily. The police are combing the city. If Diamond's vanished into thin air, that doesn't reflect well on his supposed innocence."

"I recommend looking into James McKay's past," Woodward said. "He's the group's treasurer. I wonder if he wanted to eliminate a rival for leadership."

"I doubt that. He's a businessman—"

"And a shrewd one, too. Most people would guess Mr. Diamond owns a Bowie knife. It's fairly easy to get one. Perhaps it was planted at the scene to point in his direction."

Woodward's words reassured me. My uncle didn't seem satisfied, however. "I can't see James McKay overpowering Stephan. He was a young man and very fit. McKay cannot walk down the street without being short of breath."

"I can see your point, Captain Granville."

"Dodd was gathering information about this political group, but I'd wager on Diamond as the killer." Uncle Harrison sounded bitter. "Maybe he saw Santiago on the street and followed him to that office. Tried to reason with him, but had no recourse."

"No." I rose to my feet. Both men followed, my uncle with reluctance. "My husband is not a killer. If you want a wager, so be it. My half of the Early Bird mine, because I'm convinced Ace is innocent. Are you willing to match my wager?"

My uncle clearly had not yet recovered from shock over my daring offer. "Don't be ridiculous, Lily—"

"Why? You've pressured me into getting an annulment, and hounded me about being a widow soon. As Father would say, fish or cut bait."

He straightened to his full height. "The income from the mine has doubled, in case you're not aware. It will triple if we can access the quicksilver from Sylvia's land."

"So you'd rather I put that claim on the table instead?" When Uncle Harrison didn't answer, I sat again into my chair. "Done. The quicksilver claim against full ownership of the Early Bird. If you win, you can do as you please with both. Mr. Woodward is a witness to this agreement and can draw it up in writing, if you wish."

"I'm not a gambler at heart."

"Oh come now, Captain. You and George Hearst

took risks over the past decade," the attorney said. "Perhaps your cold feet means you believe Mr. Diamond is innocent? Consider this suggestion. If you lose, you will sign over your portion of the Early Bird to Mr. Diamond but retain twenty-five percent of any profits from production. That is more than fair."

Uncle Harrison drummed his fingers on the table. "Sixty percent."

"Thirty," I said. "Draw up the contract, Mr. Woodward."

"I accept your word, Lily. But know this—your husband may hang on the gallows no matter what you do, even if he's innocent."

"He will be cleared of this murder charge in a court of law."

"You can back out any time," my uncle said but I shook my head.

"No. I gave my word."

I was determined to prove my uncle wrong. Heartbreak would follow if his prediction did come true, and Ace was hanged, but I had to find proof. Uncontested proof that Ace had nothing to do with the anarchist explosion.

"There must be evidence at the dynamite factory. What about those men you hired, the ex-Pinkerton agents? Haven't they found anything?"

"They didn't get any information out of Emilio Alvarez, if that's what you mean," Uncle Harrison said. "The other workers refused to speak to them. And the supervisor forbid them to look around the factory."

Woodward sighed. "Martin Dodd is heading out there now. Knowing him, he'll snoop with or without permission."

"The fool! He might be the next one killed."

"Always the pessimist, uncle." I smiled at them both. "I'd like to see the factory today. My husband owns half of the Colossus, so they must allow me inside."

"I forbid you to risk your life, Lily," my uncle said. "You may be a married woman, but with your husband under suspicion, it's not wise to go there."

"Thank you for that advice, but I disagree."

Woodward held out his arm. "I will escort you, Mrs. Diamond, if you insist on taking this excursion. I don't suppose it will be any more dangerous than visiting the jail."

Uncle Harrison scowled. "This entire business is too dangerous."

"You're convinced Ace is guilty, and you'd rather see him hanged."

"That's not true. I won't deny I put my own ambitions over your future. I hoped for a successful marriage between you and Stephan, and so did my wife."

"It's too late for apologies, uncle. I had no intention of marrying Stephan—"

"So she continues to refuse my nephew?"

I twisted at the shrill voice. Paloma Díaz Granville stood in the doorway, resplendent in a wine-colored moiré silk dress. A tiny hat topped her looped and braided coiffure. Two spots of apple red bloomed on her alabaster cheeks.

My uncle jumped to his feet. "Paloma. I didn't expect to see you so soon."

"You sent a telegram. Couldn't you have sent a message instead?" She surveyed me in disdain. "What could be worse news than this ungrateful child rejecting Stephan? Lily ran away like a frightened rabbit. My nephew is so disappointed."

"Lily married his business partner, Ace Diamond, against my wishes."

"*¿Por qué permitir que tal cosa—*"

"Hush, hush. There is something else I must tell you," he said and drew her close.

I held my breath, aware she had a bigger shock coming. Paloma's lightning reaction stunned me. Ignoring Uncle Harrison's whispered words of comfort, she pulled away from his tight embrace. Her black eyes darted between Adam Woodward and her husband, back to me and then once more to fix on my uncle's face.

"*No! No, no puede ser verdad!*"

"It's true, Paloma. I am sorry."

"Where is Stephan? It's a lie, it cannot be true!"

"They took his body to the coroner's office—"

271

Paloma shrieked another torrent of Spanish, pummeling his chest and screaming, her tirade unrelenting. Then she rushed straight at me. Her slap stung my cheek so hard, I reeled back against Woodward.

"*Es su culpa que haya muerto! Has matado a mi hijo—*"

I would have returned the favor, despite my bewilderment at her brazen assault, but Woodward whirled me out of reach. Uncle Harrison grabbed his wife around the waist. He ignored her barrage of kicks and punches, even when she smacked her head backwards against his face. He refused to release her. Blood trickled from his mouth into his goatee and down his neck to soil his collar, but he half-carried her out of the room.

"Stop! Do you want the hotel staff to call the police?" Uncle Harrison glanced back at us while Paloma babbled in Spanish. "Wait for me, Lily. I'll be back as soon as I can."

I pressed a hand to my hot cheek. "She took the news very hard."

"Yes, indeed. Are you all right?" Woodward's eyes twinkled. "I believe she accused you of murder. My Spanish is very rusty, though."

"She thinks I killed her nephew?"

"*Muerto* is death. And unless I'm mistaken, *hijo* is child, not nephew."

272

*'. . . there is no secret that they*
*can hide from thee. . .'*
*Ezekiel 28:3*

# Chapter Fifteen

"Her son?" I gulped a mouthful of water from the closest goblet and perched on a chair. "Stephan was her son? How was that possible?"

Woodward sat in gratitude. "I heard the rumor long ago that Juan José Santiago had a mistress. His barren wife took the child as her own. Quite a secret for Señora Díaz to bear all these years. No wonder she had her heart set on Santiago being a leader."

"But why would she think I murdered him?"

"You rejected him. That led to the City Hall explosion, and then his murder," he said, "although that's conjecture. We ought to ask Martin more about *Oso Español*. Where they have been meeting, and what else they may have planned."

"Would they meet at the dynamite factory?"

"Well, it is in a remote location. Far enough from the city to prevent any gossip like in a neighborhood around here. And from the police."

I grew restless. "When is my uncle returning?"

"I don't know." Woodward slowly rose from his chair. "It's well past mid-afternoon. It will take an hour at least to get to the factory."

I glanced at the doorway, as if that would draw my uncle back. "If your offer to escort me to Rock Canyon hasn't changed, I'd like to start now."

"All right, if you're sure. You'd better check again at the reception desk, in case your husband sent a message as to his whereabouts." The attorney sounded regretful. "I'd never have paid the bond money if I had known another crime would be committed. The police may send men out to the dynamite factory and search for Mr. Diamond."

"We'd better leave immediately. Uncle Harrison will have to catch up to us."

"I'll meet you outside in five minutes."

I raced to the stairs, wishing we hadn't wasted time talking. I couldn't allow the police to arrest Ace for the second time. In my room I surveyed my clean clothes and ruled out the fancy wedding dress borrowed from Kate. My navy suit was dusty, muddy, unwieldy. After stripping to my petticoat and corset, I clawed through my valise. Ace's stiletto dropped to the floor and almost skewered my stocking-clad foot. Heavens.

I retrieved it and laid it on the bed, along with my black riding skirt. I groaned. The side seam gaped near the pocket. I didn't have time to use a needle and thread. Tossing the horsehair bustle on the bed, I donned the slimmer skirt, hoping my hip-length jacket hid the gap. I pinned a straw hat to my curls and pulled on a pair of low-heeled boots. Then I wrapped Ace's stiletto in a handkerchief and slid it inside my boot top.

But I left the gold pocket watch under the bed's pillow. It was too precious to lose or risk being broken. It would be safer here. I snatched up gloves and hurried to the stairs.

At the reception desk, I jotted a quick note for my uncle. No word from Ace, so I headed outside. Adam Woodward waited by a small two-seater buggy.

"I have a question, Mrs. Diamond. What did your uncle mean by 'my wife?' " he asked. "I wasn't aware that Captain Granville was married."

"Yes, he and Paloma Díaz married in secret. I left a message for him to follow us."

Woodward nodded, his eyes hooded. "All right. Let's hope we can find your husband out in Rock Canyon."

He boosted me into the seat and climbed up beside me. The attorney drew the top up and locked it into place, since the overcast sky threatened rain. A cold wind blew. My jacket wasn't thick, and I wished now I'd chosen a hooded wool cloak. The team threaded a way south through traffic to Market Street. Woodward guided them west away from the city.

"Look at that line waiting for the streetcar," I said. "Goodness. The city ought to have double the number for so many people living here."

Adam Woodward focused on driving the team, saying very little unless asked a direct question. That gave me plenty of time to worry about Ace. And Uncle Harrison—had he taken Paloma up to his room to calm her? Explain the circumstances? I didn't blame him for choosing his wife before helping me, though. I only wished I could ask Kate and Charles for help. But they had their own life, their own friends, and people depended on them and their ministry.

Where had Ace gone after his release from jail this morning? Not knowing frightened me more than I cared to admit.

I paid little attention to the scenery during the buggy ride. My mind whirled with various possibilities. At least I'd be taking action instead of waiting at the hotel for news. Or discussing events after the fact. I replayed everything since our hasty wedding—the policemen's visit, my first meeting with Woodward, the visit with Ace in jail, lunch the next day with Uncle Harrison and learning all about *Oso Español* from Martin Dodd.

And then, Santiago's murder had shocked us all.

"I never expected to see that," I said aloud.

"I beg your pardon?" He chirruped to the team, heading them south along Castro Street. "The Mission Dolores is over a hundred years old."

The bell in the distant adobe's tower tolled slow, a solemn knell that echoed overhead. It sent a chill up my spine. Was it instinct or something else that hinted at upcoming disaster? For all I knew, Ace could be lying in Rock Canyon with his throat cut. I shuddered. I did not want to live without him. Not after we'd promised to share our future.

The buggy rolled over a set of jarring ruts, and I gritted my teeth. "What will we find at the Colossus, I wonder."

"I've been thinking the same thing. Not someone stabbed in the back, I hope. Or evidence that Emilio Alvarez lied. Perhaps one of the other workers will speak to us."

"Do you know his father, Pedro Alvarez? My uncle does."

"He's a ruthless businessman. Everyone who knows him is careful to steer away from making him angry. I've done some legal work for him," the attorney said. "Like your uncle, he's not easy to please. Imagine the two of them together—"

"Alvarez has given my uncle advice on production at the Early Bird mine. He disagreed with an engineer's direction, and was proven right."

I explained visiting the hydraulic mine site, watching the powerful hoses undercut the ridge and cause its collapse, how Hank Matthews had saved my life but lost his own. Woodward guided the team onto another road. I recognized the stony canyon by the sharp tang of eucalyptus trees, the grassy steep slopes and a glimpse of the winding creek along the bottom. The sun dipped toward the west beyond the canyon. Long shadows stretched behind us, and I twisted back into the cold wind. I'd read the Midwest farm-land had already frozen. November here felt more like a chilly spring night.

"Is the factory large or small?"

"Not large enough for the increase in production." Woodward frowned. "Last year they produced eleven tons of dynamite. As of today, the Colossus recorded seventy-five tons and that doesn't include what's been delivered since the last count. Astonishing."

"Then why in the world didn't Stephan pay my husband a share of the profits?"

"It's a shame you can't ask him that yourself."

"Ace told me all his investment money—six thousand dollars—went into supplies. How can that be? If the factory has been producing an incredible amount of dynamite, why was Stephan so desperate for money? Did he siphon off profits for the *Oso Español*?"

"Your husband was a fool to trust him."

Stunned by the attorney's harsh tone, I groped for an answer. "It's criminal—"

"Don't repeat such ideas, Mrs. Diamond, especially to the police. They might believe your husband had good motive to kill Santiago."

The gruesome image of Stephan's slashed throat and the blood spattered over the office flashed in front of my eyes. I also remembered Martin Dodd's nervous energy, his shaking hands and sweaty face. And all the information he'd explained about the political group, the members and their flag. Dodd seemed as shocked as the rest of us about Stephan's throat being cut. He'd been reluctant to tell Woodward what had happened, in fact.

I froze. What had he said?

My heart raced, and rushing blood pounded in my ears. Martin Dodd's words returned. *His throat was slit with a Bowie knife* . . . Not once did he mention that Stephan had been stabbed in the back. Minutes ago, I'd wondered what we might find at the dynamite factory. And Adam Woodward's odd statement didn't register. Until now.

*Not someone stabbed in the back* . . .

How had the attorney known what happened to Stephan? Either he'd been present when the killer stabbed him, or he killed my ex-fiancé. I stared into the growing dusk. I was sitting beside a liar. A man I trusted as a friend—no, not a friend. Woodward betrayed me. I hadn't learned to be cautious since the long train journey from Evanston to Sacramento. Once again my fate was out of my hands.

The buggy wheels hit a rock, which skittered away. Not waiting for Uncle Harrison had been a mistake. A huge one. Should I jump? Would I survive a leap into the steep canyon with rocks, thorny scrub and perhaps snakes? Probably not.

The attorney stopped the buggy's team near a pile of rocks. A shadowy figure emerged, but my hope died. It wasn't Ace after all. The stranger raised the tin shell of a lantern and struck a match. The light flared. I recognized the man's face at the same moment Pedro Hernandez Alvarez raised his eyes to meet mine. He smiled and then bowed low.

"Señorita Granville—oh, perhaps I should say Señora Diamond. Welcome to the Colossus Safety Powder Works, which my friend here and I now own. Once you realize that your husband will without a doubt be hanged for murder."

I glanced between the two men in cold fury. "You two are friends?"

Alvarez laughed. "Oh yes. He did not tell you? I hear you came for a tour of the factory, Señora. You'd like to speak to my son as well? I shall send for him, although it may take him a few days to return from Sacramento. He had an important dynamite delivery."

He signaled to Woodward, who prodded me to the buggy seat's edge. Not with a finger, but with a small derringer. The attorney gave an apologetic shrug.

"Did you kill Stephan?" I asked, one hand on the seat back.

"No, Señora Diamond, he did not." Alvarez pulled me out of the conveyance. My ankle twisted and I gasped. He didn't seem to notice. Or care. "Señor Woodward joined our cause for a share of the profits. Every man has his price, *si*?"

Pedro Hernandez Alvarez dragged me along a rough sloping path toward the closest building, a stable by the lingering animal smells in the air. I sidestepped a pile of soiled hay and rounded an outcropping of rock and scrub brush. The stable's door squeaked on its hinges. Alvarez shoved it open wide. Sunshine streamed into the dim interior.

"I brought you a visitor," he called out. "Hello? Are you still alive?"

Was Ace here? A few stacked crates lay in one corner. Most stalls held mules, and a few twitched their ears in curiosity. I noticed movement in an empty stall, and deep grunts. A man on his stomach fought against tight rope bindings on his wrists and ankles. A strip of cloth was tied around his mouth. He rolled over and glared at Alvarez, who walked in and kicked him. Martin Dodd rolled again, grunting in his throat. His reddish-brown beard and hair held bits of straw. Dirt streaked his face. I limped toward him but Woodward caught my arm.

"Have they hurt you, Mr. Dodd?"

"Don't talk to him. Have a seat at the desk, Mrs. Diamond. We have an important document for you to sign."

The attorney waved to one crate, the makeshift seat. Two others stacked together served as a table. I sat on the single crate's hard surface, glad to rest my sore ankle. The dull throb had increased, but I dared not check for swelling. Instead I laced my boot tighter for better support. Adam Woodward set a pen and ink bottle before me and tugged off my gloves. He then produced a sheaf of papers from his coat and smoothed them out. I squinted in the dim light to read the handwriting. Alvarez set the lantern on the crate.

"Sign over your rights to this factory. Now."

I gazed into his half-lidded dark eyes. "My husband owns it, along with whoever will inherit Santiago's half."

"You will inherit, as you well know, after Diamond is hanged."

"The police haven't found him yet."

"They will, soon enough," Woodward said. "We'll make sure of it. Come now, Mrs. Diamond. Sign it and you will be free to go."

I stared at them both. Martin Dodd lay trussed at his feet, glaring at Woodward with clear hatred. "Why should I believe you? You might slit our throats like Stephan."

"Santiago served his purpose. He also challenged my authority, which was a mistake," Alvarez said. "I do not tolerate challenges."

"Then why did you place that flag under Stephan's body in the office? Didn't that call attention to your political group?"

"We have laid *Oso Español* to rest. The flag also served its purpose."

"And your son did too, lying to the police about my husband being involved."

"The police believe what they are told. Lucky for us they failed to listen to Mr. Dodd. He was a stinging insect, harmless enough. At the time."

"No more talking, Mrs. Diamond." Woodward gestured to the document with the derringer. "Sign it. Pick up the pen. Now."

I obeyed and signed Aunt Sylvia's name. "It's worthless, though."

"What do you mean?"

Alvarez grabbed my arm, but too late. I'd already ripped the paper in half with a jagged tear. He backhanded me. I tumbled over in a heap, against the stall where Dodd lay, and heard him grunt louder. My lip was bloody, and my fingers traced the stinging welt on a cheek.

"You want to make it worse for Mr. Dodd?" He kicked the journalist, who groaned. "If you wish, I shall accommodate. I can kill him now—"

"No. Please."

He rubbed the heavy signet ring on one finger, eyeing me. Woodward stepped between us, muttering something, before Alvarez nodded. He grabbed me from the crate, shoved me forward and then waited until I crawled toward the stable door. Then I rose to my feet. I needed to maintain dignity and courage. Expecting rough treatment, I hadn't realized that every step would be agony. The winding and steep path lined with rocks proved difficult. Within fifteen minutes, we'd reached a larger building with a sign overhead.

Colossus Safety Powder Works had been printed in huge bold script, and the names E. Santiago and J. R. Diamond below that. One thing had to be true. They hadn't captured Ace so far. He was alive. Somewhere.

Or so I hoped and prayed.

*'. . . they saw that evil was
come upon them.' Judges 20:41*

# Chapter Sixteen

Alvarez pushed me through a narrow door. Inside, more lanterns illuminated the interior and shelves held wooden crates. All the same size, and stamped with the word Colossus along with numbers—possibly the product's weight. Dust motes drifted in the dim light. I wondered where they stored the nitroglycerin. Hadn't Ace said it was dangerous? But Alvarez dragged me to a small side room, with a large wooden desk and chair before an open window. A cloth-bound ledger book and stacks of papers littered the desk's surface.

Woodward shoved me onto the chair. Alvarez brought forth a long length of thin braided cord and tied my wrists in front of me. Then he secured the other end of the cord around a coat hook on the wall. I wouldn't be able to climb out the window. Or go far outside the room, unless I could unfasten the cord. I leaned back. The taut braided cord chafed my wrists. Alvarez stuffed a cloth between my teeth. Woodward tied a strip of linen around my mouth.

"Nnngh!"

"It won't matter if you scream. No one lives near for miles. But I'd rather not listen," Alvarez said. "Come, Mr. Woodward. Bring fresh paper to write up a new deed."

The minute they left the room, I stood and walked forward to the wall. Lifting my arms over my head, I worked at the tight knot. My fingers failed to loosen it. My arms shook. Voices drifted from the room outside. I raced back to sit, although no one entered the office.

Relieved, I swiveled the chair around and managed to pull the cloth over my chin. I spit out the nasty cloth. Then I flipped open the ledger on the desk, despite the tightening cord. The page had a list of figures—with other names besides Ace and his six thousand dollars. My jaw dropped at the total. Where was all that money?

I tore out the page and folded it small, then stuffed it inside my corset cover. Once I shut the ledger book, I tiptoed my way to the wall again. The voices had grown louder. I recognized my uncle's sharp tone and Paloma Díaz Granville's shrill voice.

"—*mataste a mi hijo! ¿Cómo pudiste hacer tal cosa?*"

Alvarez said something in Spanish as well. So my uncle had brought her along to the factory. Did he know she was involved with these men? I risked a peek around the door frame and then pulled back in horror. Adam Woodward stood less than a foot from where I leaned against the wall. I waited, my heart in my throat, dizzy. Once I was certain he didn't intend to enter the office, I peeked again. They'd left the room, their voices receding. I returned to the coat hook, tugging and pulling, and almost kicked the wall for being dull-witted.

I'd forgotten about Ace's stiletto in my boot. Unfortunately, with my hands tied so tight and my boots so tall, I couldn't get a finger inside the leather. Should I untie my boot and risk the ankle swelling to twice its size? I'd never be able to walk, much less run, if I had any chance to escape. Somehow I had to get one hand loose to retrieve the knife. It took a minute to lift and carry a chair beneath the hook. I could use my teeth. I hoped.

Taking care to keep from getting tangled in the cord, I stepped onto the broad seat. My fingertips dug into the braid. I wiggled and worried the knot back and forth. The bond seemed impossible to loosen. I bit down again.

The leather tasted horrible. It didn't budge more than a quarter of an inch. And no matter how hard I tried to curl my hands together, I couldn't slip one free. Frustrated, I shifted on the chair. When my boot slipped off the edge, I grabbed the cord to save myself.

The chair legs screeched. I swung, cringing, until my feet found the wooden floor. Both my knee and ankle ached now. I inhaled a deep breath. The cord had not loosened around my reddened wrists. One hand felt colder against my cheek. Would I ever get free? I didn't dare climb back onto the chair. I heard Uncle Harrison's voice and risked another glance into the large room. Woodward held his derringer and a long knife, no doubt the one they'd used to murder Stephan. Paloma and Alvarez argued in Spanish further away.

So she'd lured my uncle here. He'd fallen into the same trap, believing their lies. We would both be killed. They'd never risk letting us go and telling the police the whole story.

"I demand to see my niece!"

"Shut up," another man answered. James McKay, by the sound of his heavy breathing. "You'll see her and her husband's body too. In the canyon."

My uncle's reply was too faint to hear. I closed my eyes, my hopes failing. His body? Could it be true? How had Ace evaded death so many times before, until now? My fists clenched and I fought against screaming aloud.

Uncle Harrison cursed, I could hear that. His wife didn't sound happy either, uttering a biting string of Spanish before she switched to English.

"Pigs—you slaughtered my son because you wanted this factory!"

"A necessity," Alvarez said. "Stephan was not cooperating with our plans."

"*Oso Español* was an idea, not a plot to kill innocent people and steal money."

"Ah yes, your high standards. We chose a different route, my dear."

Paloma screeched. "*El barbáro*! Will you plant these *palos de fuego*, these sticks of fire, throughout the city then?"

"Sacramento, actually. The new Court House, the Governor's mansion," Woodward said, "and the Central Pacific railroad. The state government will not risk damage, of course, but if they refuse to pay up—we shall treat them to a display."

"And then what?" Uncle Harrison barked a laugh. "You'll never get away with it."

"We will, Señor. South America is awaiting us," Alvarez said. "We will take our savings and be well out of the country. Along with our products."

Their savings, listed on the ledger page I'd taken. All those thousands of dollars, stolen from people like Ace, thinking they had invested in an honest business. I had proof now but it was little comfort. They'd kill us all and escape.

Paloma spat more curses in Spanish. Alvarez answered, although I didn't understand a single word. I glanced around the door frame. He held the derringer up to Paloma's head this time. My uncle fumed, his fists clenched. Woodward was hunched over the papers on a side table, beside the stack of crates. James McKay had vanished.

I leaned my head against the wall. No one would come to my rescue, not my uncle or my friends, Kate and Charles. Not even poor Martin Dodd. Anger flooded me. I couldn't give up so easily. Somehow I had to get free on my own. I slid the chair back into place. After working the knot with frantic energy, I stopped and took a deep breath. I had to calm down. Once my hands no longer shook, I worked a fingernail into one loop. It started to move, so I tugged and tilted side-ways. But I halted when I heard a thump.

I crept off the chair, listening, my heart in my throat. Where had that sound come from? The blood rushing in my ears didn't help. Frozen in fear, I heard a slight rustle.

Someone grabbed me from behind. I wanted to scream but bit that back. By his strength and sweaty smell, it had to be Martin Dodd. Until I heard the drawling voice in my ear.

"Miss me, darlin'?"

"Oh!"

I twisted around, hooked my bound wrists around his neck and pulled Ace into a heady kiss. Relieved, grateful he was alive, I rubbed my hands against his scruffy face. He winced as if in pain, but grinned wide. His whisper sounded like heaven.

"Beard's a bit itchy. I'm gettin' soft. You'll have

me civilized before you can say cow chip, Lily Diamond."

Laughter bubbled from my throat. I forced myself to whisper. "Where have you been all this time? I've been worried sick."

"In the canyon, hiding. I wish I had a knife—"

"Your stiletto's in my boot." I watched him tug it free. "Shh."

Ace slit the cord between my wrists and also near the hook above my head. He coiled the rest of the braided cord and stuck it inside his dark jacket.

"Never know when that might come in handy."

Ignoring my sore wrists, I ran my hands over his unruly hair, over his shoulders and arms and squeezed his warm hands. His bruises had turned purple, yellow and green, but the swelling above his eyes had gone down and his cuts looked less raw. Ace pulled me against his chest and kissed me, long and hard. He tasted salty, smelled of tobacco and whiskey. I snuggled into his arms, so grateful, and sent a prayer heavenward. Ace released me too soon.

"We can't stay here, Lily. Come on."

"My uncle—I can't leave him." I explained about his secret marriage to Paloma Díaz, about Martin Dodd in the stable with the mules, the document they'd wanted me to sign, and over fifty thousand dollars they'd stolen. "We can't let them get away with this."

"I know what I'm gonna do. Don't worry, I'll figure out a way to rescue your uncle. But I'd rather not leave you here. Things are gonna get hot."

"Hot?"

"Shh."

Ace pulled me along behind him, out of the office and along the shelves. Every so often, he stopped and checked between a stack of crates. Wires or rope snaked between them. I had no idea what he was doing, but kept tight hold of his jacket as if I'd lose him again. At one point a huge spider scuttled near my hand. I bit back a scream. I had adored Lucretia, the lizard in my mother's garden. Why would a spider bother me? Giddy, I almost laughed aloud.

"Where's your hat?" I asked.

"In the canyon." Ace pushed me outside. "All right. Time to get help, darlin'. Take this and go on back to that stable."

"What?" I stared at his stiletto.

"Take it and free Dodd. You said he's tied up."

"Oh, yes." I slid it inside my boot. "All right."

"You better take this too," Ace said, his eyes hard, and held up his Colt. "Ever fired a revolver before? Hardly any kickback."

I stared at the weapon, hesitating. "But—"

"I'd go with you, Lily, but I got things to do here."

"You mean rescuing my uncle?"

He cupped my face. "I can't promise a miracle, but I'll try."

"But—"

"Listen to me. They'll kill us. They'll kill your uncle and his wife too," he said, close to my mouth, and kissed me. "I need Dodd's help if we're gonna get outta this alive. Be careful, and shoot whoever gets in your way if you have to, but go on."

"I'm not sure I can shoot someone."

His second kiss reassured my fears. "Give Dodd the Colt once you get him free. Tell him to meet me around the back side of the factory. You stay at the stable. All right?"

I nodded, unhappy, the Colt in my hand. Ace slipped behind a stack of crates. He was right. We needed help. But the weapon didn't feel right in my hand, despite its light weight. Hadn't I fired Father's heavier Navy revolver? I remembered the recoil, my hand and arm shaky for several seconds. The ear-splitting sound of the shot, the acrid smell of gunpowder, that loud ringing in my ears for hours afterward. I held Ace's weapon away from me, like I would a rat by its tail. Ugh. I couldn't possibly use it.

My heart in my throat, I walked back along the shelves and past the office. In another moment, I found myself outside in the inky night. My eyes soon adjusted. The first step up the slope sent a shooting pain up my right limb. I scrambled as best I could along the path. I couldn't tell which way to go at a curve, and chose wrong. I retraced my steps upward again and limped along the narrow track. Was I lost? I caught a faint scent of dung.

I crept forward, slower, until I reached the stable. The weathered wood was rough under my hand. I inched toward the open doorway. A mule brayed, scaring me half to death. I waited, listening hard, to the voices inside.

James McKay mumbled something, but I heard Martin Dodd's reply. He talked fast, as if desperate. "I'll go east, you won't hear from me again. I swear to you, I will!"

"We can't trust you."

"I'll forget everything I ever learned about *Oso Español*. About your involvement, about the money. I swear it. On my mother's grave."

McKay's voice echoed in the stable. "We can't risk it, I tell you."

"I'll take the next train back to Chicago. You don't have to do this, boss. My family has money. They'll pay you. Any amount. Name a figure—"

"Shut up, for God's sake."

"No!"

A gunshot echoed. I dropped Ace's pistol and then snatched it up again. The handle was cold. So was the barrel. It wasn't even cocked and ready to fire. That shot had come from inside the stable. James McKay had killed Dodd in cold blood.

A rush of fury engulfed my senses. My father had been murdered. Stephan too. I swung around the stable's open door and aimed the Colt. Martin Dodd lay at McKay's feet, a hole in his temple, his eyes glazed and blank. The businessman shifted his bulk, surprise on his face. Then he pointed his revolver again. At me.

"Put that pistol down, little girl."

"You killed him. How could you? He wrote articles for your newspaper!"

"What of it? Now put it down so you won't get hurt." McKay waved his revolver, a sneer on his face. "You don't have the guts to fire it anyway."

I breathed deep and pulled back the hammer. I hated the horrible sound of the click, but I pointed the barrel at his head. "The police will be here any minute. Lay down your weapon, please. I shan't ask again."

"Fat chance of that."

He fired. Something whizzed past my ear. Heart in my throat, I almost lost my balance in shock at the reverberation. I squeezed the trigger without thinking. Fired again. And then opened my eyes. McKay had fallen backward, blood seeping between fingers planted on his chest. The revolver slid from his other hand into the hay. Stunned, I stood waiting. One mule poked his head out of a stall, staring as if accusing me, but James McKay didn't move.

Whirling, I fled.

*". . . for all they that take the sword*
*shall perish with the sword."*
*Matthew 26:52*

# Chapter Seventeen

Blind to everything, I stumbled back toward the factory. Another man was dead because of my actions. I'd pulled the trigger. McKay had fired first, but perhaps he deliberately missed. Had he wanted to scare me? Or kill me? Doubled over, I fought nausea. I closed my eyes and prayed for forgiveness. Nothing changed. No wave of peace came over me.

Only grief.

Cold brushed against my damp cheeks. I hadn't even realized I'd been weeping. My breath ragged, I leaned against a slender tree bole and swiped a sleeve across my face. Somehow I'd forgotten my handkerchief behind. I sniffled.

Had I acted in self-defense? Or was it murder? I was guilty of not acting fast enough, after days of chafing against inaction. I'd let McKay murder poor Martin Dodd, remained outside that stable, listening. Afraid. What a fool I'd been, thinking that a man like McKay would show mercy. Ace gave me his Colt in case of trouble. But I failed to use it.

I hadn't learned to identify evil. I hadn't learned that while all people deserved a chance at redemption, not all would accept. And I had yet to learn how to forgive myself.

I hoped, fervently, that those who showed no mercy in their hearts would be shown no mercy after their own death. The choice had to be made here, between good and evil. I had that same choice. I'd failed my father, and now Martin Dodd. But I promised to save my husband. Ace was waiting behind the factory, expecting Martin Dodd, who was dead. The police would not come to help. There was no one else. Only me.

Stepping with care, I stumbled on. I held the Colt in one hand, reached out to the next tree and then a shrub, snaked my way from a rock pile to a patch of tall oat grass. I reached a huge boulder. Beyond it, the factory loomed ahead. I crept along one weathered side of the building and then rounded the corner. Ace was nowhere in sight. But several wagons, piled high with crates, stood near the wide open double doors. A figure circled the nearest wagon, a spool in his hands, and unwound a length of wire along the ground and between rocks. Once he stashed the spool behind a tree, he returned to the wagons.

I squinted, but without a lantern I couldn't tell who it was. The man tossed a cloth over the crates and backed away. He wasn't tall enough to be my uncle, or heavy enough to be Adam Woodworth. Was it Pedro Hernandez Alvarez? He'd mentioned taking dynamite to Sacramento. I glanced down at the Colt in my hands. I couldn't shoot, even if the man did get in my way. The man clapped a hat on his head, tugging it in a familiar way.

Relieved, I limped forward and met Ace by the wagons. I pushed the Colt into his hands. "Here, and be glad I didn't shoot you." My breath hitched in my throat. "I'm sorry—"

"What are you doing here, Lily? Where's Dodd?"

"H-he's dead." I pressed myself into his chest, my entire body shaking, my voice halting several times. "I didn't know. I didn't realize McKay would shoot him like that. It's all my fault. And then I shot McKay. That was horrible."

Ace listened while I warbled out the full story, hugged me tight and then kissed my wet cheek. "Don't cry, darlin'. It's not your fault."

"I ought to have saved Mr. Dodd."

"You'd be dead—McKay would've shot you down, too. Listen to me. We're on our own now. We gotta survive." He let go of me, checked the pistol and reloaded the empty chambers. "I ain't seen nor heard anyone yet. They're inside the factory somewheres."

I bit my lip hard. "What shall we do? They'll kill Uncle Harrison."

"Chances are they might, at that. Now hush. Stay behind me."

Sticking the pistol inside his coat pocket, Ace unwound the spool further up the slope until we reached the top. Then he sat me down behind a huge boulder twice my size.

"What is that wire, or is it some kind of rope?"

"It's got gunpowder inside. Once I attach it to the blasting caps on top of the dynamite, the fuse will be ready. Gimme a minute. This is important."

I waited, impatient, while he worked. Several long, thin lumps under his coat caught my interest. "What do you have there?"

Ace pulled one free and held out a stick. "You wanted to know what dynamite looks like. Here you go. It won't hurt. Go on, touch it."

My fingers smoothed the paper. "This is a fire stick? It looks harmless."

"Before it's lit, sure. Don't forget there's nitroglycerin inside." Ace withdrew several matches from his pocket. Ace grabbed my hand and placed them in my palm, then folded my fingers over it. "Wait here for my signal. Then you're gonna light this special fuse."

"No, I'm not." I opened my hand. "I'm coming with you."

He pushed a strand of hair out of my eyes. "It's too dangerous, darlin'. I'll fire three shots and then you strike the matches. Make sure that fuse is burnin' good. It's fast, trust me. Then you get down and stay down, behind this rock."

"I'm not staying behind!"

"I don't wanna lose you, Lily—"

"You won't, unless you leave me here. I'm coming." I folded my arms under my bosom. "Now tell me why you want to blow up the factory. That's crazy."

Ace clenched his fists. His tense and stiff body told me plenty. "They're not about to rob me of all my money, and steal the dynamite too."

"I have a list, I tore it from the ledger. It's proof—the police will force them to return everyone's investments," I said. "That detective is bound to come looking for you here. Maybe they're already be on the way. We ought to wait."

"I ain't countin' on them. Leave the matches and come on, then."

He led the way back between the rocks and down the steep path. I had to make sure Ace wasn't hurt or killed. I wasn't going to wait among the rocks, all alone, wondering what was happening. But my throbbing ankle delayed us. Ace slid an arm around my waist, helping me over the worst spots, and then stepped through the factory's back entrance. One hinge squeaked. We halted. Held our breaths, and then walked forward.

"This way. No more talking."

Ace guided me through a narrow side room,

where low tables held long thin metal tubes in holders similar to candle molds. The scent of paraffin rose from a large tub. Another tub held lumpy clay. I guessed the workers formed dynamite into sticks and wrapped them in paper here. One metal tube was cold and oily beneath my fingertip. I wanted to ask Ace how nitro-glycerin was mixed into the clay, before being stuffed into the molds, but kept silent.

A rustle caught my attention. I twisted around, but no one was in the room. Where was Ace? I tiptoed out, past the stack of crates. Someone snaked an arm around my middle and then pressed another arm over my mouth. I fought to break free but failed. And I recognized the lawyer's voice when he spoke.

"Ah, Mrs. Diamond. I've been looking for you." Woodward dragged me forward. "How did you get loose? Without help—"

I bit his forearm hard. He yelled and then cursed when I kicked his shins. Woodward swung me into the nearest stack of crates. I'd anticipated that, so my shoulder took the brunt. It still hurt like the devil. My eyes smarted at the stabbing pain.

"You betrayed me! And my uncle."

"Purely business, my dear. My loyalty lies with those who pay a higher fee," he said. "You once asked about my dreams. I lost a fortune once by investing in a business that failed due to embezzlement. Everyone else lies, cheats and steals their way into huge mansions. I've seen it firsthand. This was a sure thing, so I took advantage when the opportunity arose."

I struggled harder. "But it's immoral."

"Keeping all the profits instead of sharing with investors? True. Like I said, I paid the price to other men who cheated me. It's time I reaped the benefits."

Something Father once said about his war experience popped into my head. Win each skirmish, and you may win the battle. I'd survived James McKay. Now I had to overcome a new enemy. I bent forward, braced my feet against the floor and launched myself backward.

My skull connected with Woodward's face. Or so I assumed, given his startled cry of pain and his loosened grip. I pressed my advantage now. Once I hooked a foot around his ankle, I tugged with all my strength. Woodward tripped sideways, luckily, since I sprawled forward. Thankful he hadn't landed on top of me, I rolled away from his grabbing fingers. Somehow he managed to snag my skirt. Drawing out the stiletto from my boot, I slashed at his hand.

Woodward roared another curse. I crawled behind the crates, wove my way through the maze, breathing hard, sore, until I heard the attorney moving toward the factory's front room. Then I stood, wobbling a little, and limped my way after him. I had to find Ace. I crept to the door and listened. And waited too long, because Woodward materialized out of thin air and twisted my wrist. The stiletto dropped from my nerveless fingers.

"Let's join the others, shall we?"

He marched me forward. Blood from his hand dripped down my skirt. Once we reached the open area past the crates, Woodward shoved me to the floor. I landed hard on my bruised arm, elbow and shoulder and rolled, gasping in pain.

"I found her, Alvarez! She had a knife. That must be how she escaped."

"So the little bird has returned. With her wings clipped." Pedro Hernandez Alvarez emerged from the office along with my uncle and Paloma. He waved the revolver at us. "What, she cut you with her little knife? A tiger, is she?"

"This handkerchief is soaked through." Woodward dropped the blood-stained linen by my face. I twisted aside. "The bleeding won't stop."

"Why are you asking him for help? He is heartless." Paloma walked forward and ripped her petticoat hem. She bound it tight around his hand and wrist. "I have known Pedro Alvarez since we were children. He's a snake. If only he'd killed himself and saved us this trouble."

Alvarez slapped a hand on his thigh. "I have always found you amusing, Paloma. Suicide is for real cowards, I am afraid. Like your husband."

303

"You dare bring that up to me? You, who drove Benito to the devil! You threatened to ruin him if he did not sell you his business—"

"He gambled, my dear. I loaned him more money, but each time he gambled that away too. Poor Benito. No self-control. No sense of what you deserved. And he did not care about your uncle's history, the grand General Mariano Vallejo." Alvarez sketched a bow and pulled her against his chest. "You should have chosen to marry me in the first place."

Paloma raised her chin. "I will never regret choosing a man instead of a pig."

Alvarez shoved her against Uncle Harrison. "You married another coward. And unless Señora Diamond signs the deed to this factory, you will die with him."

Woodward laid out the sheaf of vellum on the table. Bright crimson stained the muslin bandage on his hand. He staggered, almost dropped the pen, and set the ink bottle with staring eyes. Alvarez pulled me from the floor. We all watched the attorney tumble into the same spot where I had lain. He gripped his wrist, his mouth moving, breathing shallow.

"What is wrong?" Alvarez kicked him.

"He's bleeding to death—"

"No matter, because you will sign."

He raised his revolver and pointed at my uncle's head. By the time he cocked it, ready to fire, I had grasped the pen. Blood spattered the deed's surface, but I slowly read the words the attorney had written in haste. Alvarez tapped his foot, impatient.

"Sign it, Mrs. Diamond."

"She ain't signin' anything." Ace emerged from behind a crate, his Colt in hand, aimed at Alvarez. "I wouldn't point that revolver my way, not with all this dynamite behind my shoulder. The whole place would go up like a tinderbox."

"Not like at City Hall?" He shrugged. "Emilio was careful, but his friends were not so lucky. You won't shoot. I may hit your lovely wife instead of Captain Granville."

Ace didn't blink. "Drop it, or you're a dead man."

"I know when a man is bluffing, Señor—"

Both weapons fired once, twice. I ducked under the table. My uncle and his wife had crouched by the wall. Ace lay behind an overturned crate, dynamite sticks spilling over the floor. Blood stained his left leg, but he fired again at Alvarez who vanished into the office. I'd noticed the man's shirt above the waist sported bright red.

"Gut shot, and he can't get out the window," Ace said. "I blocked it up. Take your uncle and go, Lily. You know what to do!"

"No, no! You're hurt—"

"Go on, I'll make sure he ain't gonna escape."

My uncle pushed Paloma toward me. "Go on, I'll bring him. Get to safety."

Paloma dragged me off, unaware that she tugged my injured shoulder. The pain seared through me and numbed my fingers. I heard another gunshot. She refused to let go, though, pulling me out to the large room, through the double doors and into the night.

"Let go of me, please! I must get Ace out of there!"

"Your uncle will not let him die." She grabbed my hair and hauled me past the wagons that sent long shadows east from the last rays of sunset. "They will come, Lily. Enrique is no coward. Your husband is not either. Did he want you to set off these sticks of fire out here? That would kill us all."

"No. The fuse is up in the rocks."

"Then let us go there. Now." Paloma yanked me forward toward the path. "Come along. We cannot allow Pedro Alvarez to escape from the factory."

"The police will arrest him and put him on trial for murder—"

"The police are useless. He will die for killing my son!"

She raced up the steep path. I struggled on without help, although I failed to get far due to my ankle, my shoulder and my aching back. And then I heard it. A loud sizzling, and saw the sparking fire race along the rope with alarming speed. Paloma had set the fuse, and I couldn't stamp it out. It left a blackened line behind. Would Ace and my uncle die inside with Alvarez? All because Paloma Díaz wanted revenge for her son's death.

I sank down on the path, weary, in pain, peering back at the factory. Uncle Harrison staggered out of the factory, a bulky figure over his shoulders. He sprinted past the wagons toward the rocky path. Surprised, I slid a little downward and scraped my hands on gravel. My uncle set Ace on his feet and supported him, both men limping upward. By the time they reached where I sat, a blinding flash lit up the sky. A huge boom deafened me.

Terrified, I cowered beside Ace. He pressed me into the ground. "That was only the wagons," he said in my ear. "We need to get up in those rocks."

"You've been shot—"

"Quit talkin', Lily, and move!"

Pain blurred my mind. We hurried as fast as possible, passing the line of trees before Ace pushed me to the ground again. He covered me with his body. Mere seconds before the second earth-shaking explosion. I peeked, aware of the brighter light, as if the sun had exploded over our heads. Ignoring the ringing in my ears, I hid my burning eyes. Rocks, sharp splinters of wood and other debris rained beside us, behind us, atop us. Dust filled my mouth and nose. I coughed and hacked, choking, unable to hear anything.

Not even Ace's voice, although his mouth moved against my ear.

It seemed hours before rain of debris ceased. I rubbed my itchy eyes. Coughing, I rolled when my husband's weight lifted from my back. He stood above me and shook bits of wood, gravel and dust from his hair and shoulders. Then he stretched a hand out.

I clasped it and rose to my feet. "Alvarez shot you, didn't he?" My voice sounded dim, so I repeated the question. "Where?"

"It ain't bad. Already stopped bleedin'. Bullet went right through the flesh." He fingered the hole in his trouser's fabric. "I'm obliged to your uncle for gettin' me outta there, though."

I pressed my index fingers against my ears. A buzzing sound accompanied his dull words but it didn't fade. "What about Alvarez? And Woodward—how horrible."

Ace pulled me into his arms. "It's over, darlin'. That's the best way to think about it."

The dust cloud had dissipated somewhat below us. I glanced down, aware that nothing was left of the dynamite factory except chunks and splinters of wood, bits of metal, pieces of unrecognizable flotsam. The trees and shrubs at ground level were gone, and many had been flattened against the slope. Ace touched my shoulder and then apologized when I gasped in pain. I hid my face against his chest and slid my good arm around his neck.

"It's either out of joint or broken. I can't put my full weight on my ankle either."

"How are we gonna celebrate our honeymoon, if we're both in bad shape?"

Ignoring the pain, I leaned over and planted a kiss full on his mouth. "That should hold you over, Jesse Diamond. But I still want that bath."

Ace laughed at that. "You'll get that, Mrs. Diamond. And plenty more."

*'. . . ye shall receive of me gifts*
*and rewards and great honour. . .'*
Daniel 2:6

# Chapter Eighteen

I rode sidesaddle, the little bay mare beneath me gentle yet sturdy. The sand dune was pocked with hoof prints from the gelding farther ahead. A bracing wind stirred the thin veil draped over my hat. I gave the mare her head, letting her chase the waves back and forth along the sand. Her dainty hooves lifted smaller clods in a figure eight trail. One bit of damp sand landed on my full skirt, but I brushed it aside with my gloved hand.

A large house stood on a granite outcrop, far above the lapping ocean waves. Beyond them, sea lions basked on several huge rocks a ways from shore. Their odd barks echoed above sleek heads that seemed tiny compared to their massive bulky shoulders and flippers.

My heart swelled with joy, watching a few animals slip into the water. Captivated by the mesmerizing deep blue swells, I didn't realize that Ace had ridden his horse back to join me. He reined in his magnificent chestnut gelding with fluid grace. Flashing that devilish grin, he slapped his hat against the horse's flank and pranced the animal around my mare. The wind snatched his voice when he spoke.

"So how do you like the Pacific, Lily?"

"It's very different from the Atlantic. And the Great Lakes."

"See, the new factory's been built already," he said and waved an arm east toward the hulking wooden shell. "Good luck to 'em, too. Glad I'm out of the dynamite business."

"Don't even bring that subject up, please. It's too cold." I pulled my long wool cloak around me. "Although it is a pretty day for March. We must head back, or Etta will be worried."

"Home? Or to the Mason's?"

"They're coming for dinner along with Uncle Harrison."

I didn't bother to mention his wife. Paloma hadn't left the house since Stephan's murder, but my uncle seemed happier after we sold the Early Bird back to him. Under conditions, of course, but he didn't fight hiring new engineers or using less destructive mining practices. Our thirty percent share of the profits had been a sore point for the first few months.

"I'm surprised your uncle is speakin' to us after you won that wager. Awful smart of you, darlin'." Ace sidled his horse alongside mine and kissed me, a bit awkwardly. He reached out to tweak my nose. "Cleared my name, got all that money back for the investors in the Colossus, and my six thousand dollars too."

"So when will you start the horse breeding ranch?"

"We got plenty of time yet."

I decided not to argue. Smiling to myself, I urged the mare to follow Ace over the sand dune. How would my husband take the news? No doubt he'd scold me for riding a horse in the early stages, although I wasn't certain yet. And I'd wanted to see the ocean. We had been so busy supporting Kate and Charles' growing mission, hiring carpenters to plan and build our new home, and scouting out the best locations before choosing land near Twin Peaks.

We'd enjoy a view of the San Francisco hills for years to come, and raising our children. Juliana, and later John after my father. I'd never felt so blessed and happy, in love with my husband and life itself. Peace welled up in my heart. Peace, joy and thankfulness to God for helping me through such trials. We could settle down and enjoy a civilized life in California, without further troubles.

Ace waved his hat and let out that blood-curdling Rebel yell. I laughed. Civilized, indeed.

Maybe we needed more time after all.

# Author's Note:

I came across the tidbit below on a website called "Found SF," dedicated to San Francisco history. Imagine me shouting, "Eureka!" The inspiration for a plot! And fitting, given how Rooster Cogburn, the sequel to the John Wayne film version of True Grit, also used dynamite. Funny how things work out. So I began researching dynamite. Thanks to A Most Damnable Invention: Dynamite, Nitrates, and the Making of the Modern World, by Stephen R. Bown, and the menu for a banquet given in honor of the Central Pacific railroad builders on www.cprr.org, I began writing my story—twisting things a fresh way, with a little fudging of the facts whenever necessary. I also found the history of the Giant Powder Company of San Francisco—which had the first dynamite factory in the United States. I hope you find this book is as exciting as the first book in the Double Series.

Happy hunting in your own journeys into history!

Meg Mims
*www.megmims.com*

# Giant Powder Company History . . .

www.foundsf.org/index.php?title=
Giant_Powder_Company

". . . Alfred Nobel licensed his new invention to Julius Bandmann of San Francisco, the brother of a close European business associate. Following a demonstration of dynamite in the blasting of a tunnel for the old Bay View railroad (likely the first use of dynamite in the United States), Bandmann incorporated the Giant Powder Company in August 1867.

Giant Powder Company leased property in the unpopulated "outlands" of Glen Canyon (then known variously as Rock House, Rock Canyon, Rock Ranch or Rock Gulch) from Rancho San Miguel resident L.L. Robinson, who also served as Giant's first president. While dynamite was relatively stable, nitroglycerin was not, and storage was mandated to be as far away from populated areas as possible. The factory began manufacturing dynamite in March 1868, a full two months before the official patent for dynamite was granted to Nobel.

During the first year of production by mills in Rock Canyon and Europe, the total production of dynamite increased from 11 tons to 78 tons. Production at the Giant mill in Rock Canyon continued without a hitch for 15 months. Then, on Friday, Nov. 26, 1869, at about 6:45 p.m., an explosion rocked the one-acre complex, killing the chemist and his teamster driver and injuring nine others. The exact cause of the disaster was never determined.

Because the population of San Francisco was advancing closer to Rock Canyon, Giant purchased 100 acres in the sand dunes south of Golden Gate Park . . ."

# About the Author:

Clocks and time play a big part in any late bloomer's life. And time plays a vital part in every mystery.

Meg Mims is an award-winning author and artist. She writes blended genres – historical, western, adventure, romance, suspense and mystery. Her first book, *Double Crossing*, won the 2012 Spur Award for Best First Novel from Western Writers of America and was named a Finalist in the Best Books of 2012 from USA Book News for Fiction: Western.

Meg also wrote two contemporary romance novellas, Santa Paws and The Key to Love. Her short story 'Seafire' is included in the charity anthology *Hazard Yet Forward* to benefit a fellow writer battling breast cancer. Meg is a staff writer for *Lake Effect Living*, a West Coast of Michigan tourist on-line magazine. She earned an M.A. from Seton Hill University's *Writing Popular Fiction* program. She is a member of RWA, WWA, Women Writing the West, Western Fictioneers and Sisters in Crime.

Born and raised in Michigan, she lives with

her husband, a "Make My Day" white Malti-poo and a rescue Lhasa Apso, plus a drooling black cat. Meg's artistic work is in watercolor, acrylic and pen/ink media.

**Center Point Large Print**
600 Brooks Road / PO Box 1
Thorndike ME 04986-0001 USA

(207) 568-3717

US & Canada:
1 800 929-9108
www.centerpointlargeprint.com